PASSIONATE DESIRE

THE DESIRE SERIES BOOK 2

BARBARA DONLON BRADLEY

ONE

Heather found her way blocked by a huge set of shoulders. Damn it. Sometimes her mind link with Storm got in her way. He had to know what she was up to and was going to try to stop her.

"And where do you think you're going?" His deep voice flowed over her, making her insides melt.

"Please tell me you're not going to start being overprotective already." She looked up into her mate's determined face. "I was just going for a walk."

"The doctor did just release you from the medlab. You have been through a lot, from your kidnapping two months ago to your pregnancy. I'm not being overprotective, just concerned for my mate's welfare."

"Storm, I'm fine." She tried to move around him, but he wouldn't allow that. A sigh escaped her. "I bet if I were to drag you into that bedroom you wouldn't be worried about me just being released from the medlab."

A spark entered his eyes. "I didn't hear you complaining earlier."

He was right. She enjoyed every moment she was in his

arms. Heather gave him a sultry smile. "You didn't have any complaints either."

"No, I didn't." He wrapped an arm around her waist and pulled her close. "My heart, bringing you to ecstasy is what I live for. To have you fall apart because of what I do to your body arouses me. It's why I never tire of you and always want you."

Desire started to unfurl inside. She slid her hand up his shirt, hoping she could talk him into letting her out. "So do you want to come with me?"

"You haven't told me where you were going." His grip was strong on her waist. He dipped his head so he could work his magic on her throat.

Where was she going? The moment his lips touched her skin she forgot everything but the feel of his mouth on her neck. "Can't think."

"Then it wasn't important." His tongue slid up over her mark and she felt it to her toes.

"I just want to get out." Her voice came out breathless. "Feel the sun on my face."

"Where did you want to go?" He continued to nibble in the one spot he knew would make her knees weak.

"The gardens?"

"We've never done it there before." He captured her lips, easing her mouth open so his tongue could tease hers. She melted just a little more in his arms. "We can go, but if I find we can't make it back here before I need you again…"

"Storm."

"I can take you back into that room and make you forget about the gardens altogether." He ran his fingers against her jawline in his gentle manner. "I don't need to walk."

"You promise to be discreet?" She knew he would get his way. One way or another. And this was the only way she could get hers.

He adjusted his arm around her waist and guided her outside. "Of course."

"As discreet as your mother was with that tent?" She referred to when she had first come to Vespia. He had been away on a mission and she wanted to be there when he arrived home. His mother had brought half of the palace guards with her so Heather could greet him when his ship landed, including a giant tent no one could miss.

"We did have a few moments together so I could see the gift you made me." He squeezed her waist. "That red outfit is still my favorite."

She smiled up at him. "I know." Heather looked around and found them being followed by guards as well as a few of the news people with their cameras aimed at them. A sigh escaped her. "I see we've got our entourage."

"Ignore them." He took her hand in his and let her set the pace for their walk.

Heather took her time, enjoying the leisurely stroll. She stopped whenever she felt like it to smell a flower or touch a leaf.

"Thank you." She rested her head against his chest.

"For what? Spending time with my heart?" He stopped walking and tugged on her hand. She looked up at him, then in the direction he nodded to.

Not too far in front of them was a young girl clutching a well-loved stuffed animal. She stared at them. Her eyes filled with a touch of awe and fear. The child knew who they were.

Heather crouched down so she could be closer to the child's level. "It's okay."

The little girl looked up at her mother for a moment before she took a few steps toward them. "I have a present for you."

"Really?" How did the child know she was going to be here? Storm had given in a little too easily. Did he plan this so the news people could get some footage they wanted? This way the media would leave them alone? Heather knew they had been hounding him for an interview with his mate and he kept putting them off.

The small girl pulled a bunch of wilted flowers from behind her back. Poor thing had been waiting a while to give them to her. "Wait. They were much prettier before."

"They are beautiful. Thank you very much." Heather took them and smiled.

The big, happy grin was worth her little white lie.

She stood and slipped the flowers into Storm's waist band. "You planned this, didn't you?" She said it softly and kept her face averted so the cameras trained on them wouldn't pick up what she said.

"I swear I didn't." He looked at the flowers sticking out of his waistband. "You're not going to leave them there, are you?"

"Don't have any pockets." She winked at the young girl who stared in awe for a moment before wrapping herself around Storm's leg for a quick hug. The child then dashed to her mother's side.

Heather stood. She smiled at Storm, waiting to see what he would do next.

He gave her his 'I'm not happy with you' look before he passed the flowers to one of the guards. In seconds, they had been set into a device that revitalized the flowers and placed them in a small vase. "They look much better there than in my waistband."

"I know, but did you see her face when I did that?" Heather looked at him, her eyes sparkling. "I think I made you a hero in her eyes."

"Because you stuck those pitiful things in my pants?"

"Because you didn't growl at me or become angry at what I did. You showed her honor by allowing me to put them someplace safe. That's why she hugged you."

"I'm not sure I understand." He slipped his arm around her waist once more.

"You are destined to be the next leader, right?" At his nod, she continued. "And as leader, your job will be to protect the people and the planet of Vespia. She knows that. Those flowers were very special to her. I could tell by the way she held them. You treated her flowers with care. You might not have liked what I did, but you didn't fight me."

"What makes you think I didn't like it?"

"That look of yours."

He pulled her up against his body, lifting her just enough so her feet wouldn't touch the ground. "Which look is that?"

"Your brows drop and your eyes narrow at me."

"So that one is called 'that look'?" He grinned. Storm lowered his mouth to hers. "I'm going to have to remember that one."

Heather wrapped her arms around his neck. "I have lots of names for your different faces."

"Which one is the 'I want you now' look?" he asked, his lips still inches from hers. Desire danced in the depths of his eyes. He finally closed the distance between their mouths, his tongue delving, searching for hers.

She found want filling her body. Too bad they were out in public.

It didn't seem to bother him at all. His lips left hers and worked their way to her neck. "I know of a nice, secluded spot."

"Now?" Her modesty warred against her growing desire.

"You promised to go along with me if I couldn't make it back to our rooms." He looked down at her. The longing in his eyes held such promise. "It will be discreet, I promise."

He led her to a simple bench surrounded by shrubbery and flowers. The bushes were tall and sculpted, sealing the bench in so no one would be able to inadvertently see anything. On top of that, they were surrounded by their guards.

Storm sat first. He never lost contact with her, so she couldn't back out on him. Pulling her onto his lap, he had her straddle him. Her face showed her fear.

"You okay?"

"This isn't something I think I'm ready for." She let out a pent-up breath.

"I would never make you do anything you don't feel comfortable with." He touched her face with such tenderness. "I see such strength from you I sometimes forget that a lot of our ways are foreign to you."

His honesty filled her with determination. He believed she could do this or he wouldn't suggest it. She stood and straightened her skirts so it wouldn't hamper them. Once she had them out of the way, she eased herself back down on his lap.

Storm pulled her close, capturing her lips with his. He drew her into a vortex of passion with the swirl of his tongue. She felt it in the heat of the kiss, in the heat of his mouth on her mark. It made her blood boil.

"I need you." Her voice was barely a whisper.

Storm didn't need any more prompting. He freed himself from his trousers and helped her slide down his hardened length. He buried himself deep inside her. They both shuddered at the intimate contact. "I need to feel your skin against mine."

She removed his shirt, and he opened the top portion of her dress. Slipping it from her shoulders, the gown pooled around her waist. His hands slid up her back, holding her close and right where he wanted her.

"Now, let's see if I can make you forget about everything else but us." His fingers worked their way into her folds, finding the one spot that made her desire spiral out of control.

She sucked in her breath as his fingers brushed against her most sensitive spot. Her muscles rippled against him, making him wonder if they could reach their releases without either making a move. Every time her muscles constricted on him like that he felt it deep inside.

He continued to stroke her body, and it continued to sing for him. She was caught up in the maelstrom of sensations flooding her. Heather's sheath tightened around him like a vise. Her breath came out in soft pants. Head tilted back, her eyes were not quite closed and her mouth was slightly open. This was what he wanted. She looked so beautiful when she hit her release.

Her mind reached for his as she hit the pinnacle. The intimacy they shared went beyond anything he could ever explain to anyone. Once she was released from its grip, she touched his face with her fingers.

"Ready for more?" He had his hands on her hips, helping her set the pace for her next release. Her muscles tightened against him, increasing the desire filling them both. He felt her mind brush against his so he could feel her body's reactions as well as his.

Every frisson of heat she felt, he felt. When one move made her body tighten, he felt it in his soul. His lips nibbled on her throat, working their way to her mark. That always had a deep connection for her. He swirled his tongue against it and she came apart in his arms.

———

"What the hell?" Suddenly Kuarto found himself overwhelmed by sexual sensations that kept building around him. He was supposed to be driving to his next patient, but he couldn't focus. His body hardened with the powerful release surrounding him.

Someone else's release. He had no clue who brought him

along on their sexual exploits, but he got caught up with them every time.

The truck he drove took a hard right before he could regain control, and he hit the ditch running alongside the road. He pounded his hand against the steering wheel. Every time this happened, he got swept away with whoever was doing it. He just wished it would stop.

"Whoever! We have to talk about this. I don't want to be part of your intimate liaisons, so please leave me out!" he screamed to the heavens. It just wasn't fair. He had abstained on purpose. Women just complicated things and now he was mentally sharing these massive orgasms with a woman and her mate and the man didn't leave her alone. The fates were downright mean to him.

Kuarto pulled his vehicle out of the ditch, using the magnets under the bed of the truck, and got it back on the road. A quick check showed a couple of new dents in the body, but the frame was fine. The dents he could bang out later, but he hated hurting his truck at all. He had found it in the small building next to the house when he bought it and had fallen in love with it the moment he found out it worked. Things like this weren't made anymore. Technology had seen to that.

He drove to his destination as quickly as he could. He was already late. He grabbed his pack as he stopped the vehicle. "Sorry, Ken. I tried to get here as fast as I could."

"It's okay, Doc." He gestured him to follow. "She went into labor a few hours ago but I thought she might be over-acting which is why I didn't call you right away."

"Isn't this her third child?" He walked into the house of the couple. This man was by far the dumbest male he had met. Kuarto was sure of it. "You know each child comes a little faster than the last one, right?"

"She could have held it in."

Kuarto wanted to smack the man in the head. He had no

clue about birth and really didn't seem to care. "You have the next child and let's see if you can hold it in, okay?"

"Doc?" He heard her frightened voice.

"I'm here, Sara. Everything will be fine now." He raced to her side when he noticed the fear in her eyes. Kuarto picked up his scanner and ran it over her body. Overall, everything was fine. The baby's cord was wrapped around its neck a few times but he could fix that in an instant. He talked to her softly and helped her bring the baby into the world.

"He's beautiful." The new life he held awed him. This was why he became a doctor. This rare, beautiful moment when you got to see a miracle. Once he finished checking the baby thoroughly, he handed him to his mother.

Kuarto looked at the child's father, hoping the baby would have more brains than dad. "You and the baby will be fine." He made a few notes for the records he had to turn in. "Come see me in a week so I can check and see how well your son is doing."

"A boy? Really?" She looked down at the sweet face of her baby.

"Yep." He touched the baby's tiny hand and was gifted with it wrapping around his finger. He couldn't help but smile at the new life, trusting him like this. "He looks just like his dad."

She grinned as she hugged the baby to her.

Kuarto grabbed the father by the collar when he was finished with the mom and child and dragged him outside. "You let her rest, you hear me? I don't want to rush back out here because you were too stupid to understand she needs to recuperate from giving birth. She isn't supposed to do anything more than care for the child for two weeks. That includes fixing dinner or cleaning. No yard work or farming, milking, anything that would make her lift or move anything heavier than a baby."

"Yes, Doc."

"Good." He picked up his pack and headed to his truck. "I'll know if you don't follow my directions." He climbed into the vehicle and took off. If the man did what he should, everyone would be fine.

———

Storm sat on the couch, waiting for Heather to return from the council chambers. His mother had insisted she work with the elders some every day. So he had freed her schedule so she could be with them for the afternoon sessions.

He felt a little nervous over what he was about to show her. She wasn't going to be happy, but he needed to make her see this was the only way.

She came in the door and her smile faded. "What is wrong?"

"Nothing." He patted the cushion next to him. "I have something to show you."

"Alright." She sat beside him and turned her attention to the large screen he received most of his communiqués on. Images flashed on the screen. Images of her. Heather stood when she realized where the pictures came from. "That is from the other day? How were they taken?"

"I took them."

"Excuse me?" She looked at him in shock and there was a hint of betrayal in her eyes.

"I had to." He brought up one picture of her with her eyes half open. "The news people have been hounding me about you. They wanted to interview you. I have to give them something. I thought a picture would work."

"This over them talking to me? That is so personal. I can answer a few questions about my background."

He grabbed her and pulled her up against him. Desire for her warred with anger. "They don't give a damn about your background, Heather. If they got their hands on you, they'd be asking how many sexual partners have you had, how many different positions you have tried, which one is your favorite. They want to know if you can keep me satisfied."

She glared at him.

"Why do you think mother thought it was a good idea to release your pregnancy to the public? It was to show I've not been celibate since our mating. But they want more. If we don't give them something, then they will come after you. Do you want them cornering you on your way to the council, asking you all these intimate questions?"

"I get your point." She studied his face, sensing his contradicting moods. "Are you okay? I know you're cross with me because I'm questioning this, but you seem highly aroused too."

"I had to go through the pictures. Find the right one to give them. Just watching you in the different stages of your release filled me with want, but this picture." He pulled up another still. "This one has me so hard for you right now."

Heather never saw herself the way he did. But the image in front of her revealed everything. Storm held her close in the image, his eyes held an intensity she only saw when they were both close to their release. She had her back arched, head thrown back, eyes closed, mouth slightly open, her ecstasy etched on her face. Just looking at it had her blood racing. "Is that what I look like?"

"Yes." He nibbled on her throat. "You are the most beautiful to me at that moment."

"Is that the picture you wish to release?"

"What is the human saying? 'A picture is worth a thousand words?' Don't you think that will show them that you are sexually pleasing to me?" He worked on the seals of her dress. "As much as I'd like to keep this one for myself it would be perfect. But it will be plastered everywhere. That is why I wanted you to see them first. Help me pick out the one you're happy with."

"Before or after you ravish me?" She worked on his shirt while he peeled her dress off her shoulders.

"How about during? You'll see how arousing these images are and be glad." He got the dress off her just as she had helped him out of his pants. He eased her to the carpeted floor. Her muscles gripped him as he slid in deep. "My heart."

He started a quick pace, one they normally worked their way up to. "Now watch." He set it so that the pictures would flash on the screen for about thirty-seconds each. With a flick of his wrist, he moved it from the screen to the ceiling above him so Heather wouldn't have trouble watching her own orgasm unfold.

Heather watched him maneuver her to straddle him. The next few pictures showed her fear over the thought of getting caught and him calming those worries. His tenderness when he realized her fear pulled at her heart. She remembered he didn't force her. This was her decision.

Storm ground his hips against hers, causing heat to pool in her stomach and make her forget about the pictures for a moment.

"You need to pay attention," Storm spoke softly in her ear. He slowed their pace down, making his strokes deeper instead.

"It's hard to focus on two things at the same time." She tilted her head back as the slower movements had her body humming. When she could refocus on the images, she was standing and adjusting her skirt. Then the images showed Storm kissing her. She didn't realize how heated their kisses got until she saw it happen in front of her eyes.

"You can tell the moment I enter you." Storm knew what she was looking at somehow. And he was right. Her body tightened when he penetrated deep inside. Her eyes dilated and she bit her lip.

"Mark that one." Her voice came out slightly breathless. The next few pictures were them undressing each other so that her upper torso was naked. She knew the moment his fingers started working their magic by the intensity on her face. Her forehead was pressed against Storm's, her hands grasping his arms. "That one too."

More flashed in front of her. The next picture she had him mark was the one of her first orgasm. Her eyes were partially opened and he gaze locked on Storm's face. Her fingertips touched his jawline.

She lost focus on everything as her body reacted to a thrust that sent her close to the edge. The heat in her stomach intensified as it spread to her limbs. Heather tilted her hips and wrapped her legs higher on his waist. Her mind brushed against his as she felt her body tighten just before she reached her release. She soared to the stars as spasms shook her core.

Storm continued to pump into her, his so close he couldn't help but move faster, hoping to catch the instant that was eluding him for a moment. He stiffened as he reached what he was after. His orgasm had her clamping down on him as she felt everything he did.

"And we haven't even gotten to the good pictures yet." Storm pressed kisses against her neck as he allowed the pictures to continue.

Heather wondered how many orgasms it would take before they could pick out a picture.

———

"It is a beautiful picture, Heather," said Toki. "It's all anyone can talk about."

She nodded, although she didn't quite agree with the general census. To have such a private thing plastered everywhere had her blushing a lot. "I'm just not used to it."

They ended up going with the one that made Storm so hard. It was by far the most erotic, yet tasteful photograph of her. Storm even had it framed. It hung in their bedroom, in the main room of Anseri's home and he had one made for his office. Being confronted by it all the time was desensitizing her to being embarrassed by it.

"So where is my brother, anyway?"

"He should be here any time." Heather offered her a drink. "I'm surprised he didn't ask you to meet him at his office."

"He said it was a sensitive subject, and he didn't want the information to be recorded." Toki took the glass Heather handed her. "Is this Earth iced tea?"

Heather nodded. "It has been very warm recently so I thought you might enjoy it."

Storm entered the room then, grabbed his mate and captured her lips with his.

"You two just don't get enough of each other, do you?" Toki set her glass on the coffee table.

"How would you expect me to greet my mate?" He hadn't let go of Heather but had broken the kiss. He looked into Heather's eyes. "We'll finish this later."

"Why did you call me here?" Toki stood. The passion Storm and Heather shared for each other was a little overwhelming at times.

"I believe I found Heather's brother."

"Really?" Heather was excited to finally meet her twin.

"Yes, based on the information you have gleaned from him when you've been in contact." He pressed his forehead against hers while he handed his sister a disk. "This should have everything you need to find him, Toki."

"When should I leave?"

"As soon as possible."

————

Kuarto looked around as he started up his truck. Looking at his watch, he figured he'd be able to get home without any trouble from the couple in his head.

That was what he called them now. The mind-sharing had started a few months ago, but he only found himself included every once in a while. In the last few weeks, they seemed to connect every time. It had already taken its toll on him. The time difference between them gave him some relief, since they seemed to be sleeping when he was working, but he was having trouble getting any rest at night and it was making him cranky.

The two in his head couldn't stay away from each other and the only time they shared with him was when they were hitting their orgasm, and he had worked that out to be about every two hours when they were awake. It was hard to get anything done with that kind of schedule.

A loud whine filled the air, forcing him to look up.

"Oh, that doesn't look good." He watched as a small ship billowing a whole lot of ugly black smoke, flew over his head, making a straight line for his home. "If you hit my house I will be one angry man."

He hit the gas and pushed his vehicle so he could keep up. Trying to keep an eye on the ship as well as the road wasn't the easiest thing to do. The black trail continued its path right for his home. He didn't need this. Strangers on this planet were frowned upon and having one in your backyard would make you a target. A loud boom filled the air as the ship connected with the ground. He reached the site seconds later. It had missed his house by several hundred feet, but it was still very close.

Sleek and black, the small ship's nose had buried itself in

the ground pretty deep, but he could see the door so could still get the ship to open, if he could figure out where the controls were on the outside. Kuarto looked for a seam or seal but didn't spot it. At least not right away. He rubbed his hands along the body of the ship, searching, hoping he'd hit some sort of indentation. "Ah. There you are. Can't hide from me for long, can you?"

He had been labeled brilliant by his peers. Had been the most sought-after doctor in the galaxy and hated it. So he just took off, changed his name, and found some tiny back-water planet to hide on. If these people knew who he was, he'd probably find himself drugged and sold to someone who knew his value. Which was why he didn't want this kind of intrusion. He had worked hard to keep his true identity secret and he didn't need some uninvited guest to screw things up for him.

He could have ignored this but he had two things that didn't work in his favor. One was the ship landed too close to his home for him to pretend it didn't happen. The other was his oath as a doctor. He needed to be sure the people inside were okay before he read them the riot act and sent them on their way.

He pressed the lever and watched in satisfaction as the doors opened. He had hoped to find the ship empty, thinking it could be unmanned by the size at first, but he spotted a body slumped over in the seat, which killed that idea. The pilot was encased in a head-to-toe uniform. The suit was sealed, giving the pilot as much protection as it could during the landing. That was good. He should have survived the crash.

And someone to yell at always made him feel better.

The interior still billowed heavy smoke, which hindered his vision. He needed to get the pilot out so he could see to their injuries. After being sure he could move the pilot,

Kuarto slung him over his shoulder and carried him out. His burden was a lot lighter than he expected. "What are you, a boy?"

This guy couldn't have weighed more than one hundred and seventy-five pounds, and he was a tall one. Close to seven feet. Kuarto wasn't short. He was well over seven feet, but he tried to play that down as much as possible. There weren't too many races with that kind of height, and he didn't want to think of what that could mean.

He laid the body on the ground and searched for the seal of the suit. It looked vaguely familiar. Vespian in design. Not too many people knew about that race but being the most sought after doctor did have its perks. It took a second for him to find the right spot. A grin spread across his face when he heard a faint noise as the glove he held came off into his hand.

He worked on the helmet, releasing the catches before he could remove it. His first glimpses of the face didn't make him happy. "Oh, this can't be good."

A whole bunch of hair spilled out. What he knew of the Vespians was limited. Very alpha, very big and very private. Most of the ones he had treated took his help with a glare and were gone the moment they could leave, but all of them had been male. This one was female. He didn't know a damn thing about their females.

He brushed her hair out of her face. To make matters worse, she was by far the most beautiful thing he had ever seen. "Probably my mind sharing couple's libido talking."

Kuarto had taken an oath of celibacy when he walked away from his old life. The less ties he had anywhere the better. Being attracted to someone could cause trouble for him and would complicate too many things. Knowing he was attracted to her made him leery. Better to get her on the road to recovery and on her way.

She had a strong pulse, and other than the nasty gash on her forehead, she hadn't been hurt too badly. "So, how did you get that gash in this getup?" The suit should have protected her completely.

He pulled out his portable kit and used what he needed to start her healing process. In seconds, her eyes fluttered open.

Golden eyes with a bright green ring stared up at him. "Who are you?"

"Kuarto."

She struggled to move.

"Hang on, now." He gently pushed her back down. "You've just been in a crash and it might take you a moment or two to get your body to respond the way you want."

Her eyes filled with confusion as she was able to turn her head so she could look over her shoulder to see the ship. "I flew that?"

Okay, that was not a good question and he knew it. How badly did she hit her head before she got the helmet on? "What is your name?"

"My name?" She looked up at him, fear creeping into the golden depths. "I don't know."

"That's fine." Although it wasn't. He checked the readings on his scanner to see if he could reverse the memory loss. "I'll pull the records from your database on board and will get your file. Memory loss isn't unusual with something like this."

A weird hum filled the air around them. He knew that sound, and it wasn't any better than her amnesia. Kuarto only had seconds to react. He pulled a device from his pocket and activated it before he spread his body over hers. The moment the force field activated, the ship exploded, taking any information he could have gotten to help her remember who she was.

Now he had a very pretty guest to contend with.

And explain.

———

"Sir? We've lost contact with her ship."

Storm turned to glare at the young man who just spoke. He could see the readings too. "Do you know why?"

"No, sir." The young man swallowed hard. "On her last check-in everything was fine. She was headed to the coordinates programmed into her ship. As far as we can tell, she was close when the ship stopped communicating with us."

He really didn't need this. "Give me all the data on her last coordinates."

The young man nodded and downloaded the info to a disk. He handed it to Storm with shaky hands.

Storm took the chip and walked out of the command center. It looked like he needed to go find his sister before she got into any more trouble. He crossed the open atrium to get to their rooms, wondering what Heather had been up to. Normally, she would brush her mind up against his from time to time, but today he hadn't felt her presence once.

He walked into a darkened room and felt his heart stop for just a moment. After all they had been through, he feared she would be taken from him again. Until the person behind her kidnapping was found and stopped, Storm would be vigilant.

He spotted her silhouette and breathed a sigh of relief.

"You worry too much." She stood as he walked toward her.

"Only about you." He walked up to her and wrapped his arms around her. "Why are you sitting in the dark?"

"I was meditating." She rested her head on his chest, listening to the beat of his heart.

"Everything okay?" He touched her stomach as he led her to the couch and eased her down.

"Of course." She brushed her hair out of her face and gave him an exasperated look. "Please don't treat me like I'm some sort of fragile flower. We have another sixteen months left on this pregnancy, and I'll go crazy if you start being too overprotective this early."

"Can't help myself." He gave her one of his bone-melting smiles. "But you do know how to distract me, don't you?"

She wrapped her arms around his neck. "I think I have an idea."

He bent his head to hers and captured her lips with his. He loved the taste of her. Her tongue slid against his, making him groan at the pleasure. He then moved his lips to her throat where he loved to nibble.

"You're home early." She tilted her head to the side so he could have the access he loved.

"I know. I went to speak to my mother." He worked on the seams of the dress she wore. "My sister has turned up missing."

She pulled back to look at him, stopping him for a moment. "That's not good."

"I'm sure it's nothing." He went back to the seams of her gown, opening it easily, exposing her body to his gaze. Storm found it flawless, the velvet skin begging for his touch. His fingers caressed her softness as the dress dropped to the ground. "But I'm going to go check it out to be sure."

"I'm going with you." She had already opened the seams of his uniform. All he had to do now was walk out of it.

His hands cupped her breasts. This was one thing he didn't want. She had a way of getting what she wanted even when he was dead set against it. "You know, I think these are a little fuller than they used to be."

"Don't change the subject." She put her hands on her hips. "I'm going with you."

"Heather." He lifted her in his arms, and carried her to

their bed, hoping he could distract her enough to forget her desire to accompany him. Why did he even mention it?

But Heather knew what he was up to. She smiled up at him, ready to accept him into her body like she had hundreds of times before. The moment he surged into her he could only think of the wonderful sensations their joining caused.

"You are taking me with you." Her voice, laced with her desire, was soft in his ear.

"Too dangerous." There was no conviction in his voice and he knew it, but he was too caught up in the intimacy they shared. Everything washed over him. He felt her muscles tighten against him, sending delightful frissons up his spine.

"Why?" She licked her lips as one shiver of excitement raced through her blood.

He felt her body quake as it took control of her for a second or two. Every once in a while, he stroked her just right and it fanned her desire to a white-hot flame. "My heart."

"I promise to be a good little mate and obey your every command, plus we can do this whenever you want." Her muscles had him in a steel grip. Every time he slid in and out it just heightened everything.

"Oh, you don't fight fair." He picked up the pace, causing her muscles to ripple against him. His body shook at the feel of her tight sheath rubbing against him.

"And, oh my," she stopped talking, heat unfurling in her stomach. It blossomed out, filling every fiber of her being. Her mind brushed against his as her release was on top of her. "You don't?"

Like a light being turned on, Heather's orgasm grabbed her and filled her with overwhelming joy. It spilled over into his mind, so he felt the same emotions she did. His release was just as powerful, making them both speechless. Heather floated back down, relaxing against the pillows with a smile on her face.

"Oh, and I think I found another outfit you might like."

He perked right up. Rising up on his elbows, he looked down at her. "Really?"

"I'll save it for when we return home."

"Home?" He nuzzled her neck. "Why?"

"There's not a lot of privacy on those scout ships." A sigh escaped her as he nibbled on her throat. "Remember what happened the last time we were around people and I wore one of your favorite outfits? It almost caused a riot just because I bent over the wrong way. I don't like being an exhibitionist despite what that picture shows. What I do, I do for you."

"And I like my own private shows." He sighed. "So now you're not only demanding that I take you with me, but we have our own ship?"

"I wouldn't dare make a demand like that." She brushed his hair with her fingers. "I know better."

"But if I go along with this I get to see you in that new outfit and you will do whatever I ask of you?" He studied her face, watching as her eyes dilated at the promise of his threat.

"Your wish is my command."

"You know that could get you into trouble." He lowered his mouth to her mark. Still deep inside her, he felt her body pulse as he pushed his tongue along the tissue.

She arched up against him. "I hope so."

———

Damn it, not again!

Kuarto had to come up with a reason why he suddenly had a woman at his place, not get lost in the sexual antics of his mind sharers. The name he gave them sounded so inane, but he couldn't come up with anything else. Now that he had regained control, he needed to work on what he hoped the people here would believe about his unexpected visitor.

The people in this small village all knew each other, so a stranger would attract a lot of attention. Then he remembered one of the men talking about ordering a mail-order bride. That might work out for him, since there were women from other planets willing to move to some of the more remote outposts to find a husband. Their own worlds were hard and husbands were rare. All he had to worry about was whether or not Vespians were listed. If so, he should be able to pull it off.

He pulled up the information on the brides. There were several companies who specialized in brides and they had every kind imaginable. It didn't take a lot for him to backtrack on his computer to make it look like he had been looking for a bride for a month or so, and that would help with explaining her arrival.

The young woman slept in his bed at the moment. She looked so innocent there. He watched her, hoping everyone would believe the story he would have to weave.

The only thing he needed to do now was use his precious replicator to create what a bride would bring to her new home. He rarely used the machine because of the minerals needed to activate it. They weren't the easiest items for him to get his hands on. So what he had, he used sparingly, normally for medical supplies he needed when it would take too long to order them.

Considering her ship burnt up on impact, all he needed to do was create an outfit he thought a new bride would wear to meet her husband-to-be for the first time. From everything he read, most would wear their wedding gown. Not very practical, but he did understand why, so he created a nice dress for her. Something she could wear now and still be pretty enough for people to think it was her wedding dress.

He brought it into his bedroom and placed it on her bed, hoping she'd put it on without any questions when she woke up. Glancing out the window, he saw one of the locals heading toward his home. Figured he would be the first one to show up after the crash.

He went on the defensive the moment his front door opened. It always worked on this man. "What do you want, Guapo?"

"I come to see you and that's how I'm greeted? Shameful, doctor. I heard you have a new bride and wished to pay my respects."

"That didn't take long. Or was it the crash that brought you, and made you check to see what might have caused it?"

"You wound me." He grabbed at his side where his heart was. "I worried something could have happened."

"Right. Go home, Guapo." He moved about his small office, trying to look like he didn't care what the man thought. "I'll bring her around when she is ready."

"No quick peek?"

The young woman walked into the room at that moment, wearing the dress he had left for her. Why did she have to come out right while the most untrustworthy man on the planet happened to be in the building?

"Thank you." She noticed their guest and stopped. She stepped close to Kuarto, as if she was looking for protection from him. At least she knew better than to talk.

"Guapo, my bride." Not being able to explain anything to her, he prayed she wouldn't question him in front of this little sleaze bag. It wouldn't go well if she did. Thankfully, she gave him an odd look but kept quiet during the introductions.

"She is very pretty. You are a lucky man." He studied her,

something that made Kuarto uncomfortable. "Tonight, I will come back, and we can celebrate."

He didn't think it was a good idea, but wasn't sure if the man understood the word no. The moment the man left, Kuarto focused on her. "You shouldn't have come out."

"How was I to know you were going to have a guest?" Hurt filled her eyes.

"We need to get our story straight before he comes back." He ran his fingers through his hair in frustration. He hadn't meant to hurt her feelings but had no clue how to fix it. "I have bought you. You're my mail-order bride."

"Okay." She looked at him with such innocence.

At least she wasn't going to fight him on this. "You need to be quiet as much as possible when he is here. He's not one I trust."

"Then why do you deal with him?" She looked out the window to watch the man retreat.

"Sometimes you have to deal with the worst to survive." He looked at her. "You know, we need to come up with a name for you. 'I don't know' doesn't roll off the tongue."

"What do you suggest?" She played with a piece of gold around her neck.

"What is that?"

"The necklace? I'm not sure. I noticed it when I changed."

"Maybe it says something we can use." He stepped up to her and took a hold of the gold disk. It was warm from her skin. It practically burned him. "To Toki, sister, friend, Heather and Storm."

"Toki? Sounds like a nickname."

"It does, but it's Vespian, which you are too. I'm not sure how many people will recognize that, but I don't want to take a chance with using a non-Vespian name." He didn't have the heart to tell her it meant pain. "I don't think it would be smart to give you a human name when you're not human."

"Then Toki it is." She looked up at him while he continued to hold the medallion. "I wanted to thank you for the dress."

"Oh, you're welcome." He backed off, not real sure why he had stayed that close to her for as long as he did. "Thought it would look better if you dressed the part of a mail-order bride. What did you do with your other clothes?"

"Left it on the bed."

"It might be smart to put that away. Don't want people asking too many questions because they happen to see it." He walked into his bedroom. The uniform lay neatly on his bed. Kuarto picked up the outfit, folded it, and put it into the wooden trunk he had at the foot of the bed. The cover's disheveled look reminded him what caused it. He had a woman in his bed. Too bad he hadn't joined her. He sure wanted to.

A slight sound behind him made him look around and he found her inches away. Being attracted to Toki was going to be a problem. He needed to be professional. "Okay, this is what we will tell people. You came here as my bride. The ship you came in fell apart as you entered our atmosphere and blew up after you were able to exit it. All your worldly possessions were destroyed in the explosion."

"Which is what happened," she commented.

The confines of the small room weren't helping him at all. He picked up a whiff of something before realizing it was her. That unique scent all women had. He needed to get out of the room before he did something stupid like kiss her, so he headed back into the main room of his simple home. She followed right behind him.

"It's also believable because people will think the ship was probably old and shouldn't have made the flight in the first place." He gestured to a chair. "You did get banged about a bit and I'd like to examine you." He pulled out a pocket-sized scanner. "I'm a doctor, although on this planet

I've been known to take care of just about anything that moves. My supplies might not be able to bring your memory back, but I'd like to try."

She looked at the scanner before looking back at him. "It would be nice to remember again."

He nodded and led her to the far, right wall of his home, where he had all his medical supplies. He had already treated her other injuries when he first brought her to the house. The suit had protected much of her body, the gash on her head was about the only thing he could address. Kuarto would love to know how she got the nasty cut, then was still able to seal her suit properly before she lost her memories.

He checked the wound, happy with the way it was healing. In an hour or two it would be completely gone. The amnesia was a different story. After running a series of tests, he found it temporary, but everything he tried to reverse the problem didn't work.

"Well, I have good news and bad news. Everything looks good, but the memory loss is going to last a bit longer. I'll keep working on it, but I'm not sure how quickly I can fix your problem."

"So what does that mean?"

"You're going to be my guest a little longer."

———

Storm went through a few more last-minute checks before he was satisfied. "My heart, you really should sit while I do this."

"I'm fine." She checked the supplies she had asked for.

"Maybe so, but you are in the way." He swiveled his chair so he could check final flight information. "If you want to get airborne, you need to move out of the way."

She wanted to stick her tongue out at him but continued her own work instead. She had spoken to the doctor, and gotten a medical bag to carry, just in case she needed it. The doctor had given her most of the things she needed to help Toki if she was injured, and the training to use the equipment as well.

Heather had done her research and found that the undeveloped planet where Toki was last seen was very leery of anyone just showing up. They might be able to cloak one of the smaller ships, but not a large medical one. So Storm went along with them having a ship of their own. The larger medical ship would have to hang back as they went to the planet.

"It should take us about a day to get there." He snagged one arm and pulled her into his lap. "You have everything ready?"

"Like what?" She tried to look innocent.

He nuzzled her neck. "A certain something you promised me. It's the only reason you're coming along."

"You telling me that you have no use for me other than sex?" Her voice was soft, slightly seductive, and very serious.

"Of course not." He pulled back to look her in the eyes. "But you used sex to come with me. You could have used so many angles to make me bring you, and you know I would have gone along with it."

"True, but you know what I am capable of. You gave me a unilateral 'it's too dangerous' and you know how much I hate that." Her eyes grew wide as she realized how she had been manipulated. "You're evil."

"What are you talking about?" He played with the seam of her uniform.

"You did that on purpose because you knew I would come up with the one thing you always want to make you bring me along with you."

"You're my mate, so wouldn't pleasing me be part of what you want to do, anyway?" He smiled at her. It was the one he normally gave her when he thought he had the upper hand.

She had no answer but knew she would get her revenge. He liked to play games and she had gotten very good at winning these little matches. "Whatever you say."

He didn't like the way she gave in. It always meant trouble.

TWO

uapo arrived right after they ate. Kuarto had barely put the plates into the sink, and the man was at their door. He would swear the man had his house bugged if he didn't constantly sweep for things like that. Guapo brought a potent alcohol that was popular among the local natives and something Kuarto had avoided as much as he could. Guess tonight he'd have to see how well he could withstand the effects he had heard the alcohol caused.

Guapo poured the three of them a drink and lifted his cup in a toast. "To you and your bride, Doc."

"Thanks." He lifted his glass as well but didn't drink. He was still going to avoid it as much as he could. Kuarto wanted his wits with him with this man around. Especially with the way Toki was downing the contents in one gulp. She had no clue what she was doing. "Sweetheart, you might want to take your time on that."

"I'll be fine." She smiled as she took the refill and drank it the same way. At the rate she was inhaling the alcohol, she wouldn't be worth a thing when he needed her to keep her wits about her.

"That stuff is kind of potent."

"It's okay, really."

He shook his head, hoping Guapo would leave before she said or did something she shouldn't. He wondered why he was there in the first place. There was no way he was there to help them celebrate their union.

"Doc, there is a friend of mine coming for a visit who wants to meet with you tomorrow. Can I bring him here?"

"What does he want?" Guapo always had an agenda. The man he spoke of was probably not of the best caliber, especially if he worked with Guapo. He always seemed to know the seedier side of the galaxy and had already tried to get Kuarto involved several times.

"Not sure." He picked up his drink with a smile as he watched Toki continue to down her drinks. "He has something he thinks you might be interested in and wants to show it to you."

"I guess." He became suspicious immediately. How did this guy know he would be interested in anything? What did he know? This was when he would normally run. He had done it before, and if it wasn't for his guest, he'd do it again. Now he felt trapped.

He had to go along for the time being, but he wasn't happy about it. Kuarto also wasn't sure if he wanted this man to come to his home, but since Guapo had already set up everything, the man probably already knew where he was, so moving the meeting to another location would just raise questions.

"Good. I'll bring him first thing." Guapo kept looking at a timepiece, making Kuarto suspicious.

Kuarto pulled his scanner out of his pocket and scanned his drink. He didn't see anything out of the ordinary other than watered-down alcohol.

"What's the matter, Doc?" Guapo suddenly looked nervous.

"I know you too well. I can see you watered down the

drinks." He watched the slimy little man for a second before he ran his scanner over Toki's drink as well. It was heavily laced with some sort of chemical. Kuarto glared at him as he picked up her cup and dashed the rest of the contents out the window he sat next to. "What did you do?"

"I thought she might need some relaxation, you know, so this evening would go well." He tried to look innocent, but Kuarto would have none of it.

"You were hoping to get her so aroused she'd take you on as well you mean." He stood, his seven-foot-eight frame towering over Guapo's seated six-foot-one. Kuarto put his face inches from his so Guapo could see how angry he was. "Get out now, while I still let you walk."

"Hey, meant no disrespect, Doc." He hadn't moved, so Kuarto grabbed him by the neckline of his tunic and hauled him to his feet. "I can still bring my friend by tomorrow, right?"

"Honestly? I don't want to see your face for a few days, so you work that one out on your own." He dragged him to the door. "Out."

"But—"

"Now!"

The man slinked off into the night.

He turned back to his guest. Her eyes were taking on a definite glassy look. The drug must have taken effect.

"What was in that?" She gave him a goofy grin. "Sure has a relaxing effect on me."

"You've been given an aphrodisiac." He wondered how long it would take her to pass out on him.

"Interesting." She stretched. "They normally don't affect me."

His brow creased. Was her memory suddenly coming back? "How would you know?"

"It's always been that way." She paused as she realized what she said. "I remember that."

"What else do you remember?" He stepped up to her. Her eyes had cleared a bit.

"I know my name isn't Toki although a lot of people call me that."

"So what is your name?" He found standing so close to her just made him aware of how good she smelled. He knew she didn't wear any sort of fragrance, but there was something about her essence that made him want to stay close.

"I don't remember." She reached out and ran her fingers through his hair. "Your hair is beautiful. A deep brown I've never seen before. It's not as black as mine, but I like that."

"Um, let's get back to what you do remember." The physical contact was intimate and had him wanting her too easily. He needed to move away from her, but for some reason he couldn't get his feet to listen to him.

"Sure." Her hands touched his face, then slid down his neck to the top of his collar.

"You mentioned you knew the aphrodisiac wouldn't work on you?" He had to clear his voice to keep it from cracking. Her wandering hands made his whole body catch on fire. "Why?"

She found the seam of his shirt and opened it. Her fingers slid against his skin, the soft tips leaving a trail of arousal wherever they touched. "Not sure. A snippet of a memory from when I broke my arm. They tried to give me something for the pain, but it didn't work."

The scan he did showed a childhood break on her left arm, and as much as he wanted to grasp on to that and use it to steer them to safer ground, he couldn't seem to do anything but pray she touched him some more.

Her lips followed the trail her fingers had made. He felt it deep inside, making him painfully hard. It had been too long since he had been with anyone. What was he thinking? No matter what she said about drugs not affecting her, he saw how much she ingested and knew it had to be causing this.

But the moment she peeled her dress off and stood in front of him naked, he lost all willpower.

His hands had a mind of their own when they started to explore her lean, well-muscled body. Kuarto knew by the shape of it that she took good care of herself. It always amazed him at how soft the skin could feel knowing the depth of the muscle. Hers felt like velvet against his fingertips. Her breasts, soft and pliant, begged for his lips. The heat of his mouth brought a shudder from her.

"That feels so good." Her voice sounded deeper, laced with desire.

He liked it when his partner told him what they wanted. That way, he didn't have to guess. They had worked their way to his bed, and he found he was the one being eased into it instead of the other way around.

She was in control, and he wasn't sure if he wanted to fight her. She knew what she was doing and what she wanted. Her smile was bright as she straddled him and eased herself down on his hardened staff. He heard her sigh as he filled her. Her body shuddered once again as she settled herself on him. If this was any indication, it had been a while for her too.

She set a pace she felt driven to, sliding up and down his shaft with a fever he felt himself. Kuarto gripped her hips, helping to keep her from moving too fast. They strived for release together, with Kuarto taking control. He didn't want her to hit her climax too soon. Everything intensified as he moved within her. Her muscles constricted, gripping him like a vise he didn't want to be released from.

Then he felt them. "No, not now."

The two who messed with his life were feeling a little randy, and he would be caught up in the moment quickly. Why couldn't they just leave him alone?

———

Storm sat in his command chair, making sure everything was set up properly. He had three ships following his, and he had to be sure everything was going according to plan.

Especially if he got his way. He didn't want to have to stop pleasuring his mate to have to deal with something going wrong.

Heather had asked him to make sure all the cameras were off earlier, so he had hope. She wouldn't have asked him to turn them off if they weren't going to be intimate.

He hadn't seen Heather in the last half an hour or so. She had been trained as his second in command as well as a medical liaison for the doctor, and she was very good at her job. Although he thought she would have been done a while ago, she had remained busy. When he did finally see her, he was surprised to see her fully dressed.

"Problem?" He had hoped to have her naked and under him by this point.

"No problem, sir." She addressed him as her senior yet gave him the sultry smile of his mate. What was she up to? "Just have to make sure a few things are done before I turn my attention to you."

He wasn't sure why she would say that unless she was trying to get back at him for his comments earlier. She disappeared from sight again for a moment before she popped her head out. "So have you taken care of your end of the deal?"

Storm wasn't sure what she was speaking about until he saw one of her arms, encased in a lace sleeve, wrap itself around the door frame. She had gotten out of her uniform already? He hit one button and smiled at her in anticipation. "Of course."

"Good." She had gone back into the room, taking her time and making him feel his need more. "Now, remember, you can't touch until I say so."

He had been waiting so long all he wanted to do was grab her and have his way with her, but she always gave him such a thrill with these outfits, so he stayed in his command chair, gripping the armrests hard. "And if I disagree?"

"You want me to answer that?" She popped her head out of the room she had absconded to. He still couldn't see anything. "Didn't you learn the answer to that about a month ago?"

"I hate it when you threaten me like that."

"I promise you will enjoy the outcome, my heart. I just know you, and I need to be sure you won't move when I come out of this room."

"You saying this outfit is better than the red one?" He sat forward in anticipation.

"That one has always been your favorite, but you know I strive to come up with something you'll like better."

"That was my favorite because of when you did it. It will be hard to surpass that moment." He closed his eyes as the memory washed over him. "You whipped open the simple dress and exposed something that got my undivided attention and made me wish I wasn't someone of such high recognition."

"And that is my goal every time. I want to make you forget who you are for just a moment." She dimmed the lights and stepped out of the room so he couldn't see what she had on easily.

"You know that's not fair." He stood.

"I'm just setting the mood." She took a step toward him.

"I don't need any mood lighting, my heart."

"You sure?" She pointed at his clothes. "I can't tell with that uniform on you."

"You're right. It does kind of hamper things, doesn't it?" He pulled the uniform off and sat back down in his command chair. "Did I tell you I had this chair made for us?"

"Us?" She walked toward him slowly.

"It has these great features I created since I had hoped for moments like this." He pressed a pedal with his foot and the arms of the chair slid back and down. A perfect place for her to place her legs when she straddled him, which was one of her favorite positions.

"I see." She came close enough for him to see her outfit and paused. She held her breath as she watched his reaction. It took her a while to settle on this look, knowing he would say he loved it because he loved the fact that she went out of her way to create these titillating outfits. His desire to see her happy would have him saying he loved a burlap sack if she were to wear one. As long as he got her body afterwards.

He stood as he took in the outfit. The whole thing was made of see-through black lace. The two pieces didn't cover much except her arms. The lace covered from shoulder to about halfway down her palms. It even had a small hole in the sleeves for her thumbs. The top was off the shoulder, hugging her across the collarbone, then falling softly against her breasts. She felt it exposed a bit much of the bottom of her breasts, but it didn't look right if she extended it or made it hug her. So she ended up leaving it alone.

Storm didn't say a word as he walked up to her. His hands skimmed along the edge of the lace top, grazing the soft tissue showing just below the material. His hands slid down her bare abdomen to the slight scrap of lace covering her hips. The material was a stretchy lace that hugged her like a skirt.

She had been afraid it would ride up as she moved, but it sat on her like a second skin, barely covering her mound in the front, and exposing a touch of her derriere in the back. She was so grateful there was no one else on the ship who could inadvertently walk in on them. She wasn't sure how she would have reacted if someone had.

He wrapped one hand behind her neck and pulled her to him, capturing her lips with his. The thrill from his quick movement sent a spark racing along her veins. His tongue plunged into her mouth, his desire for her evident. His fingers skirted along the edge of the material on her hips. They skimmed the inside of her thighs until he found her heat.

Her knees quaked a little as he slipped a finger or two up inside her.

He broke the kiss as he lifted her and carried her to the command chair. He climbed into the chair and sat her feet on each side of it.

"This is a beautiful outfit. One of my favorites." He pulled her onto his lap, impaling her in the process. His eyes closed for a moment as the tightness of her sheath gripped him, taking his breath away. "You can wear this to greet me every day and you'll get the same reaction each time."

He placed his hands on her hips, helping her set a pace they both would like.

"Better than the red?" She tilted her head back as she got swept up in the emotions encompassing her. Each thrust filled her to the hilt, each time inching her closer to release. Her body shook with need. Every time they came together, the mental bond between them got stronger.

"Same as the red." He kissed her cheeks, one at a time. A soft, chaste kiss as desire spiraled around them. His lips then claimed hers as he felt her body clench and rocket out of control.

———

Kuarto felt his mind partner's release grab him as Toki reached hers. It was an amazing thing to experience. Toki griped him in a vise-like hold that made his body shake as he felt his orgasm start to build. Feeling both was a powerful thing, and he was riding on the wave that would bring him to his release. It had been a while, so he knew it would be quick and overpowering. It started deep inside, muscles tightened and became stretched. The center of his want blossomed, filling him with a delicious shiver. His body quivered, and he felt the world rock as he hit his climax.

He gasped as everything around him faded and he could only feel the free-fall sensation that filled him. Wind rushed past his face, danced along his body, making him feel pure joy flow through him. He had never felt a release this profound. It had to be his little mind guests' fault, but this time instead of wishing they would leave him alone he reveled in it.

Toki sighed as she regained herself. "That was wonderful."

"Glad you enjoyed it." He started to pull out and found himself locked in an embrace he couldn't break. She was deceptively strong for a woman.

"Where do you think you're going?" she asked, her question innocent.

"I was going to give you a break?"

"I don't want one. That felt too good for me not to want to do that again." She brushed a few strands of hair out of his face. "Unless you don't think you're up to it."

He could feel himself already growing hard. "Oh, honey, I'm up to it and this time I'm going to get more than a sigh out of you."

"Promise?"

He gave her a smile as he pulled her toward him so he could capture her lips with his again.

———

The next day, Kuarto sat in his office, waiting for Guapo to show up. He knew the man would have purposely forgotten he had been kicked out last night and would hope Kuarto wouldn't bring it up. Guapo's history told Kuarto he would be pushing for him to meet with this new friend of his. Kuarto wasn't sure why and that always made him leery.

Knowing this man might know who he truly was bothered him too, but now he'd just have to wait and watch.

He had told Toki to stay hidden until he sent for her. Hopefully, she would listen to him. He wanted to be sure she was safe. He also wanted to know just how much the man Guapo wanted him to meet knew about him. Find out how much danger he might be in.

Guapo walked in the door with a smile on his face. If anything, the man was punctual. Kuarto could see the glimmer of fear in his eyes. Guapo was hoping he had forgotten that he had kicked him out the night before. There was no hope in that.

"Thought I told you I didn't want to see you today." He glared at the slimy little man.

Guapo swallowed hard and kept going like nothing was wrong. "I wish you to meet my friend."

"Go home and take your friend with you." He moved about his cramped office, dismissing Guapo. Now it was time to see what he would do.

He didn't seem happy with his comment, but instead of leaving, he just stepped aside as the man walked in.

The man who walked in didn't fit any kind of look Kuarto would have expected. He was average height with fair skin. His light clothing was clean and expensive looking, well-kept blonde hair, eyes shielded by dark glasses. Kuarto wasn't sure what he expected, but it wasn't this smallish man.

"I'm sorry he has caused trouble for you. Anything I can take care of?"

"He insulted me and my bride last night. Doubt you can fix that." Kuarto stood a good head taller than this man. He sat at his cluttered desk, ignoring them as he pretended to work on a few files.

"True, but I do have my ways." He looked at Guapo who shook in his boots. "Don't I?"

"What do you want from me?" What kind of power did he have to make Guapo afraid? Kuarto wasn't about to give him the upper hand, so he greeted him the way he always greeted strangers. He looked up from where he sat and glared at the man.

"I have heard you are the best doctor in these parts."

"And where did you hear that?" He pulled a few more documents up and filed them so they wouldn't block any other work he needed to focus on and waited to hear what he feared most.

"Around. Understand you were the best ever until you ran away from it all." The man looked about his place like he had walked into the most non-sterile environment he had ever been in.

The man knew far more than he should. Kuarto had worked hard to keep his real past hidden, yet this guy knew things he didn't want as common knowledge. But he wasn't going to give him the satisfaction of showing a reaction. "You don't impress me."

"I have something I think you might find fascinating."

"Doubt it." He wondered how fast he could get his guest to pack. They might have to get off the planet quickly.

"Try me." He handed him a chip.

Kuarto looked at the chip, then at the man before he inserted it into his computer. He watched a file pop up and opened it. Data streamed onto his screen as images started to load. The readings were off the scale. This embryo or egg was perfect, flawless. Something he would be excited to work on under other circumstances. He tried to act nonchalant. "Where did you get this?"

"You don't need to worry about that as long as it's mine."

"And you have proof?" He looked at the man before turning his attention back to the data, amazed at its perfection. In all his years, he had never seen anything quite like it. "Considering this is an egg and you're not female, I find it hard to believe that it's yours unless you grew this in a lab."

"It doesn't matter since I am in possession of it, does it?" His attitude made Kuarto look at him again. Did he think Kuarto was going to drop to his knees and beg to be able to work on this?

"It does if you want me to help you with it." He popped the chip out.

"Keep that. There's nothing on there I don't mind sharing. Once you work your way through the data, maybe you will want to speak to me." He noticed movement behind the door, which made Kuarto look in the same direction.

Guapo was the one who made matters worse when he stepped into the other room and dragged Toki into the room. "This is the doctor's new bride."

The man's whole demeanor changed when he saw her. He stiffened, narrowing his eyes at her. Did he know who she was? He sure wasn't happy to see her. "You wanted a Vespian bride?"

"I wasn't specific, so that was what I was sent." He sat back in his chair and watched a myriad of emotions run across the man's face before he slapped a smile on. Who was she, and what did she mean to him?

"Well, I'm happy for you." He turned to go.

"You can have your chip back if you want it." Kuarto was pretty sure he did, so was surprised when the man shook his head.

"No. You keep it. Let me know what you think." He looked at Toki once more before he turned and walked out.

He waited until they were well out of earshot before he spoke. "So what is it about you that upset him so much?"

"Don't know." She shrugged her shoulders. "He doesn't look familiar, but maybe we should ask him."

"No." He put a hand on her arm when she started toward the door. "He didn't seem happy to see you, so I'm thinking it's not a good idea to pursue that train of thought."

"But if he knows something…"

"We know nothing about him and knowing he's working with Guapo has me questioning his motives. I'm not sure if I would trust him."

She looked at the man and sighed before she looked back at Kuarto and nodded.

"I know you want to know who you are, but I don't think he's the best source for that information right now." He wished he could do or say something to make her feel better. It would drive him crazy if he had no clue what his life had been like thirty-six hours earlier.

She looked so forlorn he reacted instinctively and took her into his arms. She sighed as she leaned into him for support. "This is all so strange to me. What if I'm some sort of evil person?"

"That's easy to prove. Come work with me today." He should be packing up everything to get out of there, but so many people relied on him. Kuarto needed to make these last few calls before he left. He brushed a few strands of hair out of her face. "I think that will make you realize what type of person you are."

"Why?"

"Because I'm a doctor, remember? I do nothing but help people, and if you find that rewarding, then you're a good person."

She gave him a strange look. "I'm not sure I agree with that."

"You willing to prove me wrong?" He gave her his best smile. Leaving her behind wouldn't be smart, anyway, so this would keep her with him.

"I guess so."

"Good." He steered her to the row of cabinets. "I need you to load those bags with the gauze and bandages that are in this cabinet. When you're done, I'll let you know what else I need done so we can go visit some of my clients."

They worked together to gather everything he needed and then headed out to his barn. He opened the doors to expose his truck.

"What is that?" Her eyes sparkled with excitement at the sight of his truck.

"Transportation." He grinned. Knowing she was impressed with it stroked his pride.

"I have never seen anything like that before." She walked around the vehicle slowly.

"Probably not." He caressed a fender gently. "I converted it from diesel fuel to solar cells. I also replaced the tires with magnets so it would use the magnetic core of the planet to be propelled along. Come on, you'll love it."

He opened the door for her and helped her in. He leaned in to snap the straps to secure her in, his fingers grazing the soft skin under her arm. It sent a jolt of desire straight into his brain. It took all his strength to keep his composure as he checked the straps.

Once he was sure she was secure, he walked around and climbed in his side. It took him a minute to regain control. He couldn't look at her as he started the truck up, but the engine came to life at the flick of a switch and he grinned again. The sound of the purring engine never got old. Reversing the gears, he backed the truck out of the garage before easing it into drive. He didn't have to worry about traffic, so he flew down the dirt road worn into the ground by the travel of animals and other equipment.

She squealed a few times as he took a few corners a little sharper than he should have, but when he looked over she had the same happy look he had when he drove this for the first time. It didn't matter how old the vehicle was. There was a certain joy in driving, feeling the wind in his hair.

"I could get used to this."

"It's addictive, isn't it?" He had to shout to be heard over the noise of the engine. "Somehow, the man I bought the house from had this in his garage and had kept it in good condition. I was able to convert it where he could only maintain it. It has taken me several years to get it where it is now. It was a devil to drive in the beginning, trying to find the fuel was the biggest obstacle, but as I was able to convert it slowly, things started to make sense. I found so many things I could change to make it better."

"Can I drive it?"

It was his baby, and he wasn't sure if he wanted to share it with anyone, but the look on her face had to be close to the look he had when he first realized what the truck was. "Okay, but you have to treat it with respect."

"Promise."

He pulled the truck over and turned the engine off. It took him a few seconds before he could talk himself into relinquishing the seat. "Sorry, I never had to share before."

"If you don't want to." She hadn't moved yet.

"I don't go back on my word." He opened the door and waited for her to climb out.

"Are you sure?" She fiddled with the snap, not figuring out how to release it. He pressed a small button in the center of the metal clasp.

"Yes." He watched her climb out, so he did the same. Kuarto got into the passenger seat and closed the door.

Toki sat there for a few moments before she started the engine. It didn't take her long before she figured out how to work the controls and had it flying down the road.

It sure was a different sensation, being the passenger than the driver. He feared for his life a few times in their travels. He gave her directions to their first destination, happy when she finally turned the engine off.

The smile on her face made him forget his fear. He knew

what put that smile there. He had felt the same thing the first time he drove it.

"Come on, we have work to do." They walked into the thatched roof house. There wasn't much to it. Maybe two rooms in total, a small hearth where the family did most of their cooking. The mattress was a pile of twigs covered by soft grass then a linen cloth. On the bed lay his patient.

"How are you doing today?" He knelt next to the simple bed, checking her readings. The small child looked pale. Much paler than the last time he saw her. This didn't make him happy. "You been taking your medication?"

"She has, Doc. I made sure of it." A young woman had walked in when they arrived. She stood in the doorway, wiping her hands. "She was fine until a few days ago. My husband felt she was ready to help with the chores again, so sent her into the fields. I went looking for her when she didn't come back after the sun set and found her unconscious."

It didn't make sense. If she was getting better, what had caused the relapse? "Show me."

"What?"

"Show me where you found her."

The mother nodded. He gave Toki a look that asked her to stay with the young girl. He headed out after the mother when Toki sat on the bed and spoke to the child quietly. The mother led him to a section near the woods. "This is where I found her."

He walked around the area. There had to be something that was causing this. "Is this where she's been working from the beginning?"

"I guess, but we've all been working here for the last few months. This is the latest area we've cleared to use for the farm."

"Thanks." He pulled out a handheld and started scanning.

"You think it's something here?"

"I'm not sure. If all of you have been here, and she's the only one who gets sick, it could be something else. But I don't want to dismiss anything like that until I'm sure." He moved about the area in small circles until he was able to reach the edge of the land and into the wooded area nearby.

"Okay." She scuffed her feet and looked around. "Is that your bride?"

"I see news travels fast." He gazed up from his readings long enough to look at her.

"There's not a lot to keep us entertained here, Doc. You know that. We all know when someone's cow or drebo gives birth."

"True." They always knew whose house he was at if there was an accident. "Guess I didn't think it through before I sent for a wife."

"Especially since we had a few single women here who were interested in you."

He looked at her again. "Really? Who?"

"Susan is one."

"Susan? Isn't she about sixteen?" He was almost twice her age. "I could be her father."

"Doesn't stop her from having a crush on the most hand-some man on the planet."

"Please." He felt he got all the scanning done, so he set the recorder to process the information to see what might be causing the problem. "You mentioned two."

"The other one will make you laugh."

"Oh, no." They headed back to her home. "Redanda? Isn't she about eighty?"

"Eighty-three but remember her race lives to over two hundred years, so she's still young."

He didn't have the heart to tell her he suspected he was also Vespian like his fake bride. He had the height and skin tone. His eyes weren't the bright golden tone he had seen on other Vespians and his hair wasn't jet black, but he still had the outer ring around his eyes that they had and his hair was the same texture. From what he had learned about the race from the few times he had helped members of Vespia taught him they lived at least three hundred years, so to him she did seem a lot older. He'd probably outlive her by one hundred and fifty years. "Then we'll just have to order her a husband."

"I believe she is one step ahead of you on that one. I heard her new husband would be arriving in a day or two. I think you inspired her because she's excited about his arrival."

"Good." He stepped into the room to find Toki sitting on the bed with the young girl. "Did you two have fun together?"

The young girl's eyes lit up as she held up something in her hands. "Look, Mommy. Toki taught me how to make a doll from things around the house."

She turned and gave the mother an apologetic smile. "I hope you don't mind. Your daughter said the scraps I used were going out with the refuse."

"Thank you for staying with her." She smiled as she took the doll from her daughter. The girl's smile changed mom's whole demeanor. "She is as beautiful as you are. Have you named her?"

"Aswee."

"Of course. Aswee is a beautiful name." She handed it back and patted her on the head. "Take good care of her."

The young girl hugged her doll.

Toki stood and crossed to Kuarto's side. He leaned over and spoke softly into her ear. "You aren't evil."

She looked down as his words sunk in. He could feel her relief, then he heard a beep and lifted his handheld. "What I thought. There is some draxinia there. It doesn't harm adults, but it can cause children to get sick. To keep her healthy, you and your husband must be the ones to clear that area and you need to decontaminate yourselves before you're around her."

"You know, we have always needed her help in the fields." The mom looked worried.

He did. They were growing, but at a pace they could handle. His concern was what she might inhale in that spot. If she continued to get sick, he might not be able to reverse the damage. "Where is your husband right now?"

"In the northern section. He's working on clearing some rock out of an area we hadn't spotted before."

"Have him come by when he gets a chance so I can explain what is going on with your daughter." He smiled as he laid a reassuring hand on her shoulder. "I'm sure there is a way to get her healthy and still have her help with the farm."

She nodded her relief. "We'll be around this evening, then."

———

Heather watched as Storm set everything up for their approach to the planet where his sister's ship went down. The doctor had already confirmed she was on the planet and healthy. She had been moving about the place all morning.

Heather noticed Storm's more relaxed posture. He wasn't worried about what he would find when he arrived anymore. A slight chirp filled the room. Heather looked up. Storm hit a button, and the doctor filled the screen. "Sorry to disturb you, sir, but we just received a mayday call from another ship."

"Is it one of ours?" Storm didn't even look up.

"No, sir."

"Then send a message to the nearest ship of their race." He felt Heather's hand on his arm. "Hang on, Doctor." He cut the sound and looked at her. He cut the visual at her determined look. "What do you think you are doing?"

"I know I am overstepping my boundaries, but are you going to leave those people out there when we're the closest? What if it is an Earth ship with whom you just signed a treaty? How do you think that would look?"

"Heather."

"I know this isn't the Vespian way, but you need to think beyond that ideal now." She knew she was close to pushing him over the edge, but she had to try to get him to see things differently. "This is a chance to show other races that Vespians can have a heart. You can still keep to yourselves. Helping a distressed ship doesn't break your laws."

"So now you want me to suddenly retract my command?"

"All you said was send a message to the race's people. You haven't given any other command."

"They will know you did this."

"Isn't helping you think things through part of my job as your mate? Your other half?"

The frown on his face would have frightened anyone else. Heather knew better. He always seemed so angry when she interrupted him, but in the end she always got that bone-melting smile. Her heart beat a little harder when it finally appeared. He pointed to her clothes. "If we do this the uniform comes off again. That chair has more positions for us to try."

"We don't know how far that ship is." She didn't have a problem with his demand. Anything to help those people. "What if it is only minutes away?"

He turned the sound back on. "Have you contacted the race?"

"Yes. They are two weeks out. Sir, if we don't help them, they could all die. Their ship was hit with a blast that is venting their atmosphere." He sent the stats over to their ship. Heather put them up on the main screen. "They have about twelve hours of air left. If we head there at max speed, we could be helping them in three hours and be back here in twelve."

Storm kept his features clear, but she knew he was feeling cornered. She touched his mind softly. *You can turn this so you won't lose face. I've seen you do it.*

"Doctor, it isn't our normal procedure to help others, but we also can't ignore people in need. We've been making strides to work with the people in this galaxy, and this is our next step." He reset their coordinates to take them to the ship in distress. "You are in charge of this. They are not to know any other ships are with you."

"Of course." He breathed a sigh of relief. "Thank you, sir."

"You're welcome." He turned the screen off and looked at his mate. "The uniform?"

She gave him a sultry smile. "Thought you'd want to take it off me."

———

Kuarto headed back to the truck. Placing his gear in the bed of his vehicle, he turned and waited for Toki. The way she worked with that girl while he was gone was wonderful. She joined him a few moments later. "Aswee?"

"I know, she wanted a name and that was all I could come with."

He opened the passenger door for her. "Hope you don't mind, but the next stop is a bit tricky to get to so I'd rather drive."

"That's fine." She climbed into the cab. "Maybe I could drive again later?"

"I should be able to arrange that as long as we can keep to the schedule I have set." He started it up and headed toward the mountains that loomed ahead. "How did you know how to make the doll?"

"My uncle taught me." She grabbed his arm. "I have an uncle."

"Remember anything else?" Bits and pieces were coming to her, so she should get her memory back, but he didn't know what it would take for her to get everything to return.

"Um, no." She watched the scenery whiz by. "The moment I realize I remember something it all goes away."

"Don't try so hard to remember next time. We'll have to come up with a series of questions that might stimulate your memory more than shut everything down."

"Where are we going, anyway?"

"To the mines. This planet is rich in slyostica."

"Never heard of that."

"It's a crystal used in most of Earth's replicating technology." He pointed to a small black hole in the side of the mountain. "We go in there and travel down several miles. You're not afraid of small places, are you?"

"Don't know." She watched as the hole grew bigger. "Guess I'll find out pretty soon, won't I?"

He grinned. "Sure will." He steered the truck closer to the cavern opening, working his way through the tight walls of the ravine that led to the cave he had to park the truck in.

His mind started to wander on him. Kuarto had to shake his head to get his focus back. Weird sensations began to overpower him. He felt strong desire flow through him. Crap. They were at it again and it was broad daylight for him.

He tried to fight it but found himself overwhelmed.

"Take the wheel." Kuarto felt the beginning of her orgasm, and he was in the middle of maneuvering his truck into the tight space of a ravine. He was losing touch with what he was doing because of them.

Toki looked at him. "What?"

"Now, do it now." His eyes rolled up into the back of his head.

"What the—" She didn't have time to react to anything else. Grabbing the steering wheel, she tried to level it back off so they wouldn't hit a canyon wall.

THREE

S torm stepped up to Heather. "Each time you challenge me like that I try to teach you not to do it in front of other people. Yet you never seem to learn."

"Guess I'm just a little hardheaded." She watched him, noting his eyes were filled with desire for her.

"A little?" He walked behind her and brushed her hair away from her throat. "You're as hardheaded as I am hard for you all the time."

"Ha! You sure you're not just a little harder?" She reached back and rubbed her hand across his crotch. The uniform might hide what was there, but she knew better.

"Woman." His mouth was just inches from her neck. His breath stirred the delicate hairs on her throat. "I guess I'll just have to teach you another lesson in obedience." He released the collar area of her uniform so he could nuzzle her throat like he loved to do. "You do seem to enjoy them."

"Almost as much as you enjoy teaching me." She tried to turn so she could face him.

"Sorry, but you have no say in what happens. That's part of your punishment." He eased the seal of her suit down further to where he could see the soft tissue of her breasts rise and fall with each excited breath. "You will just stand there and take it like a woman. My woman."

She could only lick her lips in anticipation.

His teeth grazed the soft tissue near her collar bone. "I want you to move to the chair."

Heather didn't want to move. Her body quivered in anticipation. Then he stopped. She looked up at him in confusion.

"Move to the chair and I will continue, but until then, nothing." She reached for him and he stepped out of the way. "I mean it."

So he wanted to prove a point. She walked to the chair and straddled it. Feet planted firmly on either side. Then she planted her hands on her hips and turned back to give him another sultry look.

He was pleased by her movement, yet he hadn't taken a step toward her. What was he waiting for? A sigh escaped her.

"Bored, my heart?"

"With you, never, just trying to figure out your strategy." She stood there, proud and waiting. "You always have one when I overstep my boundaries."

"True." He did move closer then. "And you always seem to forget your place."

"I never forget that." He always fought these things even when he knew she was right.

"Then why do you question me when you know you shouldn't?" He stepped up to her, his face inches from hers.

"Was I wrong to bring up the information I did?" He used these tactics on others and they were always frightened, but she knew he did it to show his frustration. Storm would never hurt her. "Do you truly believe we should have left those people to their own devices?"

"No." He backed off a bit.

"Did I say anything while you spoke to the doctor?" At

least he was admitting the truth now. "Did they see me touch you?"

"I doubt it." He moved around her. "I have the cameras angled a certain way in case they were to try to contact us while we were engaged."

"Then why the anger?" She marveled at how he thought of everything to make sure her modesty stayed intact. "Have I ever done anything to make you look bad in the eyes of any other Vespian? Haven't I always been the good little mate who never questions her man? At least not in public. Why don't you trust me to do what is right when it is right?"

"I do." He moved close enough to touch her heart. "You make me feel things I have never thought possible. I fear that all you need to do is look at me a certain way and I will crumble at your feet and it won't matter who sees."

"Storm." She touched his face, understanding his confusion and wishing she could erase it. "That is what love does to you. I know the word love doesn't translate into Vespian very well, but it is the only word I can come up with. It grips you hard and makes you realize that nothing matters more than the happiness of the one you care for. I gave up all I knew to be with you because of the love I have for you."

"My father was always a strong man. I never saw any weakness in the way he dealt with my mother." He still saw his feelings as a weakness. She needed to get him to see it wasn't.

"Love makes you strong, not weak." She unsealed his uniform so she could touch his heart. The heat of his chest penetrated her hand. "It just changes you so much you fear what is happening. And that is what drives your anger, fear."

His golden eyes gazed into her soft violet ones. She could see the emotions at war with one another. He had been raised to always be in control, but so had she. She had learned to lock her feelings away after she had heard enough of the cruel things that were said to her because she was so different. That training came in handy now. She could talk to him without letting emotions get in the way. Hopefully, make him see love was a glorious thing, not something to fear.

"You have accepted everything so easily. How?" He used his other hand to touch her face. His fingers brushed her cheeks before they wrapped around the back of her neck.

"Because I don't show my emotions. I keep it all locked up inside. That's why I can put up with you so well."

That brought a snort out of him. His other hand eased the seam of her uniform open all the way down. She mimicked his move.

"Would you have left your world if they hadn't ordered you to?"

"Now that isn't a fair question. I knew you maybe a day or two. The question is whether or not I planned on going back home once the treaty was signed."

"Did you?" She saw that slight spark of fear enter his eyes when he asked that question.

"What do you think?" She had eased his uniform open enough that she could wrap her hand around his hard member. "Did I ever once say anything that would make you think I would want to leave you?"

"No." He tilted his head back and closed his eyes at the contact. "But you weren't given much choice."

"That's because I chose to stay."

He opened his eyes as he studied her face. She never kept anything from him, especially now that they could share parts of their thoughts. Their bond grew stronger every day and soon he'd be able to access anything he wanted.

He pulled her face to his and captured her mouth, his tongue pressing for entrance which she gave gladly. His need to dominate was so strong she could taste it in his kiss. Her uniform gone, his hands traveled up and down her body, touching and playing in all the right places to bring her arousal to a white-hot flame.

Her body quaked with need and her hand shook just trying to remove his uniform. She couldn't do it with the same quick precision he did.

He picked her up, cradling her to his chest. Storm moved to the command chair and sat down. From the way his leg muscle moved, she was sure his foot pressed a metal pedal. A slight hiss of air and he grinned down at her. Gently, he laid her on the footrest, which had now risen to be level with the seat. The back of the chair slid down and back, giving Storm a comfortable place to kneel.

He lifted her legs, so he was in between them, then surged into her. The angles built into the chair put her hips at just the right spot. She didn't need to angle herself to allow him better penetration. He went in deep and her body shook.

"Storm." It was all she could say before everything shattered around her. Wow, that didn't take long. That white-hot flame consumed her, burning away everything but the joy of her release. Her body gripped him, causing delicious shivers to race through his blood as he continued to move in and out of her. Another wave started to hit her with his movements. She arched against him as this one crested and carried her away.

He pumped faster, his breath coming out in harsh gasps. "My heart." And he lost control. He pushed into her deeper and faster, his legs jerking a little as his orgasm grabbed him and sent him soaring. He lay on top of her, his heart beating hard. He placed soft kisses on her eyes, her cheeks, then took her lips with his in a long leisurely kiss. "We're taking this chair home with us."

She laughed, a deep throaty laugh that had him getting hard again. "You sure it's the chair and not the mind sharing?"

"Oh, the mind sharing has something to do with it." He

nibbled on her throat. "But this chair made everything fit perfectly. Even now, I'm at an angle so I don't have to break contact for me to play with certain parts of your body I couldn't reach before."

"You calling me short again?" She gave him a mock glare. "I could start calling you giant man."

He pushed himself up on his elbows and grinned. "I like that. Everyone will know how large I am."

"Not what I meant." His mouth closed on one peak and brought an "Oh" out of her.

"See?" He licked it, watching it pebble up under his ministrations. "Before I had to leave the warmth of your body to pay homage to your breasts."

"I think I do," she said, her voice slightly breathless. She was beginning to like the chair too.

———

"Why didn't you tell me you had a medical condition?" Toki yelled at his unconscious form. Fear gripped her as she struggled to maneuver the truck. She cringed as she scraped the left wall. He wasn't going to be happy about that. "Damn it, wake up! I can't do this alone."

He started to come to, although still dazed for a few seconds. The moment he saw a large rock formation looming ahead and the fact they were heading right for it, he jerked the wheel to the right and moved the truck out of the way.

"Pull over," she shouted at him over the noise of the engine.

"What?"

"Pull over." She pulled the wheel enough to get him to find a safe place and stop.

"What is wrong with you?" He glared at her.

"With me?" She grabbed his hand and placed it over her heart. "You feel that? That's a heart beating in fear. Why didn't you tell me you had a medical condition that could incapacitate you at any moment?"

"I wish it was that easy." He turned the engine off. He stared out at the rocky horizon. "I have suddenly picked up some sort of mind meld."

"How would that cause you to black out the way you did? Your eyes rolled up into the back of your head. Scared me half to death."

"The meld only happens when the couple's being intimate. Right at the moment they have an orgasm I'm invited to attend. Can't fight it. Believe me, I've tried. Most of the time it happens early to late evening, so there is no real danger. I'm assuming it has something to do with their planet's cycle. It's never happened this early."

"Just how far away is this mind link coming from?"

"I don't know. I haven't been able to get a whole lot from my counterparts while we're connected. I do know they are mates. There's an intimacy between them that goes beyond casual sex and I'm connected to the woman, but I feel both." It felt good to finally tell someone.

"Both? Really?" She seemed fascinated by it. "So she must have a bond with her mate and somehow you got sucked into it all?"

"That's the best I can come up with."

"Interesting." She climbed out of her side of the truck, walked around the front, and opened his door. "Get out. I'm driving."

"What?"

"You just said you never know when it's going to happen. What if they're just taking a breather?" She held onto the door and waited for him to move.

He wanted to argue with her, but he knew she was right. What she had said had happened at least once before. It took him a moment or two before he slid out of the seat. "Only because I don't want you or my truck...what happened?" He stopped when he spotted the damage, rubbing his hands against the scratched fender.

"Unconscious man behind the wheel with a scared to death woman trying to steer from the other side of the vehicle. Be glad that was all that happened." She slammed the door shut and started the engine back up. "Where to?"

"We can go back."

"These people are expecting you and as long as you're not doing some sort of surgery, I should be able to cover for you if it happens again. Let's go."

The sun was setting by the time they made it back to his home. He fixed a quick meal with her help, and they were ready for their guests.

She was quiet while they waited.

"You okay?"

"Yes." She smiled at him. "Sorry, I was just wondering what it would be like to have the problem you do. You feel their release, right?"

"Oh, yeah." He felt uncomfortable talking about what was happening to him. His desire for her would be magnified when he tried to explain the mind meld. Even now, it was making him think about sex with her.

"Do you have one as well?"

He didn't want to answer.

"Sorry. I didn't mean to embarrass you." She walked to the window and looked out, not saying anything else.

He knew it was only natural curiosity. If anyone else had found out he would have been hit with a whole lot more questions. "No. I get the erection, but then I'm stuck with it until I can do something about it or it finally goes away."

"I have seen no evidence of a woman here." She turned from the window.

"That's because I have been celibate since I moved here. That's one of the reasons this has become a problem for me." He saw the flash just before it entered the room. He dove for her, pulling her down and away from the window.

She glared up at him, his weight pressing her down into the floor.

"Stay put." He inched to a small panel near the door. He pressed one button and heard a satisfying yelp. Kuarto knew he should have had the force field on before but Toki distracted him. "We should be fine now."

He stood and walked out the door. She could hear him shouting at whoever took a shot at them. He was positive it was Guapo by his tone. Kuarto came in with a smile on his face. "Don't think he'll do that again."

"You don't seem upset."

"That man is an idiot and a bad shot. He's also tried this before, not with me," he added when she looked at him in shock. "But he has a history of trying to frighten people when he doesn't get his way and is never successful."

"What about the family you asked to visit? Is it safe for them to come?"

"Guapo's already long gone. He isn't known for sticking around once he has been found out. The force field I activated will keep him at a safe distance if he tries again." He pressed a few keys on the panel he had accessed earlier. "But to be safe, I have programmed our guests' DNA into the system so they can pass through where that bane in my side can't."

Toki thought about his erection. If they weren't going to have guests any minute, she would offer herself. He was a wonderful lover and had enjoyed being with her last night, yet she knew he would never press the issue again because of his celibacy. She would always have to be the aggressor.

Knowing he could possibly always have a hard-on could work in her favor. She felt the thrill of the hunt race through her. Now all she had to do was get past any defenses he might throw up to get in her way.

The young girl and her parents arrived and Toki sat and played with the child while Kuarto spoke to the parents. It took him some time to convince them to see what danger they were putting her in and agree to try to keep her out of the area, or make sure she had an environmental suit on if she was to work there.

He offered them some of the meal they had made, but they begged off and headed back home.

"Do they know of your problem?" she asked as they left.

"What?" He looked at her. "No."

"They sure flew out of here like they did. Or they knew something was about to happen." Her eyes widened when she realized she recognized the pattern. Another tiny part of her brain unlocked.

"I have my perimeter defenses on. We should be fine."

"Do you have a safe room, just in case?"

"Yes. It's under the garage." He handed her a satchel. "Fill it with all the medical supplies you can. From those cabinets there." He had one as well. They cleared out the cabinets quickly and stacked the bags against the wall. He had a few more things he wanted moved before they snuck out the back and down into the garage and opened the door. He turned on the light and headed to another door. They walked down a set of narrow stairs that were cut out of the rock the house sat on.

Toki found herself standing in a small underground hanger.

"This looks more like a ship." She touched the hull to be sure she wasn't imagining it.

"It is. Mine. One of the reasons I bought this place. The opening is about a mile back, so no one knows it's there. I was able to hide this baby here undetected." He went to the side of the ship and pressed a panel that allowed it to open.

Once she was inside, he secured the door. "I came here to get away from it all, but sometimes my past still finds me, so I knew I needed to be able to get away at a moment's notice and this ship gives me that chance."

There was a loud boom, and the ground shook. He raced to a row of screens and activated one. A grin spread across his face when he saw someone, probably male, dancing around on fire. "Stupid Guapo. Serves him right."

"Guapo, the creepy one from last night?"

"One and the same." He turned on other screens so he could see what was going on all around them. His house still stood, which was good because he'd go after whoever tried to destroy it. It didn't look like much, but it had all the state-of-the-art security equipment and it had taken him some time to load it. "That man who was here today with the file. He wasn't happy to see you, so I'm thinking he hired Guapo to come after you. Which is why he's being tenacious."

"He could just want your little bride." She leaned on a console and stared at the screen.

"True, but he would just try to steal you, not kill us both." He watched as Guapo looked around. "Damn, the fire is going out."

"Aren't you afraid it will kill him?"

"We're not that lucky." Kuarto turned from the screen to look at her. "Guapo's from a planet where it takes a fire from a much hotter flame to do any permanent harm to him. He won't look pretty for a while, but he'll be fine." He pulled the chip out of his pocket and sat it on the table. "So I guess the mystery man doesn't want to hire me."

"What are you going to do with it?" She picked it up and started to play with it.

"Throw it away."

"Why? Aren't you curious about what is on it?"

"Already looked at everything important when I opened it up the first time. I have a photographic memory."

"Must be nice." She placed the chip back on his table.

"All the information also loaded into my mainframe the moment I opened the file." He pulled up the file so she could see it.

"You strike me as a brilliant man. Why are you hiding here on this desolate planet instead of being out there making a difference?"

"I did do that for a while. I was the most sought-after doctor in the quadrant because of my research." He sat at the table. "I was a little too good at my job."

"And what was your job?"

"I was studying DNA. I had come up with a way to correct any errors in the DNA strain of any race while it was still an embryo. I could cure everyone with the insertion of a simple chemical I created. But the research had other applications."

"Military ones."

"Of course. My research could make the perfect soldier. The government could alter anyone's DNA and they would be able to fit into society undetected, only to have that enhanced soldier part activate when it is needed, then they would be able to switch back to a normal citizen of society. The thought that they could turn anyone into an assassin is what made me leave with all my research. I made sure that research is safe and they have no way of duplicating it."

"And that is why that man wants you."

"Yes. He knew an awful lot about me. I'm pretty sure he wants me to fertilize that egg. To create something to his liking." He turned the monitor with the research off and looked at her.

"Do you think it's to make a perfect soldier, too?"

"I don't know. The fact that he found me worries me. If he can find me, anyone can. I might have to find another hole in the wall to hide in."

"Why not ask for protection from one of the planets you

feel you can trust? Surely one of them would be able to protect you."

"I don't feel I can trust any of them." He went to one of the bags. "You didn't get a chance to eat anything earlier, did you?"

"Not really."

"I grabbed what I could of our meal. We do have some entertainment to watch, so why don't we enjoy our meal and watch the show?"

FOUR

Heather rested her head against Storm's chest as they waited for the doctor to finish his mission. As much as she would have liked to have gone with the doctor, she knew better than to ask. Knowing there was a chance she could have gotten hurt would have kept her at Storm's side.

Storm had finally accepted the fact that she was only trying to help, but he still felt she needed to be punished.

She grinned as she thought about how he had punished her so far and she hoped he wasn't done. He could punish her like that all the time.

"Why are you smiling? It makes me think you got your way again."

How he could see her smile was beyond her, until she noticed the mirror-like surface nearby. "I was thinking about my punishment. You think you could punish me like that again?"

"You're not supposed to enjoy your punishment."

"Oh? And how am I supposed to hate it when you bring me to such heights of joy?" She lifted her head so she could face him. "If I were to punish you the same way, you'd beg for more."

"You're right." The intercom system beeped. Storm answered. The doctor appeared on the screen. "Done, doctor?"

"Yes, sir." He smiled. "Everyone is fine on the ship. The breach has been sealed and one of their other ships is on the way to help them. I truly appreciate you allowing us to do this. The people on the ship turned out to be from Earth."

"What were they doing so far from home?" His jaw tightened just a little. That anger at giving in was back.

"They say they are a research ship exploring the area. Security downloaded a copy of their system to see if they are telling the truth. That information should be in your computer in the next minute or two."

"Thank you, doctor." The screen went blank and he sat back in the chair. Knowing he didn't like giving in had Heather shifting her weight, wanting to at least give herself some space so she would have a chance to fight before he pounced on her but his hand held her in place. "You are not going anywhere."

She sighed, and she had just gotten permission to put her uniform back on.

"You were right."

That got her attention. She sat up and looked at him. "Excuse me?"

"If we had ignored that ship Earth would have been up in arms about it. And my mother would be displeased with me even though I was just following policy." He frowned at the grin on her face. "But that doesn't mean I'm happy about it."

"Of course not." She tried to wipe the grin off, but she was too happy to know he actually saw her side this time. "So what is my punishment this time?" Her hands went to the seals on her uniform.

His hands stopped hers from moving. "As much as I

would love to bring you joy again, I have work to do and you're looking tired." He gently touched the dark circles under her eyes. "The doctor will not be pleased with either of us if I don't let you get some sleep."

"Oh," She couldn't keep the disappointment out of her voice. She was as bad as he was when it came to sex. "I'm not really tired."

"Doesn't matter." He stood and picked her up off his lap and placed her next to the chair. Using his foot, he pressed another lever. "This thing has a sleeping position, too. It will give you a chance to rest while I work my way through those files."

The back of the chair reclined, bringing the footrest up. He pointed, letting her know where he expected her to go.

"You're not going to join me?" She didn't move.

"Not right now." He placed her on the seat and kissed her softly on the lips. "Dim the lights."

The cabin darkened.

"I'll wake you when we get to the planet."

She didn't think she needed a nap but arguing with her mate wasn't a smart idea in the wake of his confession, so she rested her head against the headrest and closed her eyes. Anything to keep him happy.

Storm started pouring through the information the security force beamed over. He looked behind him to make sure his mate had dozed off and wondered what was going on with his sister and why she hadn't contacted them.

———

"He's a bit tenacious, isn't he?" Toki watched as Guapo walked around the perimeter of Kuarto's force field.

"Not normally, but maybe his new friend has forced him to do this. I'd taunt him, but I fear it will make him stay out there longer." Kuarto turned off the screen. "He's not the smartest person I've met."

Kuarto realized he was locked in his ship with a beautiful woman. As much as he would like to be with her again, he didn't feel it was right for him to take advantage of her.

"So what should we do now?" She watched him. Once she was sure she had his attention, she worked on the closers on the dress and let it slip to the floor.

He swallowed hard. It was going to be hard to resist her when she stood in front of him naked like that. "Look, I–"

She stepped up to him and placed a finger against his lips. "I know you're going to try to be a gentleman right now and probably blame the drugs I was fed as an excuse for what happened last night, even after I explained that the drugs don't affect me."

"Then why are you doing this? You don't have to." His fingers itched to touch her like he did last night. To feel the velvety smoothness of her skin.

"I know. I want to because I want you." She worked on his clothes, peeling away the simple layer. "And from what I can see, you want me too."

He couldn't deny he was erect. He wanted to blame the sexual interval his mind sharers had hours ago, but his erections never lasted this long. This was because of her and how much he enjoyed being with her last night. He wanted her but was too stubborn to admit it.

He had kept his distance from women because he didn't want anyone to be hurt due to knowing him. He knew a lot of the governments he had worked for were looking for him, and it wouldn't take them long to find him. Especially since this friend of Guapo's had found him. If he had a love interest, they could use her as leverage. Something he didn't want. But here stood the most beautiful piece of flesh and blood he had ever seen and he found saying no to her difficult.

She stepped up to him and wrapped her arms around his neck, pressing herself against him. It spurred him to action. He wrapped his arms around her and lowered his head. His mouth claimed hers in a fevered kiss. Last night showed him what he had been missing.

The ship had a single bed and it beckoned. Inching her backward, he reached the bunk and eased her onto it. He had been thinking about their intimacy all day. She had been in control last night. He didn't have to do anything, but this time was different. He was in control and couldn't wait any longer. "Forgive me."

He drove into her, her body accepting him all the way. Once he was buried deep inside, he found he could think again, but only about bringing her pleasure. The heels of her feet pressed against his buttocks, urging him to set a pace. He started moving in and out of her, first slow, then quicker as they found a tempo that fit them both.

Her tight sheath hugged him, increasing the spirals of desire circling in his blood. Her breath came out in sharp gasps as he drove deeper and deeper into her. Her body gripped him hard just as she spiraled out of control. She spasmed against him and he fought not to follow her. Last night he had been interrupted. That wasn't going to happen tonight. He could feel it.

She gave him a well satisfied smile. He pulled out and pumped into her again. Her grin widened.

———

The small armada Storm had brought with him stayed behind, setting their orbit around an uninhabited planet near the one Storm and Heather headed to. He maneuvered the ship to a large field close to where his sister's ship went down. Once they got off their craft, Storm sent his mate to the house while he went to what was left of Toki's ship to see what he could learn.

Heather approached the house to find it eerily quiet. This couldn't be good. The door was opened, so she pulled her weapon out and entered cautiously.

"I wouldn't go much further."

She stopped the moment she heard him. Turning with her weapon in hand, Heather spotted the tall handsome man who stood in the darkened interior, holding his own blaster on her. Was this her brother? "Can I assume you're the doctor here?"

"And you are?"

"My mate." Storm stood behind him with his weapon trained on her brother. "And if you harm one hair on her head, yours will come off."

He turned to face the new voice, acting like he expected it. "Considering this is my house, I should be the one giving the threats. Who are you two, and why are you in my house?"

Toki stepped into the home, drawing everyone's attention.

"Toki!" Heather smiled when she saw her. "I'm so happy to see you."

"You know her?" asked Kuarto.

"She is my sister," said Storm. He studied his sister. "You okay, Tiko?" He used his own pet name for her.

She looked at Heather, then Storm, confusion etched on her face. "Do I know you?"

Heather looked at Kuarto. "What happened?"

"Her ship crashed, and she lost her memory. She's remembering bits and pieces, but that is it."

"Toki, I'm your brother's mate, Heather." Heather took her by the hand and led her away from the men.

"What is my name?"

"You never told me," Heather laughed. "You said I would

never be able to pronounce it. I started calling you Toki, which means pain in Vespian."

"Pain?"

"You liked to interrupt us whenever you could. Hence a pain to both of us." Heather looked at her mate. "We're going to need the doctor."

Storm nodded. He pressed a small device near his collar and contacted the doctor, letting him know the situation so he would know what to bring. He did warn him to come alone and to make sure no one could track him.

Heather continued to talk to Toki, hoping she would trigger something that would free up her memory, but it didn't work. It remained locked deep inside.

———

"So what happened to her ship?" The man gave Kuarto such a glare. "They don't blow up on their own."

"Don't know. I pulled her out and before I could go back inside to get any information to find out who she was the damn thing went kaboom." He glared back. "Does that make you feel any better?"

"What?" His brow creased in a frown. Looked like Toki's brother didn't like it when someone stood up to him.

"Acting like I'm some sort of devil when I'm the one who pulled her out before the ship exploded. You should be thanking me for saving her life." He growled. "Vespians are not the most mannered group of people."

"You might want to watch what you say," said Storm.

"Why? You take offense?"

"No. But you're talking about yourself." He pointed to Heather, who still sat with his sister, talking. "You're her twin, born from Vespian parents."

"Her? My sister?" He shook his head. "I was an orphan."

"So was she."

Storm spotted the doctor approaching the simple home with his portable medical kit. He bowed to him, then moved into the house to help his sister.

"How are you people able to get through my security?" They acted like there was nothing protecting his abode.

Storm pointed to the device he spoke into earlier. "It has many functions, including the ability to override most security systems."

He didn't like that. If the Vespians had a way to override a security grid like his, then it wouldn't be long before other planets would too. What he needed to do was get his hands on one of those devices. Big and brooding wouldn't allow it, but his mate might. He watched her with Toki. She was the opposite of her mate. Where he growled and postured, she smiled and laughed.

How could she be his sister? He had no family. Didn't want any family. It just complicated things. "Are you sure we're related?"

"You think I'm lying to you?" Storm crossed his arms over his chest. "My mate is the one who swears it's you. Although, I don't know why. She's the one who you're going to have to question. Understand I will be watching you. One wrong move and I will be the one you'll have to deal with and no one likes being around me when I'm not happy."

"A bit protective, aren't you?"

"You have no idea."

The ship's doctor stepped up to Storm. "She should get everything back in a few moments."

"Good. I want to know what happened to cause her crash." Storm walked over to where his sister and mate stood.

The doctor stood next to Kuarto. "I'm surprised to see you, doctor. I thought you had died."

"I did, and I want to keep it that way." He kept his voice

down, surprised the man recognized him. Was he going to have to reinvent himself again? Too many knew who he was.

"Too bad." He looked at his hand-sized pad and entered a few notes. "These people could use your help to unlock the mystery that surrounds them."

"What are you talking about?" He watched Heather with his fake bride. When he glanced at the overprotective male, he found the man staring at him.

"You'll figure it out as they explain their story." The doctor tapped him on the arm before heading back to the single-person ship he had arrived in. "Your secret is safe, but I hope you will reconsider. We need you."

He watched the three of them together. Just by the way Mr. Overprotective dealt with Heather Kuarto could see she was his world. He was always close, touching when he could. Toki was treated like family, still familiar but with a difference.

"Storm!" She looked at her brother and smiled. Her memory was back. "Heather! I remember!" She gave Heather a hug.

"Good. What happened to your ship?" The man had a way with words.

"That was the strange thing. I don't know. I didn't feel anything happen, but the ship suddenly went into a tailspin, like it had been hit by something. I got banged up but was able to lock my uniform before I lost consciousness. The self-protection aspect of the ship must have kicked in then and made sure my suit would protect me."

"And him?" Storm hooked a thumb at Kuarto.

"Kuarto took me in and protected me when I truly needed it." She looked at Heather. "That's him, isn't it?"

"Supposedly," Heather looked at him. "Although, I'm not so sure now."

"What are you talking about?" He had stepped up to them when Toki started talking.

"You are supposed to be my twin, but you look more like these two than me." She gestured to Storm and his sister. "There's no question you're Vespian, you have the height, skin tone, hair color, although a little lighter, and that outer color ring in your eye. Then there is me, much paler than any of you. Short for a Vespian, violet eyes verses those golden ones. I don't fit and sure would like to know why."

"I might be able to answer that question if you let me take samples from everyone. It will give me a base to figure out why you don't look like the rest of us. You'd be amazed what you can learn from DNA."

"I'd appreciate it." She touched Storm's chest, then turned her attention back to him. There was a way about her that had him liking her instantly. Her simple touch had Storm relaxing his stance. "What's next?"

"I'll need a DNA sample."

"Take it." She offered her arm. By the gesture, he knew she had been through a lot of tests in her lifetime.

He took what he needed from each of them then started his work. He was amazed by what he saw. Storm and Toki were definitely twins. The DNA proved it. He put his in next, which proved what he suspected. He was Vespian. His readings were very close to Storm and his sister. Heather's was where things changed. Although she did have Vespian blood nothing else about her actually matched.

"So what have you learned?"

"That I have seen this before." He pointed to Heather's readings.

"Really? Where?" she asked, her voice hopeful.

"Here." He brought up the file with the egg given to him by Guapo's boss. Her face lost all color.

"My egg."

"Your egg." He turned back to the screen. She couldn't be lying, the data showed it was hers.

"That means he's here on your planet." Instinctively, she stepped close to Storm, wanting his protection.

"I was told by the person who gave me this file that he was the proper owner of it."

"He can say whatever he wants, that egg is mine." Anger filled her. "He tried to steal my fertilized one but was unsuccessful. That was what he got away with because I couldn't stop him completely."

"If there is a chance he's here, then we need to leave." Storm grabbed her hand and started for their ship.

"That well-dressed man was the one who kidnapped you, Heather?" Toki's question stopped Storm. He turned to face her.

"You saw him?"

"Yes." Toki nodded. "Kuarto thinks my presence was why he had someone attack us earlier."

"It is far too dangerous here for you, Heather." Storm wrapped his arms around her, ready to pick her up and carry her if she tried to fight him.

"But this could be our chance to get it back."

"I will not run the risk of him being able to get his hands on you again."

"Do you have a perimeter alarm? Kuarto? Right?" She pulled against Storm's grip.

"Yes. We'll know the moment someone is approaching. Why?"

"Storm, please. I need answers."

He glared at her and wanted to say no. Yet he didn't. Storm looked at Kuarto. "What did he want from you?"

"I think he wants to fertilize the real egg, and I believe he's having trouble getting that done."

"Wait, real one?" Heather rubbed her forehead in confusion.

"This is a clone. I knew the moment I saw it. I think he

wants to make sure he gets it right before he touches the real one." He turned from the screen. "You're pregnant?"

She looked at Storm before nodding.

"How pregnant?"

"Several months, why?"

"Would you both be willing to let me do some more testing?"

Storm's brow dropped and his eyes narrowed. Heather knew he would explode at any moment, but she wanted to know why he asked the question. She didn't say anything, just looked at Kuarto, hoping he'd get the hint and answer her unasked question.

"Why?" asked Toki. She had asked for Heather.

"Most of the time, a clone will respond like a real sample from a host. Why didn't it here? If you're pregnant, why can't the other egg be fertilized? What I would like to do is get a few more samples and see how you could do what he hasn't been able to do."

"No." Storm's voice was flat.

"We need answers." Heather looked up at him.

"There is no way I will allow you to do that type of research anywhere where the information could be stolen. Especially since that man could be close." He looked down at Heather, anger still etched on his face. "You'll have to come back to Vespia."

Kuarto didn't respond. Going to Vespia wasn't something he wanted to do.

"Can we get back to the fact of why I don't look like any of you?" Heather pinched her nose. "I'd like to know the answer to that one."

"You, my dear, are very rare." He welcomed the change in subject. "What were you told?"

"I was an orphan raised on Earth. When I mated with Storm, I learned my parents were from Vespia and they sent me away to keep me safe." She was able to step away from Storm for the moment. "I've been different all my life."

"Interesting." He pulled up two DNA strands on the computer screen. "This is Storm's and his sister. You can see how alike they are. This is typical for DNA from twins. This is ours." He pulled up another set.

Heather sighed when she noticed the big differences in them. "But I was told I had a percentage of Vespian blood. Was I lied to?"

"No. You do have some Vespian blood, but there isn't as much as the rest of us. It looks like that blood was inserted into you. It's not part of your genetic makeup." Kuarto studied her readings intently. "I've never seen anything like this before."

"Of course not." She rubbed her forehead again. "I really hate being such an oddity."

"Oddity?" Kuarto looked up, realizing he could have handled that a little better. "Sorry. I bet you have had your share of tests and requests for samples because of your uniqueness. I didn't mean to add to that. I sometimes forget my manners when I find something so fascinating."

"Most doctors get that way, so I'm used to it." Heather stepped up to his computer and studied the information there. "What is that?"

"This?" He pointed to a marker in her DNA. She nodded. "It shows you were created."

"Excuse me?" Shock filled her voice.

"You weren't aware?"

"No." Heather sighed. "Explain what you mean by created."

"You were genetically engineered." He watched as she took in the information.

Heather wrapped her arms around herself. "I'm even a bigger freak than I first thought."

"My heart, you're not a freak." Storm pulled her back into

his embrace and glared at Kuarto. "It just shows how special you are."

She looked up at him, gave him a sad smile, and touched his face with soft fingertips. Kuarto found their interaction fascinating. It was like they knew what the other was thinking.

"Why would they say they were my parents?"

"Because I don't think anyone knew this." Kuarto found all of this amazing. He brought up his information and put it next to hers. "Look, if I separate your Vespian DNA and put it next to mine, what do you see?"

"They look almost identical." There was a hopeful sound to her voice.

"Exactly. Just like twins should. It proves we came from the same parents." He merged her DNA back together. "You just have a whole lot more of what ever blood this is than the rest of us."

"How could we come from the same parents if I was genetically engineered?"

"That's the question I need to answer, isn't it?"

"How could any of this be possible and nobody knew this was being done?" Storm still had his arms wrapped around Heather protectively.

"I know the mighty Vespian race was manipulated and they didn't even know it. This is going to take some time to unravel but I will find out what happened." He received another glare for his comment. "What I'd like to do is get back to the reason he has one of your eggs."

"I don't know. I was kidnapped several months ago by him and he tried to manipulate my mind into believing I never mated with Storm."

"Heather."

"Storm, he needs to know this." She turned in his arms so she could place her hand on his heart. "He took me right after we found out I was suddenly fertile. Up to that point, I was sterile. In the end, he said I was not what he wanted, but it was our child."

"Then why did he take the empty egg instead of your embryo?"

"Because I misdirected his computer. I seem to have a talent with my mind and was able to make him think he had gotten what he wanted. I knew it wouldn't take him long to figure out he had been tricked, but luckily I was rescued before he could try again."

"Then I was right. He wants to fertilize this egg." That explained their behavior around each other too. Their minds were connected in some way.

"Why?"

"That is a really good question."

FIVE

Storm watched his mate interact with her brother and found he was jealous of the attention she gave him. He never had to share her attention before, and he didn't like it.

"It's her brother." His sister leaned close, her voice soft.

"I know, doesn't make it any better." He crossed his arms over his chest.

"Spoiled much?" She looked up at him.

"Go away, pain."

An alarm went off. Storm's first thought was to protect his mate.

"We're about to have company," said Kuarto. "You two need to make yourselves scarce until I figure out a way to explain you."

Storm nodded and led Heather out the back door. He kept out of sight but did peek so he could see who was coming. His blood went cold when he recognized the man as the love interest in Heather's fantasy. So Ialog hadn't disguised himself when he tried to make his mate think her life with Storm was a coma induced dream. He tightened his hold on her.

Heather tapped him on the arm. "Can I breathe?" she whispered.

He relaxed his hold on her but made sure she couldn't be spotted by shielding her with his body.

"I'm surprised to see you," said Kuarto. Storm could hear a chair scrape against the floor. Kuarto probably stood up.

"Yes, well. That was an unfortunate accident." There was a pause, making Storm wish he could see what was going on easily. He would peek when he felt it was safe.

"Unfortunate." Kuarto's voice held a flat note. "It is fortunate that I don't put a hole through you for what you did."

"What did I do?" He could hear the feigned surprise in Ialog's voice.

"So are you saying you didn't tell Guapo to take care of my bride? Which made him try to kill her last night?"

Bride? Storm looked down at the surprised face of his mate. He didn't remember his sister mentioning anything about being the man's bride.

"Like I said, an unfortunate accident, but I have made sure Guapo will not cause you any more trouble." There was a pause in the conversation. "I hope no one was harmed."

"I'd like you to get off my property now."

"Doctor, I need your help. No one else can do what you can."

"It can't be done. That egg is sterile. I read the research and know you have cloned it, but the clone can't be fertilized and if you have already tried to fertilize the real one before you started working with clones you've destroyed whatever chances I might have had."

"I never touched the real egg. I was very careful with it because it is a one of a kind and I don't think I could replace it."

Storm would make sure he never got his hands on his mate or anything of theirs again. If he had gotten his way the first time, it would have never happened.

"Good luck finding someone to help you."

Storm could hear more movement.

"Doctor, I could make it worth your while."

"Doubt it."

Storm wished he could see into the room, so he knew what they were doing, but he was afraid he'd be spotted if he tried.

"Please think about it. I would welcome you and your bride with open arms."

"Let me put it this way. Don't hold your breath. After the stunt you just pulled, you're lucky I haven't just shot you then asked questions."

Storm felt something sweep over him just before Heather slumped in his arms.

"Anyone else here, Doctor?"

Did Ialog feel that weird pulse as well? To be on the safe side, Storm moved away from where he had been standing, cradling Heather against him.

"Why? You planning on making sure there's no witnesses so you can finish the job Guapo couldn't?"

Storm tried to focus on what they were saying, but he was worried about Heather. She lay lifeless in his arms. What just happened?

———

Kuarto felt a strange shift in the air around him just as the man asked if there was anyone else around. He didn't need the man snooping around. "You know, I don't even know your name if I wanted to get back in touch with you." Anything to get his attention off looking for other people, afraid he'd find Storm and Heather.

"The name is Ialog. But I'm learning a lot find my name hard to pronounce, so most people have been calling me Al."

"Okay, Al. If you want me to even think about doing this

for you, then I recommend you leave now. The longer you stay the quicker I will say no."

"Then I'll look forward to hearing from you." He smiled like Kuarto had already said yes.

"And how will I find you if I want to?"

"If you start looking for me, I'll know it."

———

The moment Storm felt it safe, he came in with Heather in his arms. He looked like a frightened child. "Help her."

Kuarto pointed to his bed while he grabbed his scanner. "I felt something. I think we all did. Is that when she lost consciousness?"

"Yes. She just went limp in my arms."

He sat on the bed and checked her vitals. "She's fine. Just in a deep place in her head. Not sure what happened yet, but it won't take me too long to figure out." He stood to grab another piece of equipment and found Storm in his way. "I know you're worried about your mate, but I can't do my job if you keep blocking my movements."

Toki grabbed Storm's arm and pulled him aside. "Let him do his job. He's very good at it."

Kuarto lifted Heather's lids to find her eyes rolled back in her head. What was going on inside? He checked a few other things before he noticed a change in the readings. Wherever she was, she was coming back from. He waited for her to regain consciousness.

Heather's eyes fluttered open to find everyone staring at her.

"Hello?" She looked at the three faces watching her. "Why is everyone staring at me like I'm some sort of freak again?" She sat up on her elbows. "What did I do now?"

Storm crowded past Kuarto to be next to her. He touched her face. "You didn't do anything more than scare me to death. You passed out in my arms and I have no clue what caused it."

"Great." She looked at her brother this time. "I have this ability to just draw the oddity to myself. Do you know what happened?"

"Sorry, but none of us do. There was an event. I can't think of any other way to describe it. I felt it here." He touched his head. "Storm was outside with you. When he came in, you were unconscious."

"Storm?" She looked at him. "What did you see?"

"You were in front of me, so I couldn't see your face. I was listening to the conversation your brother was having with Al. I wasn't focusing on you. You went boneless in my arms."

"What do you remember?" asked Kuarto.

"You trying to squeeze the air out of me." She looked at Storm. "Then all of you staring at me."

"Nothing in between?"

"No."

"The children?"

"They're fine." She placed her hand on her stomach and smiled.

Toki took Kuarto's spot on the bed and spoke softly to her so Storm could talk to him.

"What happened to her?" Storm was quiet in his words, but Kuarto knew he wasn't happy with what he had heard so far.

"I have no answer." He crossed his arms over his chest. "You want to take my head off because I have no answer?"

He was gifted with another glare from Heather's mate.

"Storm." All she had to do was say his name, and she pulled his attention from Kuarto. He went to her side in an instant. "Was it him?"

"Yes." He knew what she was talking about without her

having to mention Al's name. "Do you not remember anything about him?"

"I'm sorry." She shook her head. "I try, but he always seems to be looking away from me." She tried to stand and found her balance off. "Whoa!"

"Hey." Kuarto was at her side in seconds. Using his scanner, he checked her vitals. Why was her equilibrium off? "I didn't give you permission to get up yet. I'm still running tests."

"We're going to have to work on your bedside manner." Heather took Storm's hand and stood. This time, she didn't lose her balance. "Wow, that's a little strange." Her eyes glazed over and she fell back onto the bed.

Kuarto grabbed another piece of equipment, shouldered Storm out of the way, and placed it on her forehead. It beeped when a large spike of energy raced through her mind.

"Doctor?"

"Give me a minute." He checked to see what the energy spike was.

"I want to know what is going on now!"

Kuarto stood and faced Storm, who was inches away from him. He could dish out the same type of treatment Storm was giving. "Just because you're my sister's mate doesn't mean I have to like you. Right now you're getting in the way of me trying to treat her. If you keep that up, I will ban you from this house."

"You wouldn't dare."

"Gentlemen," Heather's voice came out soft and slightly strained. "While I'm flattered you're fighting over me, can we stop with the male posturing for the moment? Kuarto, he's used to having people jump when he uses that tone, so please forgive him. Storm, perhaps it would help him if you gave him my medical history. I know you always carry the chip with you. It would explain a lot."

Storm glared at him before turning over the chip she spoke about.

Kuarto took the chip and went to his system to catch up on Heather's background. The chip was something that fascinated him. He'd never seen anything like it. It was small and clear, like a crystal. It was pretty enough someone could wear it as a piece of jewelry and no one would know what it was.

The details of her file he would look at later. Working through Heather's information, he found she had been pretty healthy most of her life. The data from when she met Storm was what he needed to go through. As the device in her back started to disintegrate, he learned that her Vespian doctor found abnormalities in the way her body reacted. That's when he figured out she was built to protect herself. The dreams she had when her life was threatened was one of them. The way the data for her true race stopped loading when it was close to completing her DNA strand was another.

The other doctor never mentioned her being genetically engineered, but the data was all there. How did he miss it?

So why did she have such a surge of energy? Could she still be absorbing the enzymes from the device and that was what caused this? According to what he read that should have happened several months ago. He needed to run a few tests of his own to see what was going on.

Kuarto crossed to the bed Heather had been placed on and sat next to her. "I'm sure you've had your share of being poked and prodded, but I need to run a few more tests."

She nodded.

"Not here." Storm's voice was flat.

"Exactly where do you wish me to do this? The sooner I run them, the better off we are." He found Storm one of the most annoying men he had ever met.

"Our ship has everything you need." Storm scooped up his mate and headed out the door.

"It's her safety that makes him act this way," said his sister. "I promise he can be quite charming when he's not worried about her."

"I sure hope so, because so far I'm not impressed. He's rude and obnoxious, and I don't see what she sees in him."

"Trust me, they belong together," Toki laughed. "Come on, if we don't keep up, he just might come back after us."

"Let me make sure I have everything I need and wipe the computer clean so the grouch won't want to blow up my place."

"Follow first, then gather your things." She grabbed his hand and pulled him behind her. "Have no idea where he parked the ship and he could be just obnoxious enough not to tell us."

"But he needs me."

"I know my brother, believe me, he knows ways around that." She took off at a trot to catch up with him.

He sighed and followed suit. The sleek black ship surprised him. He didn't realize how close Storm and Heather had landed to his home without setting off a perimeter alarm. The interior was pretty simple, a large command chair, surrounded by consoles and screens. The screens were already on and Storm was barking out orders to the computer system.

Heather didn't look any better, and that bothered him. She should have perked back up like she did the first time.

This time, Storm stayed out of his way, although he did glower at him and watch his every move. Everything he found centered around her mind. That seemed to be where the problem was. "Have you two been able to read each other's thoughts?"

Storm had been speaking to the doctor on the other ship. The moment Kuarto spoke, he muted the sound and turned to face him. "Doctor, I know you don't know Vespian proto-col, so I will let that go, but please refrain from blurting any old thing out. We don't know who we can trust."

"My heart." Heather held up her hand, which he took and placed on his heart. "You need to let him do his job his way. Remember how it was when you were trying to teach me all the little intricacies of Vespian protocol? It was a mess."

"Are you chastising me in front of people?" He said it with a smile, but Kuarto wasn't sure how happy he was about it. His eyes had a hard edge.

"You can punish me later, when we're alone."

That brought a big smile to his face and all of his features softened. "Then I should let your brother get to work on healing you so I can have my way with you." He turned back to the screen and finished his conversation with the doctor.

She nodded. Keeping her voice soft so she wouldn't be picked up by the communication system, she answered, "Yes, we've been able to read each other's minds to a point."

"Care to elaborate?" He gave her a shot which brought back the color to her face quickly.

"We can sense what the other is feeling emotionally. Like I know when he's really mad. We sense each other's distress." She paused for a moment as a soft blush filled her cheeks. "We've also have shared each other's orgasm."

"But actually talked to each other?"

"I don't think so. I know I have said things to him and he seems to have heard me, but we've never carried on a conversation except when I was kidnapped. Then he was able to enter my mind and be a part of the fake world Ialog had created for me."

"Really?" He looked up at Storm, who had finished his conversation with the doctor and joined them. "How did you do that?"

"My uncle. He's our religious leader, and he knew what

to do. Drank some very rank potions he gave me and we had her ring to help me find her." Storm gave the information under duress. "Why?"

"I'm wondering if that will help us now. I'm not sure what is going on inside her head and I need to. I can give you some medication that will allow you to connect with her. I need to know what you see. There could be some sort of blockage going on that won't show up on any medical scanner."

"Blockage?" he asked.

"Everything I have read said Heather has an ability to protect herself. It's highly possible that's what is going on here. She was fine until Al showed up and I'm wondering if he was the trigger to causing all of this."

Storm nodded. He climbed into the chair with her and held her close. "Physical contact helps us reach each other better."

"I'm going to give you both the shot." Kuarto knew better. It was an excuse to touch her. "Heather, you just relax and allow the drug to let you sleep. Storm will join you soon." He pressed the hypo against her throat and watched as she drifted off. "Your turn."

Storm closed his eyes as the medication took effect.

"You should be able to hear and talk to me, Storm." What he gave him should keep him alert but allow Storm to reach into Heather's mind. He had given Heather a different shot, so she would get a little rest and would give him a chance to focus on Mr. Overprotective.

"I can."

"What do you see?" Kuarto placed a reader on him so he could keep an eye on his vitals.

"Nothing. It seems hazy or smoky in here."

He wondered why her mind would cause that. What was it trying to hide? "Keep looking. Center yourself on finding Heather."

Storm remained quiet for a few moments before he went deathly still. "Damn, he's here."

"Who is?" An alarm on his monitor beeped as Storm's heart started beating faster. Whatever he saw frightened him.

"Al. I can see him standing in a corner."

"Has he seen you?"

"Don't think so. Looks like his eyes are closed."

"Force the haze toward Al. Try to make him disappear from sight." That could be what the catalyst was. If he left a small piece of his mind behind from when he had kidnapped Heather, he'd know when he got close to her because it would activate. No matter what sort of disguise she might have used. It could have started to activate when he came to the house which made her shut everything down.

"Okay, he's gone from sight."

"Then continue to find your mate."

"Is that what caused the problem?"

"I think so, but we need to look around more to be sure."

"Why not just destroy it?"

"Sometimes that type of tactic is the worst thing to do when it comes to the mind." That was something he expected from Storm. "What if destroying that takes her with it?" That shut him up. He was easier to deal with when he wasn't awake and agitated. "Do you see your mate yet?"

"No, just a lot of space. Wait." A smile spread across his face. "There she is and she's waiting for me."

Storm stopped talking to him, so he was probably talking to his mate. He needed them to look for another source. If Al put one in there, it was a possibility there was a second or third.

Storm smiled at the sight of his mate. They stood together, hand over each other's heart for a few moments in silence. "Are you okay?"

"Yes." She looked around. "I don't quite remember why we're here again."

"You passed out on me. The doctor had a visitor I recognized as the man who tried to be your love interest when you were trapped in that fake world. Do you remember what he looked like?"

"No, but he was in my mind for a while. It was possible he did something to block me from remembering any encounter with him."

He was afraid of that. She could have met him many times and not even be aware of it. "I passed a sentinel further back. It looks like Al. Did you create it?" He didn't think she did since she didn't remember what the man looked like, but that could be her mind's way of showing she did know who he was.

"Sentinel? No, I don't remember creating anything like that."

"The doctor believes your mind can show us why everything shut down. That sentinel might be one reason and he wants us to look for others."

"Do we know what we're looking for?"

"No." He took her hand in his and walked with her. "By the way, I do like the way you're dressed."

"How am I dressed?" She didn't even look down to see what she had on. She just looked at him.

"You're not."

"Then we're dressed the same." She smiled at him. "But why would we need clothes in our minds, anyway?"

"We don't. It's just I know how modest you can be. You were dressed the last time I was here."

"But that was different. I was seeing something someone

else created." She hugged his arm as they moved around. "If we're going to come here more, I think I should decorate."

Out of nowhere appeared Storm's chair.

"I see I'm not the only one who likes the chair."

"I never said I didn't like the chair. You never gave me a chance to tell you what I thought of it. Besides, that's not something I thought up."

"What do you mean?" He tried to act innocent, but he knew he had been thinking about that chair the moment she mentioned decorating in her mind.

"You know exactly what I mean. I can see it in your face."

He couldn't argue. He pulled her into his arms and gave her a quick kiss. "We'll get to that in a little bit, then. We need to finish looking for whatever caused you to shut down."

Heather wasn't actually looking, but it was her mind they were in, so it was possible that she couldn't see what he could. "What is that?" Storm pointed to an odd object hanging above their head.

"Protection." It came out quickly and automatically.

"Is that what keeps you safe?"

"Yes."

Okay, don't mess with that. There was a second one, almost identical, and very close to the first one. "And that one?"

"What one?"

"Do you not see the second security device?"

"No."

He looked around and didn't find anything else. It was time to tell the doctor what he found. "Doctor, I have found two items that Heather didn't recognize. One was that sentinel I had already told you about. The other is a mimic of her protection device."

"Thank you, Storm. You can come out now." He received no reply.

Storm heard him but had no plans of leaving his mate until she was ready for him to go. He waited for her.

"You okay?" She touched his face.

"I am. The doctor gave me permission to leave you."

"But you're not ready, are you?" Those bright violet eyes gazed up at him with such trust.

"I'll leave when you're ready for me to go." He touched her soft cheek.

She watched his face, not saying a thing. He was ready for her to fade away and they'd be back at the ship. Instead, she smiled at him. "You realize he will know."

"Know what?" He touched her heart. His started beating a little harder.

"Storm, he's my brother. The one who seems to join us every time we're intimate."

"Oh, that." He had her in his arms now, nibbling on her neck. "Does it bother you that he will know who has been plaguing him? And are you sure he actually joins us each time?"

"You heard him beg us to leave him alone." She tilted her head so he could nibble on her throat. "I'm just not sure I'm ready to admit we've been the ones to take him along with us each time."

"He's going to figure it out sooner or later." He picked her up and walked to the chair. His desire to have her was stronger than keeping the doctor out of their minds. It might not be the smartest thing to do, but he needed to prove she was his. "Why not now?"

She had no answer, so he made the choice for her. He climbed onto the chair and brought her with him. He laid her down, hit the lever with his foot and surged into her the moment the chair had shifted to line them up.

He felt her desire spiral. Her sheath tightened around him. She moved with him as the friction they created became all-encompassing. Storm took his time, though. He wanted her and her brother to know how loved and cherished she was. If Kuarto was going to find out now, it had to be right.

He did long deep strokes just the way Heather liked them. He could feel the heat start to build in her belly. Her muscles gripped him harder, making each plunge in more delicious than the last. Her release grabbed them and flung them to the stars. Their minds entwined, her joy was his.

Just as they started their return to their bodies, his started, sending them back out. The powerful release left them a little breathless. White hot joy filled them as they floated together.

He was there with them in her mind, glaring at them. "Damn it! I should have known! It was you two all along!"

SIX

Storm's eyes opened first. He touched Heather's face with his fingertips and watched as her eyes fluttered open. Then he looked at her brother. Anger came off him in waves.

"I should have known it was you two. It makes perfect sense." He paced. "There were those comments you two made."

"Of course it does." Heather sat up and looked at him. Storm was amazed at how easily she spoke about this. Her modesty normally had her blushing like crazy. "Why would it be anyone else?"

"Why bring me along? I don't need to know what your intimate life is like."

"It wasn't on purpose. I don't know how to stop it right now."

Storm held her in his embrace, the chair cradling the two of them. He was there for her if her brother pushed a little too hard and upset her.

"Then that will be the first thing we fix. I'd like to be able to feel my orgasms, not anyone else's." He stopped pacing for a moment and jammed his hands on his hips. "And just how often do you two do it? It seems like about every two hours when you're awake."

"That's close," said Storm. He couldn't help but smile. One of the things he loved about Heather was the fact she could keep up with his sexual appetite. His desire for her was a constant thing. Knowing her brother came along with them had bothered him, although he would never tell Heather that. Knowing they were close to keeping their intimacy to themselves again filled him with happiness.

"I'm amazed you two can still walk."

Heather placed her hand on his for reassurance. He knew what Kuarto had just said flustered her. "Doctor, our sex life is none of your business."

"It is when you share it with me. I can't get any work done. Do you know what it is like to be swept up in that in the middle of a surgery? I had to schedule my life around your sex life."

"You are upsetting my mate." Storm wasn't going to allow him to make another comment if it was going to hurt Heather. She had been through enough.

"I'm sorry, Heather. Sometimes I do forget myself." He glared at Storm. "This started about two months ago for me. How long have you two been sharing?"

"It's been about that long. Once the device dissolved, my mind seemed to expand."

"My heart, we actually started sharing before that. Remember?"

"He's right. We did notice we could feel each other's emotions. In fact, I could tell when Storm was looking for me pretty early in our relationship, but it was nothing like it is now." She leaned her head against his chest.

"Have you tried to link with anyone else? Besides your mate and I."

"No. It's not something to take lightly. I didn't just start picking up thoughts. And even now, I'm not sure if I can reach Storm when we're not intimate."

"You can. Storm being able to enter your mind a few moments ago proved that. You just have to practice more to control it."

She looked up at her mate and grinned. "That could be fun."

He leaned down and captured her lips with his. "Can't wait."

"Let's keep the libido in check, shall we?" Kuarto leaned against the console near Storm's shoulder. "The first thing I think we need to work on is creating a barrier between my mind and yours. That would make my life a little easier."

"Will you come back to Vespia with us?" Heather asked.

"Why?" He straightened when she asked him.

"Because it would make Storm happy." She looked up at her mate. "When Ialog kidnapped me, it was from Storm's mother's home on Vespia. Storm knows I'm not safe anywhere, but he would feel better if he could control some of the situation. Knowing I have markers in my head means he's still watching me for whatever reason. I know that makes me nervous. I can't imagine what it is doing to Storm."

Storm couldn't have been as honest as she was. His goal was to protect her as much as he could. Something he hadn't been able to do.

"And if I don't want to go?"

"Then we'll go home." She gave her shoulders a shrug. "We came to get Toki, not force you to go to Vespia. Her ship shouldn't have crashed, and Storm was concerned. That's why we're here."

"Why did she come here, anyway?"

"To find you," Heather said. "She was supposed to ask you if you'd be willing to meet with us. Allow Storm and I a chance to speak to you about what we've been dealing with.

See if you would help us. That hasn't changed. I still hope to get your help."

"Why me?"

"Because you're my brother." Her honesty came out so easily. It always amazed Storm. "I knew you were a doctor from the mind melds."

"How? I felt the orgasms. They were mind-blowing. I don't know how you could do anything more than just feel."

Heather's head dipped. Storm bet she was blushing. "Nevertheless, I knew you were a doctor and just about the only person anyone close to me would trust."

Storm watched Kuarto, wondering if Heather's words would convince him to help.

Kuarto didn't say anything as he looked at the three of them who were waiting for an answer. He looked at Toki. "You have been awful quiet."

"This whole conversation has been pretty much one sided." She shrugged her shoulders. "My input isn't important."

"Don't mind her. That's her training speaking," said Heather. She tilted her head as she looked at him. "Did I hear Ialog call her your bride?"

Storm had wondered the same thing. That was something he had wanted to ask about, but he hadn't had a chance.

"Um, yes." He suddenly looked nervous. "There aren't too many people who come to this planet, so a stranger stands out. It was the only thing I could come up with. It was to keep her safe."

Storm wasn't sure if he was telling the truth. He looked at his sister to see if she would give anything away, but she remained quiet. He knew he would be able to break her later and put it on his list of things to do.

"I see." Heather turned her head to look at Toki. "And what do you have to say?"

"The same." She remained still. Storm could tell she was

hiding something. "I didn't remember anything until you two showed up and the doctor freed my mind."

Storm noticed she kept her answer simple. Had something happened between them? Heather seemed to think so. He wondered what his mate was going to do next.

"So then if you don't want to come with us we'll be on our way." Heather stood, but her feet still didn't want to work properly.

Storm stood as well so he could wrap an arm around her waist to help her move. She hadn't been able to stand on her own since their run-in with Ialog. He didn't like it.

"We need to get out of here before he realizes I'm here."

"You need to rest," Storm said.

"I know and I will, once we're underway." She leaned her head against his chest again.

"No arguing." He eased her back into the chair. "We'll be home in about twelve hours, and the doctor will be the first person you see when we land."

"I'm sure I'll be fine long before we land." She rested her hand on his chest. "It's only because he's close."

"Are you arguing with me?"

"Does that mean you'll have to punish me?" Her voice held a hopeful note.

"You two are incorrigible." Kuarto rubbed his head.

Storm knew if he had tried to persuade him into coming to Vespia, Kuarto wouldn't have believed him, but there was something about Heather that had the opposite effect on people.

"I don't feel I need to go to Vespia to do what needs to be done, but I do understand your worry about what Ialog can do, so I'll go, but I need to get a few things before we leave. And if it's not too much, I'd like to have your sister help me pack my equipment."

Storm looked at his sister to see what she wanted. She nodded slightly.

"Of course." He wasn't sure if it was the smartest thing to allow, but she was a grown woman and could make her own decisions.

Kuarto nodded and headed off the ship.

"Are you sure about him?" Storm wasn't sure if he could trust the man the way Heather could.

"He's my brother, Storm. Of course, I'm sure about him."

———

"You sure didn't say a whole lot." Kuarto found her silence through that whole thing strange. It didn't fit what he had learned about her.

"As you can see, when my brother is involved, you don't always get a chance to say a lot."

"Is he always like that?" He glanced at her profile. "I wanted to give him several injections that might have shut him up forever."

She laughed. "He comes across kind of strong if you're not used to him, but he is a good man. Your sister sees through all of his blustering."

"If you say so." Kuarto wasn't so sure.

They got back to his place pretty quickly. He gathered everything he would need and knew he had to destroy any records he had of Heather and what he had learned about her. He also needed to delete information he had on the egg. Once he cleaned the system, he went out into his garage.

"I wish I could take my truck with me." He rubbed a hand against the banged-up fender. He hadn't had a chance to fix it yet.

"I could speak to Storm." Toki placed a hand on the same fender. "Ask him to have one of the other ships get it for you."

"Other ships?"

"He never travels alone. Vespian protocol."

"I'll move it into my ship. It will keep it safe and make everyone think I have left for good. Then I can come back for it at another time." Once that was done, he was ready to go. They started walking toward the ship.

"You've been very quiet." He wasn't sure what was going on with her.

"Happens when I get around family. They have a tendency to stick their noses where I don't want them to."

"So you think your brother is going to question you about us." He watched his step as they worked their way through the woods.

"I'm sure of it."

"Just tell him the truth." He lifted a branch that blocked their way. Once she passed him, he walked around it and let it go.

"And what is the truth?" She looked up at him with a touch of concern on her face. "My brother will ask me and if he's not happy with my answer he'll come after you and I know I want to avoid that as much as possible. You two don't play well together."

"What would he want to know?" He didn't get what she was hinting at.

"I'm sure the word bride will come up in the conversation."

"What happened between us is private." Storm better not try to interfere in his life.

"In case you haven't noticed, he's extremely protective of the people he cares about."

"That I have noticed." He was quiet for a moment. "What will you tell him?"

"I don't know. What can I tell him?"

He wasn't sure about his feelings for her. One of the reasons he was going to their planet was because of her, but did he want to admit that? At the same time, should he keep her in the dark when he wanted to spend more time with her? He must have been quiet a little too long.

"Look, I don't want you to feel obligated to me."

"We make a pair, don't we?" He started laughing. "Neither wants to say how we feel because whatever has happened between us is so new we don't know what to call it." He wished he could read her thoughts. It sure would come in handy right now. "I can't promise anything."

"I can't compete." Her voice was soft.

"Compete?" He looked at her. "What are you talking about?"

"Them, you. The mind-sharing thing. You know."

"Oh, honey. I don't want you to even try." He took her hand in his. "I've been quite happy with what we shared. I don't want what they have. I want what we could have."

She gave him a bright smile, and he wondered if he said too much. The ship came into view and he questioned his decision to leave once more. He knew his sister needed him and even in the short time he had spent with her, he knew there was a connection between them. He wanted to help her. Her mate, on the other hand, annoyed the life out of him and he wished he wasn't part of the picture.

The doors to the ship opened and allowed them to enter. Kuarto found Heather and Storm cuddling on the command chair. He sat against the backrest, with Heather using him as her mattress. She was curled up on her side with a happy smile on her face.

"This ship isn't much on rooms since it's one of our scout ships. Heather recommended we give you two the one sleeping room, since I still have to pilot the ship." Storm didn't sound like he was happy with what he was saying.

"Thank you, Storm," said his sister. She disappeared into the room Storm pointed at kind of fast. It made him wonder if she was trying to avoid the questions she said her brother would ask.

Kuarto wanted to be sure Heather was okay so he walked up to the chair and crouched down beside her. "You've gotten some of your color back. That's good to see."

"The ship's shields are helping with that," Storm commented.

"Probably. If she bounces back after we leave orbit, then it is the close proximity to Al that is causing the problem. Something else we're going to have to address."

"I don't want her anywhere near that man." Storm started the procedure for takeoff.

"But what if he were to come for her?"

Storm's face darkened in anger. That was the wrong thing to say. "He had her before, and that will never happen again. I'll die before he touches her again."

"Storm," Heather patted the chest she leaned against. "It's always good to check every angle."

"You are supposed to be sleeping, and why would you want to argue with me in front of other people?"

"He doesn't count. Family has never counted." She stretched in his arms. "And it's hard to sleep when you're growling in my ear."

"You seem to be doing much better." Kuarto checked her eyes and pressed his hand against her pulse. Her eyes were clear now, but her pulse was still off.

"Feeling better, too."

So that answered one question. "Have we broken orbit?"

"About five seconds ago."

"Thought so." He touched her hand. She still felt a little cold. "You taking any vitamins?"

"No, why?" She shifted in her seat.

"It would be a good idea, considering you're pregnant. Your body is feeding three now and that's going to put a drain on you as time goes on." He stood up. "I'll put together something for you to take that will help."

"Thank you." Heather snuggled against Storm. "Why don't you go get some rest and we'll work on this later?"

He nodded, gave Storm an 'I don't care look', and headed to the room where Toki waited.

Once he was out of earshot Storm spoke. "I don't remember a family clause in you arguing with me."

"You sure?" She looked up at him with innocent eyes. "Could have sworn. Guess you'll just have to punish me later."

"If I was a betting man, I'd say you enjoy the way I punish you a little too much. You've mentioned it quite a bit on this mission."

"I just know you weren't done punishing me before we landed here."

"I don't think you've learned your lesson yet, either." He brushed a few hairs from her face. "You seem too anxious to start them again."

"Then you'll just have to teach me over and over until I do learn my lesson." She kissed the palm of his hand. "You are a very good teacher."

"It's a good thing you're my heart or I might have to really make my point."

"Don't you do that about every two or three hours, according to my brother?"

"Did that upset you?" He never meant for their sex life to be a topic of conversation with anyone, even if they were family. He remembered how she felt about the picture. It took a lot for her to allow him to release the image.

"No. He means no harm, and I know that."

"How can you trust him so quickly?"

"The same way I knew you were my mate. His heart is pure. Kuarto might not understand our ways yet, but he isn't a man who would betray us. I have touched his mind and know how he thinks."

"He could have hidden that part from you."

"Can you hide any part of your mind from me?"

He had no answer. His mind was an open book to her.

"Now, we need to discuss my punishment. Since my brother has been slightly loud in his demands, I think we need to wait until we're home before you get to be sure I see the error of my ways."

"You are enjoying it too much." He hugged her to him for a moment. "I'm going to have to come up with something to prove how serious I am about you arguing with me in front of others."

"Oh? Like what?"

Her excitement made him laugh. She was his world. "I was serious before about you getting anywhere near Ialog. I won't let it happen a second time."

"What if it is the only way to end this?" She sat up so she could watch his face. "Would you deny us a chance to live out our lives in happiness because you fear what he might do to me?"

"I couldn't live with myself if something were to happen to you." He gripped her shoulders.

"You are far too overbearing for anything to happen to me anyway, so let's not even think about it." She saw the fear in his eyes. Her thoughts followed his, but she refused to let it get to her. Her mind had always let her know when she was in danger, and she believed it would always protect her. "Kuarto has made me realize that I'm not utilizing my abilities the way I should, and you get to be my guinea pig."

"What do you mean?" He didn't sound impressed.

She brushed her mind against his, filling it with her desire to be with him.

"Oh."

"Exactly. I want to see what I can do with my mind. We know I can let you in, but can I enter yours at any time? Can I create a world just for us?"

"What about other minds?" His question was one both

had thought about. "Will you try to enter someone else's mind as well?"

"I don't want to violate anyone's trust." He could sense she didn't feel comfortable answering this one.

"You didn't answer me."

"I know. Whatever my answer is will upset you. If I say no, you will demand I cover every angle no matter what, but if I learn to do that, there will be a part of you that will feel like I'm betraying you somehow. Even though we know I'm not."

"I've never had to share you before." She always knew what he felt. "It's not something I'm used to."

"I'm sorry about that." She smiled at him as her hand touched his heart. "You are my life and I have to share you with an entire planet. It's not that difficult for me because I know who you come home to every night."

"So you are saying I will get used to it?"

"No, but it's not like you will have to share me with all these people. You will be involved in any decision I must make about this."

He shifted her, so that she was lying on the part where her legs had been seconds before. "I feel the need to dominate you at the moment."

She smiled at him. "And if my brother comes out of there screaming in protest?"

"I will deal with that. Besides, that is the first thing you need to address. Try to put up some sort of shield so we can have our privacy." He dipped his head down to hers and captured her lips with his. Using his tongue, he worked his way into her mouth, enjoying the taste of her as their tongues danced together. She made him feel alive at moments like this. If he had his way, she would be beneath him all the time, sharing her body as often as he liked. He still got that, she never denied him, but knowing he could demand more if he wanted gave him a feeling of control he didn't always feel with her.

How did he get involved with the one person who could make him feel so out of control at times? His hands worked at the seal of her uniform, wishing they had been alone so she could have slipped on that little black number she had created for him. He loved the outfits. Each one made him rock hard the moment he saw them. Knowing she thought of his arousal each time she created one let him know how much he meant to her.

Her soft skin reminded him of how delicate she could be. Although she would never complain, he knew he needed to be gentle with her. Her body was going through changes because of her pregnancy and he had to be mindful of that.

He felt the brush of her fingers against his chest as she worked on his uniform as well. It didn't take either of them long before they had shed the uniforms and were flesh to flesh.

"Which would be easier for you? A shield to block him out or one to lock us in?" He surged into her, not being able to wait until she created what she needed to.

"Not sure." She arched against him when he did that. A soft sigh escaped her. She needed this as much as he did.

He felt her mind reach out to his, bringing him into her thoughts. The intimacy was phenomenal. She wrapped them in a blanket of sorts. Since it was her first try, she wasn't sure if it would work.

He moved within her then, drawing a rare sound when his stroke hit just the right spot. He felt it all the way down to his toes. "My heart, that soft sound is more arousing than any outfit you create for me."

A blush filled her cheeks, but she didn't break eye contact as her muscles pulsed against him. She might be a quiet partner most of the time, but she still knew how to let him know what she wanted and how she felt about some of his comments. He had to admit he liked the way he could still say things that brought color to her cheeks. Most Vespians don't blush.

The vise-like grip she had him in sent desire racing through him. He pushed in a little deeper, getting a shudder out of her. Taking it slow, he slid in and out, each time pushing deeper. He heard her breath hitch. She was close. Knowing her body so well now, he knew how to prolong her balance on the precipice. Knew what it took to send her over the edge.

Every part of her being cried for release. He quickened his pace, giving her all of him. In seconds, he felt her quake around him, her body tightening muscles that already had a strong grip on him. His orgasm was just as powerful, pulling him along with her.

He rested his head against hers. His breathing felt a little forced. Like he had run a marathon. They remained like that for a while, the joy they found in each other's arms all they wanted to feel.

SEVEN

"I'll be right back."

Toki grabbed his arm. "Where do you think you're going?"

"I want to check one more thing on Heather while I'm thinking of it." Kuarto stopped when he felt the heat of her touch.

"Make a note of it. You're not going out there right now." She shook her head. "Listen, I don't need a mind link to know what is probably going on out there right now. My brother and his mate alone, with nothing to do, except explore each other. Don't be dense or stupid. You go out there now and you'll see my brother angry."

"Angry? The man has already growled and glared at me. How much more can he do? Besides, he doesn't strike me as a man who cares about what other people think."

"You're right." She nodded. "He doesn't, but anything that might upset his mate sets him off. Believe me, I have been at the receiving end of that anger and it is no fun."

"He doesn't frighten me."

"You want to see real anger? Go on out there."

He stared at the door for a moment before he sat on the

bed next to her. Since it was the only real piece of furniture in the room, he didn't have much of a choice. His desire for her was starting to outweigh his resolve to not take advantage of the situation. It was one of the reasons why he had thought of checking in on Heather. Especially after the conversation they just had. Knowing what his sister and Storm might be doing dominated his thoughts. He wanted to do the same thing. What he found interesting was he hadn't been dragged into it with them. Unless Toki was wrong, Heather must have done something to block their bond.

Toki tried to act relaxed, but he could see she had been thinking the same thing he had by her body language. She wanted him and he wanted her. Why was he fighting this?

Because he felt like he was being pushed into something he might regret later.

His brain kept him from acting.

"You are a very stubborn man." Toki stood and slowly opened her outfit. Dropping it to the floor, she stood in front of him, almost daring him to touch her.

He found himself standing, his hand reaching out to gently cup a breast. Body won out over mind as he took her in his arms and lowered his face to hers. She welcomed his tongue into her mouth. A sigh escaped her when his hands roamed her body, caressing the tips of her nipples, dipping into her belly button, sliding down to find the soft, springy curls covering her mound.

He felt the heat of her hand as it closed around his hardened member. She had loosened his trousers enough to slip her hand inside. Kuarto realized he was overdressed and shed his clothes quickly. Then he continued his exploration of her body. He ran his fingers through her curls and found sensitive flesh responding to his touch. She quivered as he stroked her.

She always had to start their intimacy. His oath of celibacy kept him from being the aggressor, but once he started to respond to her advances he took control. She wanted him and he wanted her. Why did he fight it each and every time?

Toki remained passive. She wanted him to take from her, to dominate her the way he should. He felt powerful to have her at his mercy this way. So he took his time. His lips left her mouth and blazed a trail down her throat to her collarbone. He continued to place kisses down the soft tissue until he captured one of her nipples in his mouth. He suckled and stroked her, drawing moans from her throat and wetness from her core. Switching to her other breast, he used two fingers and slid them up inside her. She spasmed around the intrusion.

Her head dropped back as an orgasm grabbed her.

He dropped to his knees as his mouth continued a trek south. His tongue lathed her belly button. If his fingers caused such a reaction what would happen when he used his mouth? Bracing his hands on either side of her hips, he worked his way down. The heat of his mouth on her core made her knees buckle for a moment and he was glad he had a secure grip. His tongue swirled against her. Her hips made a little pumping action in response.

He wanted to continue to work his magic on her, he could feel she was getting close again, but his own needs began to make demands and he knew he couldn't wait any longer. The bed was just a few feet away so he stood and carried her to it. Pressing her into the bed, he hesitated for just a moment.

"If you stop now, I just might have to get my brother after you." She wrapped her legs around him, giving him the silent message of what she wanted.

He slid in deep. "Can't have that, can we?"

She sucked in her breath as he filled and stretched her. "Oh my, that feels so good."

"You haven't seen anything yet, sweetheart." He set a pace that had them both breathing hard quickly.

———

Toki felt her heart beating hard in her chest. You would think she had never been with a man by the way her body was acting, but he had a way about him that created magic when he touched her.

Every time he buried himself deep inside, she felt all of her tighten, and soft frissons of heat spiral through her blood. A couple more of those, and she was going to dissolve into a thousand tiny pieces. He did something to her. Something she didn't understand.

No man before him had been able to affect her this way. Everything he did, she felt deep inside. She had been told since she was a child that her role was destined. She would never meet a mate, never know the joy of a family until she had fulfilled her duty as religious leader. So why him? Why now?

He moved within her, bringing her attention back to the sensations exploding all around her. He slid in and out and she felt her world shrink to just her and him. He moved, and she reacted. She felt her body tightened against him, her muscles creating a vise for him to move through.

Each time he pulled almost out, she felt her body lock on his, creating a grip so tight she wasn't sure he could move right away until he drove himself back in. Everything was slick and wet, giving him just the right friction.

"Please." She didn't mean to beg, but she needed the release that seemed to be just beyond her reach. Kuarto pumped into her once more and she felt her world splinter as the orgasm had a hold of her. Everything shifted. Her body cinched up, muscles creating a heightened lock on him. It only took one drive into her body to send her over the edge, and from the way he was breathing he was right behind her.

He held her as her orgasm took hold. A hitch in her breath and her world disappeared, until all that was left was him holding her as fireworks went off in her head. He held her tight, making her feel cherished.

"You are phenomenal." He kissed her forehead.

"Why would you say that?"

"Because no one has ever had me forget about everything but us before." He braced himself on his elbows so she wouldn't take all of his weight. "Each time, I can only think of what you do to me when we're joined so intimately. I have never lost my focus before, not like I do with you."

———

The ships set down in the compound. Storm did his post flight shutdown before he opened the door for them to exit. "Welcome to Vespia, Doctor."

Storm was the first to exit the ship, then his mate, followed by his sister, with Kuarto bringing up the rear. Kuarto couldn't help but notice that Storm going first was unusual for most leaders. They would be one of the last ones out, but Storm was protecting them. If anything were to go wrong they would still be safe inside the ship.

A small group of people greeted Storm and Heather as they disembarked. Toki walked past them and headed to a different group of people. She bowed before stepping up to one of the women there and pressed a kiss to her cheek. "Mother."

"Good to see you healthy." She touched her cheek. "We were all worried when we lost touch with you."

"Storm came to the rescue as usual."

"That is your brother." She wrapped an arm around her waist. "And who is this?"

"This is Heather's brother. He has been going by the name of Kuarto." She gestured for him to step up. "Kuarto, this is the leader of our ruling council and my mother."

"Ma'am." These people didn't seem to use their birth names at all. If it wasn't for Heather, he wouldn't know anyone's name.

"So formal, just like his sister." She smiled at him. "Most call me Anseri. Heather taught me that most off-worlders like to call people by name."

Heather and Storm approached them. Both bowed before Heather stepped up, took her hands and gave her a quick kiss on the cheek. Storm did the same thing.

"You look radiant, my dear."

"Thank you." Heather smiled at Storm as she gave him a quick hug. "Must be all the tender care he gives me."

"I was going to say your pregnancy seems to agree with you, but if giving your mate credit for your glow is what you want to do, then I won't stop you."

"I think it's a combination." She looked at Kuarto. "You ready?"

"For what?"

"To meet our parents." She took his hand and guided him over to another couple who came with Anseri. "They are here, and I'm sure they want to see you."

"Kuarto, this is Streya and his mate, Helia." She bowed to them, showing them the respect of their positions.

"You were able to pry their names out of them?" He said it so softly no one else would be able to hear him.

"I didn't know our mother's name until she had gotten hurt." Heather shook her head. "It's pretty bad, isn't it?"

He greeted his parents, which felt weird since he didn't even know them. These total strangers were the ones who gave him life, yet as he studied them, he didn't see any family resemblance, which he found odd. Habit had him hitting his scanner, which sat in his pocket. If they were his parents, he needed to prove it to himself.

Heather bowed to them once again as she led him back to Toki and Storm. "You can spend more time with them later if you wish, but we need to get back to our group so we can let these people get back to work."

"What do you mean?"

"As long as the ruling council is visible, the people working here show respect by standing and waiting, and whether you believe it or not, you are part of that council as the son of two of the members." Heather joined Storm and took his hand. She looked to her brother to make sure he followed procedure as he joined Toki. She was the minister of protocol for the planet and had taught Heather everything she knew. Heather knew she would keep him in line.

Storm guided her to the waiting vehicle. Once everyone was aboard, he maneuvered it out of the landing area and headed to the main plaza. It didn't take long to arrive and touch down near a large white building.

Heather took Toki aside. "I can assign him a suite if you need me to."

"No secrets, huh?"

"I had none with you people."

"True." She looked at Kuarto. "I don't know what he wants, yet. Perhaps have rooms ready for him, just in case?"

Heather nodded. She spoke softly to one of the workers at the main building where the family lived. They would take care of anything he needed.

Storm stepped to her side. "Ready to go to our rooms?"

"Yes." She smiled up at him. "I'm feeling kind of tired right now."

"You okay? You had plenty of rest on the ship."

"I know." She felt her legs give way. Suddenly, she found herself surrounded. "I'm okay, just a little weak."

"Let me be the judge of that." Kuarto used his scanner.

Checking her readings, he found most of it was just a mineral deficiency. He set up his hypo and gave her a quick shot. "That should help, but we need to get you through a full physical. You're the first non-Vespian to carry one of their children, I'm sure there are a few extra drains on your system that no one has expected."

"Non-Vespian?" asked Storm's mom.

"It's a long story and I will fill you in on everything we have learned, Mother." Storm glared at Kuarto for making the comment but Heather noticed he hadn't said a word about what he had learned about her, so he had protected her. They all were bound to slip up from time to time.

"We have a full medical facility in the main building. Why don't we go there first so my son can explain things while you give Heather that checkup." Storm's mom led the group to the building and the medical center.

"It could wait until the morning." Heather had hoped to make light of her small mishap. It probably wasn't anything big.

"We're here." Anseri pointed to the med area.

Heather nodded. She knew better than to fight with the woman.

Kuarto checked out the medical area. It was state-of-the-art. Heather thought he'd be a happy man. It didn't seem to impress him, though. He took his palm-sized scanner and placed it next to one of the terminals. Within seconds she saw readings, her readings, on the screen.

"Neat little toy there." Storm watched her information fill the screen. It showed everything about her pregnancy. "Can you program it to show whatever you want?"

"Yes." He studied the information he brought up on the screen. Storm stood nearby with a frown on his face. Heather feared the two of them would be at each other again.

"Heather, how long did you say you'd be pregnant?"

"Um, I was told eighteen months was the normal timeline for Vespians." She found it an odd question.

"I see." He continued to go through the information. "Is there a way for me to access information on some of your history?" He looked at Storm when he asked that question.

"Yes. Why?" Storm seemed suspicious as well.

"Need to see what I can learn about your, our race. That's all."

What wasn't he telling everyone?

Storm walked to the terminal and pressed a few buttons. "What are you looking for?"

"Information on our race's pregnancy." A look passed between them, which made Heather nervous. They were actually working together.

"Anseri, I think we all need to let Kuarto do his job. Perhaps I could rest in our rooms?"

"Of course, my dear." She guided Heather and her daughter out of the center.

Toki leaned into Heather as they headed down the hallway to their rooms. "What was that all about?"

"I'm afraid to guess."

———

Storm wasn't sure what Kuarto was up to, but he had made sure no one knew about Heather's heavy dose of ancient blood, and Storm was grateful. He wasn't sure what Kuarto was after, but he planned on finding out as soon as he felt it was safe.

"So why the files?"

"Eighteen months doesn't seem to be the right timeline for Heather's pregnancy. I'm trying to figure out what is going on."

"So what do you think the timeline should be?"

"Not sure." He skipped through most of the information

Storm brought up. "It could be her body's way of protecting itself, but I won't be sure until I do some more research."

"I'd rather you not go through this here."

Kuarto looked up at Storm. "Right." He loaded everything onto his scanner and turned to face him. "Then take me to a secure system so I can do my job."

Storm started walking and Kuarto had to grin. This man just expected him to follow, and he shook his head as he did. They walked through a large outdoor center before they headed to the tallest building in the area. They entered the building and walked toward the right. It didn't take long before he found himself in the middle of a science area where he could do all the research he wanted without anyone interrupting.

"Now I need you to explain yourself."

"Really don't have a lot of information. Heather's DNA is more of this blood line than Vespian. If I knew what race it is from, I would be able to see how quickly she'll give birth."

"What do you mean?"

"Right now her readings are showing a shorter gestational period."

"How short?"

"That's part of the problem. One time I look at her readings and it looks like it will happen in a few months, then the next time it looks like it will be a normal Vespian pregnancy. I think her body is still protecting itself, but if it is doing that then I need to have all the info I can because I won't be caught unawares when she suddenly goes into labor."

Storm stepped up to the terminal and pressed a few keys. "This is all of our standard medical information." He pointed to the data Kuarto already had. "This is some of the odd things that happened along the way." He released a different file so he could view it. "And this is all we have on the ancients. This is the race where Heather's DNA comes from. They are a race that came to this planet thousands of years ago. We don't know much about them, but I have freed all the data we do have. Kuarto, this info doesn't leave this terminal." He brought up a third file, then stepped back.

"What is this language?"

"Ancient. Whatever is in the language is something we haven't been able to translate yet." Storm just stood there looking at him.

"And how am I supposed to read it, then?"

"You have three choices. One, try yourself. Your family has always had the ability to either read, write or speak the language. You should have one of those talents. Two, you could go to your parents, I believe your mother can read it. Three, Heather. She can do all three."

"Anyone else have that talent?"

"Only my mate." There was something in the sound of his voice.

"You love her very much, don't you?"

"She is my heart." Such a simple statement spoke volumes for the Vespian in front of him.

Kuarto knew his sister felt the same about him. When you watched them together, they were always in close physical contact. He guessed he was starting to warm up to the man some.

"What can you tell me about Al?"

"Not a whole lot. Heather and I were forced together from the moment we met. Someone was trying to assassinate her. There were several attempts on her life before she was kidnapped. We never knew who was doing it. When she was kidnapped was when we first learned about Al. I saw him in the dream world he had created for her, trying to be a love interest. But in the end she saw through all of that." Storm paused for a moment. "I wasn't sure if Ialog was his real name, or the face I saw was his real face until we saw him at your place."

"Heather said something about him not wanting her but her child all along."

"That was what he told her. How he knew she would be pregnant by the time he kidnapped her baffles me."

"So you don't believe that either."

"No."

———

Heather stretched and sat up. The nap helped, but she wondered where Storm was. When they weren't working, he normally was by her side.

Her mind reached out to check on her children. That had become a habit pretty quickly. They couldn't string thoughts together yet, but she let them know she was here and loved them.

Since she did have time to herself, she went to the computer terminal and pulled up some of the files she had marked to read about the ancients. Now that she knew she had so much of their blood in her, she felt she needed to know more about them. Most of the files were just about the people, great stories that would inspire anyone, but every once in a while she found a file that was a little different. Sometimes it would have technical information or the way one of their rituals was performed.

She wasn't sure what she was looking for, but she felt driven to continue to look. Storm had set up several alerts to let them know if anyone tried to access some of these more obscure files and she saw them flashing on the screen. At least she knew where he was now. Storm was with her brother, probably driving him crazy.

Since she knew her brother would be looking for the same files she would be, Heather set the system to highlight any file he opened for longer than a few moments that she hadn't already looked at. Next she programmed the computer to look for anything on ancient pregnancies. Since the ancient language was something the computer didn't know, she also asked it to pull up anything that hadn't been translated yet for her. She'd get to reading them sooner or later, anyway.

After she loaded several files onto her handheld, she settled on the couch and started to read. The stories were always entertaining. She loved reading about the people and the way they saw their world. In one of the stories, she found the writer speaking of a massive compound where the ancients would gather. According to what she read, they said the compound was somewhere near the elders' hall. So how come no one had ever mentioned it before?

She sensed her mate coming. He must have felt it when she woke up.

He came in the door and looked around. "Heather?"

She lifted a hand and waved at him. He came around the edge of the couch and kneeled on the floor.

"You hiding from me?" He braced his arms on either side of her.

"Is that possible?" She smiled at him. "You have this uncanny knack of finding me no matter where I am."

"True." He leaned down and captured her lips with his. "But you also have this uncanny knack of not being where I expect you to be."

"I'm supposed to be unpredictable." She wrapped her arms around his neck. "Got to keep you on your toes."

"You do that every moment you are awake."

"I've been doing some reading and found a few references to an old, ancient compound."

"Yeah. There's an old myth. Supposedly right under our feet, but no one has ever been able to find it." He pressed his lips to hers again. "We've even done a scan to see what was under our main compound, but nothing has ever shown up."

"So is it okay if I look around for it, too?"

"Not without me."

"Storm."

"With you pregnant? I don't think so." He pulled her into a sitting position, then sat beside her. "By the way, your brother wishes to run another scan."

"But he ran one when we arrived."

"I know, but he's having trouble with his equipment, so wants another set of readings to compare with."

She sighed. "Fine. When?"

"Now would be great."

She sighed again. "I don't like it when you two get along." She offered him her hand. "Let's go."

He led her to the small room he had left Kuarto in.

"This isn't a medical lab."

"No," said her brother, "but I don't need the lab." He pointed to a chair. "You, young lady, have a few habits that mess with my scanning."

"What are you talking about?"

"You seem to have the ability to shield yourself from the scanners." He held up his palm-sized machine. "I ran this over you today and it showed nothing but a healthy person."

"What is wrong with that?"

"It hid your pregnancy from me. This might not make any sense, but it showed you pregnant yet didn't show for how long, when you were due or the number of babies. It was like everything went into some sort of stasis."

She gave him a confused look.

"I think your body is protecting itself. Habit to keep you safe. But I have gotten the proper readings before, so I'm thinking they only register when you feel happy and safe."

"Which is why you wish to run the tests again?"

"Sorry." He gave her his best smile.

"You're worse than Storm." She adjusted herself in the seat. "Fine. I'll think happy thoughts of throttling the two of you and you run your tests."

"That isn't fair," complained Storm. "It wasn't me causing all the trouble. Why would you want to cause me bodily harm?"

"You two didn't get along until we landed on this planet. Now all of a sudden you're a united front against me. I have the right to fantasize what I wish to do to the two men who will now try to control my life completely. One of you is bad enough, but two?"

"Done." He set his scanner near the terminal and watched as the readings came up on the screen. "Much better." He showed her the screen where it displayed all the data he had been missing before. "You mentioned that the Vespian pregnancy cycle was eighteen months, right?"

"Yes. Why?"

"You do realize it's based off of their eighteen-hour day. If you compare it to the Earth time of forty weeks with a twenty-four-hour cycle you're only talking an extra thirty-five days."

"It still sounds like a long time."

"It will fly by."

Heather sure hoped so.

———

That evening, Storm found himself staring at his mate and her brother working on another project. Ever since the man came into their lives, he seemed to be monopolizing her time and he didn't care for it. His sister had joined them after they had eaten.

"Mother sends her regards."

"Had to explain to the council what happened, huh?"

"Yes." She looked at Heather and Kuarto. "They are expecting you to show your findings on what happened to the ship soon."

"I know. I have already sent my preliminary findings to them."

"What did you find?"

"Your ship was shot at. Right now, I'm going to assume it was Al. The ship showed as Vespian and he felt threatened."

"How could he detect it? I had my shields on."

"Don't know, but he seems to have access to more advanced technology than ours, so we have to assume the ship wasn't shielded from him." Storm kept his eyes on Heather. "I'm not sure how my ship was able to land without any trouble. He should have shot at it as well."

"Perhaps your mate was able to protect you from being detected. Kuarto said she has a very powerful mind. Instinct could have kept you safe."

"Kuarto's been talking to you about my mate?"

"No. He said it to you in my presence a couple of times." She sighed and changed the subject. "What are they doing?"

Heather and Kuarto sat on the floor cross-legged, facing each other. Eyes closed and hands up and out. It looked like some sort of weird pantomime.

"They are trying to build some wall between them so he won't be joining us anymore."

"I'm sure everyone will be happy when that is done, then."

"Yes." He looked at his sister. "I haven't asked, but I want to know what happened between you two."

"I told you."

"That he saved your life by protecting you with that mail-order bride scenario. I got that." He touched her arm. "But my mate seems to think there is more there."

"What has she said?"

"Nothing." He tapped the side of his head. "It's a feeling I get from her."

"It shouldn't matter what I do and who I do it with."

"Normally, I agree, but you are a special case like my

mate. You have a predestined position here that I have been told you are fighting. Mother is concerned as well."

"No one needs to worry about whether or not I will fulfill the job I'm destined to do." She didn't look at him as she spoke. "If I remember correctly, no one thought you'd be able to fulfill your position until Heather came into your life."

"True, but having a mate doesn't affect my position, it does with yours."

"Can we not talk about this right now?"

He let the silence hang between them. She said she would do what was expected of her.

EIGHT

"**W**hy do you have that damn chair in your mind?" Kuarto pointed to the chair Storm had created for them.

She just grinned at her brother.

"I don't want to know, do I?"

"Nope. So, how do you think we should do this?" She looked around at the openness of her mind. Other than the chair, the area was empty. "I don't see a place where you would be able to access my mind."

"Then the first thing we need to do is figure out where I join the two of you." He backed out of her mind and then tried to access it again. Using his mind, he reached out to her. "You got to let me in again."

Heather's mind heard him and her consciousness marked the spot. "So, this is where you come in at."

"Not much to look at, is it?" He stood beside her in her mind.

"No. What is next?"

"Close it in."

"With what?" She looked at him.

"Personally, I think you need to block most of your

thoughts from spilling out, but still allow me to contact you in case of an emergency. We also need to make sure whatever you use to block me out will not block your mate. Don't think he'd forgive me if I took that away from him."

"Don't think I would forgive you, either."

Together they worked on building the wall and door, so he could have peace of mind. Once they were done, Kuarto was ready to get to the next thing.

"That is just so boring." Heather looked at it, trying to figure out what she wanted before it started to look more like a grotto with vines covering it. "Much better."

"You're learning how to do this pretty quick." He looked around. "Now, where is the sentry?"

"I don't know. Storm is the one who sees it, not me."

"Then we need him."

She nodded and lost her focus on him for a moment. He found it interesting how everything rippled around him while she brought Storm into the picture. He watched them interact in her mind and they behaved the same way here as they did in the real world. They were always within touching distance of each other. In fact, here he could see a give and take of their auras with each other.

"Heather said she can't see the sentinel, but you can. Show me so we can take care of it."

Storm walked him right to it. He was surprised he didn't see it before, but it was possible that because Heather couldn't see it, he couldn't either. He worked with Heather to build a thick shield around it. Nothing to make it feel threatened or to cause it to wake up, but enough to keep it from seeing anything when it did wake up. The second one wasn't as easy to work with. It looked like a security camera. Unless they removed it completely there was no real way to shield it from seeing what it wanted.

He had Heather create a second one then showed her how to tie it into the first one. Whatever it was after would also be picked up by the second sentry and he had her create a link with Storm's mind so they would know when it went off.

Once they were done, they backed out of Heather's mind.

"How do you know how to do that?" she asked.

"I have worked with many races and have had to learn things you wouldn't expect to help them. The mind is a beautiful, creative thing, and it's amazing what you can do with it if you try. There is a lot more for you to learn, but we need to do a section at a time. Don't want you to take on too much." He stood. "Where did your sister go?"

"Probably her room. We sort of abandoned her," said Storm.

"I can give you directions if you like," said Heather.

"I think I'll go rest." He felt drained from working with her. "Working with the mind takes a lot of energy. I'm sure I'll catch up with her later."

"As you wish." Heather still sat on the floor.

Storm offered her a hand up. When she stood, he pulled her into his embrace and whispered. "We're going to have to test that out now."

Kuarto rolled his eyes and got out the door before he saw something he didn't need to see.

―――――

Storm glanced at the door for a moment before turning his attention to his mate. "So do you think it will work?"

"We'll have to see, won't we?"

"I was hoping you would say that." He lowered his head so he could capture her lips with his. "Having your brother around has cut into our time together."

"Don't tell me you're jealous of him." She pulled back a little to look at him.

"Of course not." He nibbled on her neck, focusing on his

favorite spot. "But I am jealous of the time he has taken up. I'm used to being the one monopolizing your time not someone else."

"And who has my undivided attention right now?" She tilted her head so he could get better access.

"My heart." He wrapped his arms around her and picked her up. Walking into their bedroom, he deposited her on the bed. "Now let's test that block you set up."

He pressed her back onto the mattress.

"Aren't we a bit overdressed?" She touched the collar of his shirt.

"It might seem like that, but I have plans. Wonderful plans I think you're going to like." He kissed her again. "I thought I'd explore you some more."

"Explore, don't you have my body memorized by now?"

He laughed. "I do. But like a fine meal, you have many layers. Lately, I have been focusing on just devouring you instead of savoring some of your more interesting parts. It's time to savor the finer aspects of you."

He watched her eyes dilate as his words sunk in. He grinned. Today, he just might get her to make a sound or two.

He nibbled on her throat once more before he worked his way to her collarbone. His attention to the soft tissue there caused goose bumps to rise on her skin. The simple dress was easy to open, exposing her breasts to his gaze. He wanted to focus on one thing at a time, so didn't open her gown any further.

He felt her hands on his shirt, opening it up so he could slide his arms out and she threw the garment across the room. Her hands traveled the planes and valleys of his muscles on his chest, his back. He reveled in the feel of her hands gliding along his skin.

His mouth traveled over her collarbone, down the delicate flesh to capture one of her tips with his lips. The heat from his breath had her pebbling up. She arched her back, begging for more under his ministrations. He moved from one breast to the other, giving the second the same attention as the first.

Her mind reached for his, bringing him into the feelings racing through her body. The heat of his mouth had her blood boiling, making her want more. Her excitement was breathtaking, and he wanted to increase it as much as he could. He reached for her skirt and pulled it up until he hit soft skin. Then he teased and caressed his way up her thigh until he found her moist heat.

She was ready for him, and he hadn't even started his explorations.

Heather hadn't been idle while he made her body sing for him. She had opened the seals to his pants and had wrapped her hand around his hard member, running her fingers up and down the length of him.

His fingers found a sensitive spot within her folds and got a sharp inhale of breath and the moan he had been waiting for. Then he heard the six little words he wanted to hear from her.

"Storm, please, I can't wait anymore."

He opened her gown and pulled it from under her. Just as quickly, he pulled his pants off and climbed back on the bed. "I love it when you beg, but you know I haven't explored all the places I wanted to."

"Next time." She got up to face him. "Not now."

He hesitated to see what she would do. Heather crawled across the bed toward him, hunting her prey. He grinned as she came after him. Being the dominator most of the time, he looked forward to those moments when she became the aggressor.

Heather's body hummed with desire. Each time he touched her it got stronger. She teased him one time that she would get to a point where all he would have to do is look at her and she would explode, and there were times when she almost did.

He sat there, grinning at her.

"What are you thinking?" she asked as she reached him.

"How beautiful you are."

She pushed him down onto the bed and climbed on top. "I don't know why I couldn't wait this time, but I must feel you inside me."

She eased herself down on him and sighed as he filled her. Her head dropped back and her eyes closed. She felt Storm's arms wrap around her, to keep her upright. Small tremors raced through her and she hadn't even started to move. "Oh, I'm in trouble."

She felt Storm's concern until he felt her orgasm take control. He hadn't realized how close she was until her release encompassed them. It was overpowering, squeezing them in an embrace that took their breath away. She could feel his struggle to maintain control as she lost hers. Everything felt over sensitized.

Storm touched her face once she came back to him. "You okay, my heart?"

"Yes. Not sure what caused that." She pressed her lips to his. "Got to say that was amazing, though." Heather hoped she wouldn't be losing control that quickly again. She started to move and found everything building just as quickly as before. It wasn't long before she moaned and clenched against him. She couldn't breathe it was so intense.

"My heart, you're killing me. I can't keep holding back if you keep this up."

"I can't help it." She sounded breathless. "Every time we cause any friction I feel like I'm going to explode."

"Then I'm going to take control of this problem." He

flipped her onto her back and drove inside again. He set a pace and allowed her to just enjoy.

She felt another orgasm coming and her world splintered. Storm continued to pump in and out of her, pushing her higher and higher as her world shattered around her over and over again. Heather felt mindless as he drove into her. A small part of her registered that he was close and soon would be joining her, but all she could do was feel.

When she felt his release join hers, everything vibrated. It started deep inside and slowly slid up her spine before entering every fiber of her being. It was glorious. She felt like she floated. No body to weigh her down. It took a long time before she could focus on the room again.

Storm had taken her into his arms and pillowed her head against his chest. She must have moved because he became alert that she had rejoined him.

"My heart, good to see you have come back to me."

"I'm sorry." She lifted her head to look at him.

"Don't be. That was amazing. I don't know if I can handle that all the time, but I'm willing to give it a try." He pressed his lips to her forehead. "You seem to be okay now. Not having one release after another the way you were a few moments ago."

"I never felt anything like that. Do you think it had something to do with the walls we built earlier?"

"We'll have to ask your brother." He brushed a few strands of hair out of her face. "You think the wall worked?"

"I didn't feel him join us."

"You really weren't able to feel too much beyond the orgasms racking your body."

"Hey, I knew you were there." She propped herself up on her elbows. "Your release was what sent me over the edge."

He laughed and rolled her so she was beneath him. "You can't blame me for that. Your releases almost killed me. I felt each and every one of them and fought to keep myself from following you too quickly. That was a true test for my stamina."

"And you came through with flying colors."

He grinned. "I did, didn't I?" He captured her lips with his.

"Do we have time to see my brother or do you want to see if we'll have an encore of the multiple orgasms?"

"That is a tough question. I would love to see if you will melt in my arms like that again but maybe we should see your brother. Find out what is causing it before we get too addicted to it."

"I'll contact him."

———

Heather answered the door for her brother. "Thank you for coming."

"Your mate doesn't like it when his requests are ignored." She gave him a questioning look as she stepped aside so he could enter. "Been doing a little research while I was waiting."

"So you knew we would contact you."

"No, but just assumed you'd want to know if it worked, which it did. Didn't feel a thing." He tapped the side of his head. "Where is that mate of yours?"

"Security. His shift starts in about an hour, but since he hasn't been here, he went in early." She moved to the couch. "Um, did the work we did have any side effects?"

"Sometimes." He sat on the couch. "But it's so rare I didn't think about it. Did you have a side effect?"

"Yeah." She sat down beside him. "How long does it last?"

"Well, I guess it depends on how intense it was. The few who had them found different results. It depended on what activated the side effect." He turned to look at her.

"I'm assuming yours had something to do with being intimate?"

She nodded. Looking at him, she tried to pick the right words. "I felt like a, I don't know, a bottle rocket. I went off and off and off and didn't come down for a long time."

"Bottle rocket?" It took a few seconds for his translator to explain the archaic phrase. "Oh. I'm sure it will fade as time goes on." He wasn't sure what to tell her. "Are you saying you didn't enjoy it? I might be able to give you something to dampen your reactions if so."

"Oh, don't get me wrong. It was phenomenal. But I don't know if my body can take too many of those. I'm exhausted and I have work to do."

"That good, huh?"

She blushed.

"What do you do here, anyway? I'm sure Storm has some sort of job where he orders people around."

"I'm split between two places. In the morning, I work out with my security team." She saw his look. "Don't let this form fool you, I'm very good at what I did when I was on Earth. In the afternoons, I sit on the council."

"That has got to be boring."

"Not always the most stimulating of conversations, but I have things to keep me occupied." She kept her ability to read, speak and write ancient to herself. He probably only knew what Storm told him and if she said too much she'd hear about it later.

"Why would they have you on the council? You're not Vespian."

"In the beginning, I was put there to learn about the people and so they could learn about me. Now, though, the public is aware of my family ties to our parents. They were the ones who requested I be put on the council permanently." She stood. "I do have some time before I have to be in council chambers.

Would you like to go for a walk? I normally will walk before I have to be there each day. Seems to help keep the babies calm when I'm sitting in those chairs for a long period of time."

"Are they bothering you?" He took out his scanner.

"No. It's just after working out I think they get excited and the walking helps soothe them so I can sit for several hours with the council without being uncomfortable."

"Lead the way."

"Let me change into my council clothing and I'll be right with you." She disappeared into her bedroom and came out wearing a long, simple gown. It cut straight across her shoulders leaving the skin bare, with long sleeves. The bodice hugged her torso to flair out at the hips. This one was a cream-colored gown.

"So you have different looks depending on where you are working?"

"I wear a uniform when working with Storm. This or something very close to it when I'm on the council." She led him out into the garden area. Her shadows, as she had come to call them, joined them the moment they left her and Storm's rooms.

"I'm surprised Storm doesn't have his own place for the two of you." He glanced at the four guards following them.

"He did. But his mother convinced him to move back into the palace. She had set aside a wing for him in hopes he would marry and have a family someday and she offered that to us when she learned of the pregnancy. I don't know what she said to him, but he went along with it when I expected him to say no. He feels his mother meddles a little too much when we're that accessible."

One of the Vespian children approached her. Heather crouched down to speak to the child quietly and received a hug for her words. Another waited patiently to hand her some flowers. She hugged that child as well. She didn't want either to think she liked one more than the other since they were sisters and always vied for her attention.

"I read you mated with him for the good of your planet. What made you stay with him?" Kuarto looked up at the giant screen and saw a flash of a woman.

"He's my heart." Heather stood. Did he see the picture of her that just flashed on the screen?

"That's what Storm said about you."

She smiled at him. It didn't surprise her in the least. She started walking again. "So what's going on between you and Toki?"

"What makes you think there is something going on?" He seemed slightly uncomfortable all of the sudden.

"Little things." She nodded to a young woman studying while she waited for her next class. The young woman came over and apologized for interrupting them but needed help with some ancient and knew Heather could help her. Although she hadn't mentioned her talent to her brother, Heather always helped anyone who needed it. She took the time to answer the question and show the young girl how to figure out similar passages with a simple technique. The young lady thanked her and bowed before going back to her bench. "You two look at each other a certain way. There's a connection there. It's new and very fragile, but I can sense it."

"I like how you didn't miss a beat in our conversation."

"Storm calls me tenacious because I can come back to a conversation hours later, right where we left off." She smiled. "It annoys him a lot."

"How do you deal with the dominating male ego? He has been very aggressive and a royal pain."

"He's not that bad." She sniffed the flowers she had been given.

"Are we talking about the same man?" He touched his

chest, pretending he was shocked. "The one who growled when I spent too much time with you."

"You don't know him yet. He is a wonderful man, just a tad overprotective when it comes to me." She touched his arm. "He has changed so much since we met. If you knew him then, you might understand him better."

"It would take a lot for me to understand him."

"At least you're not trying to out posture each other as much as you were when you first met. I thought we'd have to put you two in separate corners."

"We weren't that bad."

She laughed. "Yes you were."

The picture flashed once more, staying on the screen long enough for Kuarto to know who it was. "Is that you?"

"Yes." No reason to deny it.

"Wow." He saw the image flash again. "I'm amazed Storm let that picture be released."

"It was his idea."

"Really?" He walked beside her for a moment. "Why?"

"You see, that was my question. It has a lot to do with me being raised on Earth. You know how it is between me and Storm, but very few others do."

"And he felt this picture would show you in a different light. Make them understand that although you weren't raised here doesn't mean you lack a sex drive."

"Pretty much."

"Yet you don't want to look at it."

"It's just strange seeing yourself that way." Someone else approached her, letting her know she was due in the council's chambers. Heather thanked him and turned to her brother. "I'm going to have to get to work. You can join us if you like. The council is open to everyone."

"I guess I could for a while. I need to wait for your husband to unlock the computer for me to use, anyway."

"You don't like the secretiveness of the people here, do you?" She headed to the main hall.

"No." He walked with her. "That type of secretiveness was why I stopped being a renowned doctor and went into hiding. Too many secrets and too many people trying to tell me how to live my life and who to give my expertise to."

"You might not believe me right now, but this planet keeps no secrets from the people, only from off-worlders." His silence made her smile. She felt the same way when she first came here.

They entered the main hall, and she headed to her chair. Once she was seated, the other elders filed in and took their seats. People started to enter, and she put on her best smile as she listened to their stories and concerns. A few of the people did ask for her opinion, but she spent most of the time working her way through a few more columns of ancient. She ran across another passage about the underground compound.

There had to be an entrance. The information all pointed to the reality of the compound, but nothing mentioned an entrance. As she listened to the people, she also scanned the writing on the wall to see if she could find anything else.

Just as she found a passage that caught her attention, she spotted Storm standing just inside the door. He kept his gaze on her as she gently touched her mate's mother's arm. After she received permission to leave her seat by a slight nod, she got up and went to Storm's side. He looked anxious. The same look she had seen when he was worried about her.

"Is there a problem?" she whispered.

"My sister seems to be missing."

"I'll tell your mother."

He nodded and touched her face with gentle fingers. Heather returned the gesture before walking back to the dais and approaching Anseri's chair. She leaned over and whispered in her ear. Anseri gave the slightest of nods before

Heather took her seat again. They were close to finishing this particular session, so Anseri waited until the complaint had been given and a solution was found before she requested a break.

"It is time to take a recess." Anseri stood. It took the guards a few minutes to clear the room. Once the room was emptied, she approached Storm. "When was the last time any of you saw her?"

"Earlier today. She was in our chambers while Heather's brother helped her with a particular problem," answered Storm.

Heather signaled for her brother to join them. She spoke to him softly, pretty sure he wasn't aware of what was going on. "When was the last time you saw Toki?"

"The same time you two did." He looked confused. "Why?"

"She is missing."

"Run your computer checks." Anseri turned to Heather. "We need to continue, but you are excused if need be."

Heather looked at Storm. He gave her a slight nod. Which meant she could do what she felt she should do. "I'll stay."

She was staying more to be supportive of her mate's mother than anything else. Knowing Storm, he would be doing all the research and she would be just as bored in their rooms as she would be here, and at least here she could continue her search for the elusive compound. It would help keep her mind off Toki being missing.

Storm took her brother with him when he left.

Heather took her seat once more and wondered where Toki could have gone. She didn't know how to reach out for minds, so she didn't try, but perhaps her brother might know that talent and teach her.

Storm's mother kept a professional image, but Heather could tell by the way she spoke to the people she was fighting to maintain her composure, her fear for her daughter a palpable thing. She had just gotten her back and now she was gone again.

Anseri continued to see those who had waited, but Heather wasn't sure that was a smart thing to do. She focused her attention on her mate's mother instead of the ancient stories she enjoyed reading. If she showed any sign of cracking, they would have to clear the hall.

As the appointments thinned, Heather nodded to the head guard to see if he could shorten the session so Anseri could get an update on her daughter. She was frightened and needed information, and the only one who could give her that was Storm.

Finally, there was no one asking to speak to the council and Heather took her mate's mother away from her seat. She wasn't walking in any particular direction, just guided Anseri to a quiet corridor. "Are you okay?"

"I'm fine, Heather. I have been through worse."

"Not me." She walked with her, heading down a hall she had never been in before. This must be where the elders came in and out of. "I've never had to worry like this before."

"You don't need to worry. Storm will find her." She looked around. "Where are we?"

"I don't know." Heather looked at Anseri. "Thought this was the entrance you guys used when you came into the chamber."

"No. this isn't familiar at all."

"Great, I'm now finding nonexistent hallways." She turned them around and headed back the way they came. It didn't take her long before she realized there was ancient written on these walls as well. Excitement grew when she read a few of the lines there.

This could be the corridor that led to the underground compound. How did she find it so fast? She just started looking for it and hadn't found any information on its location. "I think I know where we are. What do you know about the ancient compound?"

"You think you have found the entrance?" She smiled. "Do you know how many times I have heard that?"

Heather stepped up to a wall with a small indentation about waist high. Checking the writing above it she followed the instructions and placed her hand into the groove. The door panel slid aside. "How many of them could do that?"

"None."

Heather started through the doorway.

"Don't you think you should wait for Storm?"

Anseri's words stopped her.

She didn't want to wait but knew if she went charging through without any sort of protection she would anger her mate. Storm would never forgive her if she got hurt because she was impatient. "Do you have a communication device?"

"No."

"Me either and I'm afraid if we leave to get him, we won't find this corridor again." She looked into the new opening, wanting to go down it so badly, she kept stepping toward it before she stopped and looked at Anseri. "Sorry. My curiosity has the best of me."

"I'm sure you'll be able to find this place again." She turned to face the way they came in only to find her passage blocked. Anseri turned back to Heather. "Looks like that is the only way to go now. There is no entrance here anymore."

Heather walked to where her mate's mother stood, staring at the wall where the archway they came through had been. "Storm, isn't going to be very happy with me, is he?"

"Don't think so."

Heather knew she was safe. Her dreams hadn't revealed any danger in months. She wanted to see where the other opening led and now had the chance. Storm would just have to understand.

The moment she stepped into the opening the hallway lit up. "Don't remember that happening before."

They continued down, with Heather stopping every once in a while to read a passage or line written on the wall. "According to this, the compound is this way."

"It's written on the wall?"

"We used something like this on Earth for frequently visited places like hospitals and major landmarks. Colors would guide you to your destination." She touched a few more alcoves and found herself in the biggest command center she had ever seen. The lights came on along with most of the equipment.

"Glad to see you found me, Heather."

Fear pierced her heart. She turned around, looking for however the voice belonged to. "Who's there?"

"I am the main system of this compound."

"You talk?" Technology had gotten very advanced, but computers who were intelligent enough to carry on an inter-acting conversation was still a little beyond them.

"Yes."

"Um, Heather?" Anseri stood in the doorway. "It won't let me in."

"That is the leader of the ruling council. Check your data banks, I'm sure you have information on her and know she means no harm."

The force field holding her dropped so she could enter the room. She looked around in awe. "This is phenomenal."

"I know." Heather grinned. Maybe now she could get the answers to the questions she had. But first, she needed to find out what was going on with Storm. "Can you tell me where my mate is?"

"He is in the main council chamber screaming your name." The image of Storm and her brother looking agitated and shouting at the ceiling filled the screen.

"Oh dear." He was going to be very angry. "You might

want to show him how to get here or he might tear the whole place down to find me."

Within a few moments, she could hear him bellowing her name.

"In here, my heart."

"What do you think you're doing?" He found his way blocked when he tried to enter the room. She could leave him there until he calmed down, but by the way he was glaring at her, she feared it would have the opposite effect on him.

"Computer. Clear them for entrance. The angry one is my mate and future leader of this planet. The one behind him is my brother."

The force field dropped, and Storm stalked into the room. He was pissed. He stepped up to her and started to crowd her backwards. "What do you think you're doing?"

"Trying to find answers." She held her own as he tried to intimidate her. Backing down wasn't in her nature. "What have you learned about Toki's disappearance?"

"Nothing." He ran his fingers through his hair. "It seems there was nothing recording when she disappeared."

"Computer, do you know who I am talking about when I speak of Toki?" She still looked up at her mate, waiting for him to realize where he was.

"Toki." A life-size three-dimensional image popped into existence near one of the computer bays. Storm stepped back from her when he heard the new voice. His sister's image caught his attention.

They walked around it as data streamed beside the image. The data moved with them.

Heather saw her real name displayed. No wonder why she didn't want to tell her, it was very close to one of their swear words and Heather would have slaughtered it.

"You found it, didn't you?"

She nodded but wasn't sure if he saw since they were all

staring at the display. "Can you do this with each of us?" Within seconds, their images loaded. Heather was amazed. She had never seen anything like it before. She walked around her image. It showed the twins, her human name as well as her Vespian name. Along with vital statistics, it also showed mental ability, physical abilities, and her potential.

"Let's get back to Toki. Could you show us what happened to her?" A screen next to her activated to show Toki walking across the garden area. Someone approached her, and she walked off with them.

"That can't be true."

Heather placed an arm on Storm to calm him down. "Computer, can you show us everything she did since arriving on the planet this morning?"

The images started from the moment her feet hit the tarmac. It showed them walking at normal speed. Heather sped it up several times so they wouldn't have to watch it in real time. Hours passed in minutes. They were now in their rooms when Kuarto helped her with the wall building. Heather sat on the floor with him across from her. Storm and his sister spoke. She slowed the speed down, although it was still going too fast for them to hear what was being said.

"She doesn't look happy." Heather leaned into Storm. "What did you say to her?"

"Just reminded her of her obligations."

All three of them were in Heather's mind when Toki said something to herself and left the room. "Computer, what did she say?"

The computer backed up the section in question and replayed it in real time.

"Everyone went to the party but me." A sigh escaped her as she exited their rooms. She went out the entrance that would allow her to walk through the gardens on her way to her rooms. She noticed a man following her.

"Look, I'm not in the mood. Go find someone else to pleasure."

"But you are the one I wish to speak to." The man she spoke to stepped out of the shadows and Storm just about leaped at the screen.

"How did he get on this planet? Our security should have stopped him."

"Ialog has an ancient device that can override any security program you have in place." The computer answered Storm's question. "Do you wish me to pause the recording while I rectify that?"

"You can do that?" asked Storm.

"Yes. I was built by the same people who built that device. I can override any of their technology, but I only take commands from an ancient."

"Let's finish the recording first," said Heather. "We need to see how we can get her back as quickly as possible."

The image started back up. "Come on, Toki."

"How did you get here?" She looked at him innocently.

"Do you know who I am?"

"Sure. You're that man who came to see Kuarto. Wanted him to do some work for you."

"So why are you here?" He watched her like he was waiting for her to make a mistake.

"The future rulers wanted my husband to care for Heather while she is pregnant. Since they were sterile before, they were worried she could have complications."

"Why him?"

"He's the best." She tilted her head and looked at him. "Isn't that why you want him?"

"So where is he now?"

"Working with Heather." She looked down for a moment, like she was searching for words. "I snuck out because I needed a little air."

"Did your husband tell you that he decided to take the

job I offered and you're supposed to come with me while we wait for him?"

"No, and I think he would have said something." Before she could move, he grabbed her by the back of the neck. He snapped something onto the top of her spine.

"That should make it easier for you to keep up."

She tried to walk back toward the doors she came out of but found she didn't have control of her motor responses anymore.

"Sorry. This special device will allow me to keep better tabs on you." He pressed a button and had her walking in the direction he wanted. "We'll send a message to Kuarto to let him know where you are as soon as we're in orbit."

"You can stop the video now." Heather crossed her arms over her chest and confronted her brother. "He took her to make you work for him."

"Then I have got to go."

"No." Storm blocked him from moving. "Then he'll have you right where he wants you."

"I can't leave her with him."

"She's my sister and I'm not any happier about this than you are, but we need to think of a plan before you go charging off."

"Do you have your data with you?" She looked at her brother.

"Sure." He pulled out his scanner and handed it to her.

"Computer, can you analyze this data?"

"There is data on a lot of people on this device. Can I assume you wish me to analyze anything pertaining to you?"

"Yes." Heather wasn't sure if she wanted to know what it could find. "Wait. I want the data on my eggs."

"A clone from the original. Sterile."

"Why?" How can the egg be sterile? She thought maybe it was part of her protective mechanism, but she would think this system could see through that.

"I'm not sure what you are asking."

"I am with child, but I was sterile before. So was my mate. How can I be pregnant yet have sterile eggs?"

"Because your mate carries a catalyst. Your eggs were designed to only carry certain DNA. Without the catalyst, you would show sterility."

"I'm not sure I understand now."

"If we were to remove an unfertilized egg from you right now, it would read as sterile. That is a result of your ancient blood. If that was to be fertilized, it would take a particular DNA strand. Not a common one. Your mate has that DNA."

"What about Al?" Kuarto asked.

"Al?"

"Ialog. The man who took Toki. Does he have the DNA strand?"

"No."

"Then how does he plan on fertilizing the egg?" Kuarto asked.

"Perhaps he has the DNA in a test tube somewhere," said Heather.

"Or perhaps he doesn't know this important piece of information." Storm looked at her brother. "We can use this tidbit in our favor too."

"I can almost see those tiny wheels in your head turn. What do you plan?"

"Still working out the details." He turned to Heather. "You should have never come down here without me."

"Couldn't help it." She touched his heart. "Your mother and I ended up in a corridor and the computer didn't give me a chance to go back and look for you."

"This system has been waiting for her to come for a while. I've been following her for years, waiting patiently for her arrival. Then I waited for her to start looking for me. Now all she needs to do is ask the right questions."

"Right questions?" She looked at her mate. "What sort of questions?"

"That one I can't answer. Think of it as a security code. Without the right question, I can't unlock the rest of the system to you."

"There's more?"

"Much."

"Why me?"

"Because you are ancient."

"Which I don't understand. How did I end up with so much ancient blood in me?"

NINE

Storm set up for Kuarto to leave the planet and be sent to the first space dock available. Al said he would know when he was looking for him and he hoped it would be quick. He needed to make sure Toki was okay. It was his fault she was taken. The one thing he had worked hard to avoid was haunting him now.

He spotted a young man sitting on the other side of the bar. He had been watching him for a while. When he walked outside, the young man followed. Was he the one Al had waiting for him? He wasn't much of a contact. After the kid had been sitting there for an hour or so, Kuarto had the bartender send him whatever he was drinking.

The young man came over once he got the drink. "Why did you send this?"

"Because I got tired of you staring at me." Kuarto looked at him for a moment before turning his attention back to the bottles lining the bar in front of him.

"Sorry. You Kuarto, right?"

"Yeah, what is it to you?" He took a sip of his coffee. The kid was a bit stupid too.

"My boss wishes to speak to you." He sat down next to him.

"There are a lot of people's bosses who which to speak to me." Kuarto looked at him. Why hadn't the kid approached him? Why did he wait for Kuarto to make the first move? "What makes yours so special?"

"His name is Al and he has something that might interest you." He placed a small holographic chip on the counter, pressed a button and an image of Toki loaded.

"Anyone could have made this." At least he knew she was safe when the video was made. He kept his relief to himself and acted bored instead. "She ran away from me a few days ago."

"She didn't run away." The young man pressed a button on the chip so he could hear her voice. "Al wanted you to hear this."

"Al told me you had taken his job offer and said I should go with him and wait until you could get away. He feared the Vespians would try to use me as leverage to keep you on the planet. I wanted you to know I'm safe and waiting for you." Then her voice ended.

"So you saying Al took my bride?" He glared at the young man. "Not what I would consider conducive to get me to work for him."

"He was hoping she would be an incentive to get you to say yes." He picked up the device and slipped it into a pocket.

He looked at the kid in the mirror behind the bar. Kuarto was already suspicious of the way his contact was being handled and he was going to get to the bottom of things in his usual style. "He has made it hard to say no."

He stood in front of Toki and hoped he hid his relief at seeing her okay. He had to continue with his act and hoped she would pick it up quickly. Al walked into the room before he had a chance to speak to her.

"Good to see you, Doctor." Al took his time walking around the room, looking and touching different things randomly. "Glad you decided to join us."

"You made it sort of difficult to say no." Kuarto watched him, wondering why he was acting a bit strangely. Another thing that made him suspicious. "I thought she got her memory back and ran away by the way she just disappeared."

"Sorry about that, but I needed your expertise and she was the one thing I thought would sway you." He looked at Kuarto then, making him wonder what he suspected. Was he on to them this quickly? He did seem to know Toki. Did he know she was Storm's sister?

"You're lucky I ran into your man." He was going to continue to play along, since he had a job to do. "I was going to go home and tell the people who sent her she ran away and see if they would let me get another wife."

She looked at him, confusion etched on her face. "But I didn't run away. He told me you wanted me to go with him."

"He lied." He offered her his hand, which she took. "I don't work for liars." He walked toward the door but stopped when her hand pulled from his. Turning, he found her rooted to the spot. The fear in her eyes warned him something was up.

"Show him your neck, my dear."

She turned around and showed the device on the back of her spine.

"That is my insurance that you will help me. She might be your wife, but I have control of her body, if you try to leave before I'm ready."

"And how do I know you'll let us go once you get what you want?" That piece of metal answered his questions. Al did know and probably had figured out her amnesia was a ruse.

"You don't, so don't anger me. I can be quite giving when you do as I ask. Not so much if you push me the wrong way."

"Threat taken." He stared the man down. He wasn't about to change his ways and act like Al frightened him when he didn't. Kuarto wasn't thrilled with the turn of events, but still believed he could get them out if he had to. "Understand, I do this under duress, and as a hostage, I'm not obligated to help you in any way. Too bad you didn't wait until we left the planet on our own. I don't like Vespians. Find them too bossy and demanding. But you're the same way." He reached for Toki's hand once more. "So where are we staying, or do you plan on not letting us sleep until you get what you want?"

"Show them to their room." Al walked from the lab he had ready for Kuarto. He wondered if he pushed just a little too hard.

The man who he had met at the space dock took them to a darkened room. Kuarto turned on lights and closed the door on him before he could say a word. He knew they couldn't talk freely, but he wanted her to know he was there for her. "You okay?"

"I'm fine." She stepped deeper into the room and looked around. "I am sorry for the confusion. I wasn't aware you didn't know what had happened to me." She discreetly pointed to several listening devices.

"I blame him, not you. I should have known you wouldn't have left me the way I thought you did." He also spotted the camera recording them. "Has he tried to do anything to you? Hurt you in any way other than that device?"

"No. Frightened me a bit and this thing hurts." She gestured to her neck.

"Let me see what I can do."

She gave him a confused look. "You sure you want to upset him?"

"I don't care right now. He can see and hear everything we say and do, so we have no privacy. The least he can do is let me make my wife more comfortable." He stepped up to her and brushed his fingers across her neck. Little goosebumps jumped up on her skin. That skin was red and angry around the device. He gave her a topical treatment. Drugs didn't work on her, so he wasn't sure if anything he did would help. The redness faded a bit. "Better?"

"Much." She turned and gave him a smile. Did she say that because of the cameras?

He had been so worried about her he didn't think, just reacted to seeing her so close. He closed the distance between them, softly pressing his lips to hers. She responded, opening her mouth, offering herself to him. He pulled her into his embrace, twining his tongue with hers. She tasted so good. He took his time savoring the moment between them. He finally broke the kiss.

"I'm sorry you got caught up in the middle of all of this." He rested his forehead against hers.

"What could you have done different?"

"I don't know, but I'd like to think I could have protected you." He tightened his hold on her. He felt her chuckle. "I see."

"What?" She looked up at him.

"You think I spent more time with those Vespians than I should have, don't you?" She probably thought he was acting a lot like her brother.

"The men were very manly and I do remember you posturing a couple of times against that Storm fellow." She rested her head against his shoulder.

"It's hard to ignore all that testosterone." He wrapped an arm around her and walked her back to the door of their room. "I guess we should get to work so we can go home."

"What does he mean testosterone?"

"Storm." Heather couldn't help but smile. "He has to maintain the illusion that we never told him she was your sister, and that her amnesia is real."

"That kiss sure seemed real." They sat in the ancient compound watching what was going on with Toki and Kuarto.

"I noticed that, too. But you know it was all for show, right?"

"Was it?"

She knew he wasn't happy with the fact his sister could be in a relationship. He hadn't come right out and said it yet, and that was what she was waiting for. "What do you think?"

"Never mind." He stepped away from the screen. "Have you figured out what the question is you need to ask the computer to unlock the whole system?"

"Not yet. I keep throwing out one here and there but haven't figured out what the computer is looking for." She gave him a hug, knowing he changed the subject because he wasn't ready to talk yet. "Don't worry. I'll get it."

"I'm sure you will." He grew quiet for a moment.

"You okay?"

"Of course." He gave her one of his heart-melting smiles. "Just wondering about how you are doing. I know Kuarto gave you the vitamins to help you, but you still seem to tire easily."

"I know."

"Even now you have a faint hint of darkness under your eyes."

"We'll just tell them you wouldn't let me get any sleep."

"Are you kidding?" He shook his head. "My family would force me to stay away from you if they thought I caused you any trouble."

"You know I wouldn't allow that." She leaned into him, feeling light-headed. Her legs gave way, but Storm's strong arms kept her from hitting the floor.

———

"Heather." He didn't know what to do. "Computer, can you help her?"

"What she is going through is very normal."

"What is normal when there is no one else to compare to?" He spoke to the computer. "We haven't found any records on an ancient pregnancy."

"I have all the information you need." The computer paused as it prepared data for him. "Please put your hand in the receptacle."

"And exactly what am I supposed to do with my mate?" he yelled at the system. "She's still not quite on her feet yet."

The computer created a soft chair for him to set her in. "Please put your hand in the receptacle."

He placed Heather on the seat, then walked to the spot he thought the computer meant. The indentation in the panel had him wondering about it since the first time he realized it was there. He felt a jolt enter his palm, race up his arm and fill his head. The images were hard to keep up with. The data that followed he just let flow, hoping he would be able to make sense of it all later. He was going to have a massive headache afterward.

Heather stirred in the chair.

"My heart." He crouched beside her. "It seems the vitamins aren't helping that much."

"Sorry." She touched his face. "I know it frightens you, but it's like I'm being drained all at once."

He felt the information fill his brain. "It's the babies. They're stretching their mental abilities by trying to contact you. They just don't know how to not use all their power. That surge makes you shut down. Once you show them how to touch your mind without using every ounce of their being, it should stop."

"And how did you become an expert on ancient pregnancies?"

"The computer." He helped her to her feet. "It downloaded everything into me."

"Downloaded?"

"I can do the same thing for you, Heather."

Storm watched in amazement as the information entered her. She stopped moving while it happened, then blinked and smiled.

"That was amazing." He touched her face. "You didn't have to touch the receptacle. Do you know how to communicate what you need to so the twins won't short circuit you?"

"I do." She rubbed her stomach for a moment before resting her hands there. "It's nice to know what to expect now. Do you think the children were the culprits of me passing out the first time when we thought it was the sentinel waking up?"

"I still feel Al had something to do with that, but the second time had to have been them. You shutting down might have frightened them and they wanted to let you know they were okay." He wrapped his arms around her, placing his hand on hers. "I still can't believe this. Computer, you mentioned that I have the catalyst that allowed us to have children. Can you explain that?"

"That information can't be unlocked until Heather comes up with the right question."

"You need to come up with that question."

"I know."

———

Toki hated the whole situation. Kuarto was being belligerent with Al. Something she wasn't sure he should be doing. She sat near him as he went over some of the research he had already done. She wondered how they were going to get out of this.

"Can you get me my scanner?"

She hoped he was teasing. All of Heather's data was on it. There was no way he would give that info to Al. Would he?

"Now?" She got up and walked to the table that held his gear. Pulling it out, she hesitated as she held it in her hand, trying to figure out why he would want to give all the data to Al. It didn't make sense. Kuarto shouldn't have brought the thing with him. She dropped it into his hand, but not before she gave him a dirty look.

He winked at her. The scanner information loaded onto the screen and she watched, waiting to see if he would stop Heather's info from going into Al's system but there was no file on Heather on his scanner. What was going on?

"That's what I thought."

"What do you mean?"

"The information I had on the clone is gone."

"Those Vespians erased all of Heather's files from my scanner, which included any info I had on that egg."

Al walked in just as Kuarto spoke.

"That egg belongs to Heather." Kuarto confronted him.

"Yes." He was so nonchalant about it. "I believe I can

unlock the information you need, if you let me have that for a few minutes."

Toki wanted to grab the thing and go running but could only watch in frustration as Kuarto handed it over. He had a stupid smile on his face. One she wanted to knock off. Why was he putting Heather in danger like this?

"I thought you said you came by that egg honestly. She didn't strike me as one who would share easily."

"I was owed, and that was my payment." He placed the scanner in a small alcove and moved to the computer. He pressed a few buttons. "I can pull up your old data before you went to Vespia, but it looks like I can't access anything you recorded on the Vespian planet."

"The research on the egg is all I need, anyway." He held out his hand for his scanner. "Just download it to the station I'm working at."

Al hesitated for an instant before dropping the little device into his hand. Toki thought he was going to keep it for a minute.

Kuarto put it into his pocket and walked back to his computer. He looked to make sure she followed him. "Oh, if you want me to continue my work you need to do a few things for me."

"You don't have room to negotiate."

"Really?" He crossed his arms over his chest. "Who do you have who can do this if I don't? Isn't that why you kidnapped my bride?"

His lip thinned when he realized Kuarto did have the upper hand. "What do you want?"

"Take that stupid device off my wife and remove your security equipment from our room. Once that is done, to my satisfaction, I will continue with the work you want me to do." He waited.

Toki couldn't believe he would be so bold.

Al walked up to her and ripped the device off her neck. It

hurt like hell, and brought tears to her eyes, but she didn't make a sound. To have control of her own body again was worth any pain she had to withstand.

Kuarto was at her side as soon as Al left, giving her a shot to help the damaged tissue heal. He also sprayed a topical on the area. "I'm sorry. I should have expected him to be a bit mean in removing that. I gave you what I could to help take the edge off. The spray will work like a Band-Aid, covering it from your hair and clothes so you won't be irritating it when you move. Don't know if it will help you. I've also put an accelerant into the dose to make the tissue heal faster."

"Thanks." She leaned into him for a moment. "What can I do to help you?"

He pointed to the screen where the data from his scanner was. "I'm sure the information that he was able to save is a jumbled mess. You think you could work your way through it so we can reorganize the info for easier access?"

"Sure." She still wasn't sure about what was going on. "Can I access it from a different terminal?"

"I'll make sure you can." He sent the information to the screen she sat in front of and they went to work. Kuarto had been working on his computer for a while before he looked at the information and sat back. "What I need is the real thing."

"Excuse me?" Toki asked.

"What?" He looked at her and smiled. "Sorry. I have a tendency to talk out loud to myself. I wish I could work on the real egg. Just having the data doesn't help me." He started moving different files around until he was satisfied. "Let's go for a walk. I need to let my mind digest everything."

"You sure they'll let us?" She stood when he did.

"What is Al going to do? We can't leave this planet. In fact, I have no idea where we are, anyway. Do you?"

"No. I was out until we arrived."

"And do you know where the spaceport is?"

"No." Confusion filled her voice. "What are you getting at?"

"We don't know how to escape, so a nice walk won't hurt us." He took her hand and led her to the door. Two guards stood there, blocking their way. "I need to think."

"Think in your room, Doctor."

"Can't. Get Al." He crossed his arms over his chest, mocking the guards' stance. When they didn't move, he spoke again. "Look, you either let us go out for a walk, or I'll knock you out, and go for my walk anyway. I don't care if you feel you must follow us because you're not sure. Call Al and ask for permission. But I'm staying right here until we get to go for a walk."

"I'm only following orders."

"I'm warning you." He pulled out a hypo.

The guard he threatened touched his ear as he got a command. "You have permission to take your walk but stay near the buildings. The perimeter security is programmed to fry anyone who tries to cross it."

"Like I'm going to go anywhere." He took Toki's hand and started walking. The air was cool, but the bright sunlight kept them warm. "You don't see too many of those."

"What?" She looked where he was pointing.

"Binary stars." They took their time. He seemed to be waiting for something.

"You are as crazy as Storm is. You know that?" She chose her words carefully, not knowing if what they said could be picked up by the security system.

"Yes." He smiled at her. She felt her heart skip a beat. "I've been around a little too long to put up with people trying to push me around. I proved that with Mr. Overprotective and will prove it to Al as well."

"I am sorry."

"About what?"

"If I hadn't been feeling sorry for myself that day, I wouldn't have been anywhere near the gardens and given him the opportunity to kidnap me."

"I have a feeling he was waiting. If it hadn't been then, it would have been another time." He wrapped an arm around her. "It's not your fault, so don't blame yourself."

They noticed someone walking toward them.

"Is that him?"

"No. Too short and the clothing is female."

"I haven't seen any women on this planet." She continued to watch as the figure grew closer. "It can't be."

"What?"

"It looks like Heather." She wanted to run to see if it was her, warn her of the danger, but Kuarto kept her in his grip.

"Trust no one and nothing you see." His voice was soft, so soft she barely heard it, but it kept her at his side.

The figure was female and as it grew closer her features were visible. "Why would Heather be here?"

He hadn't responded, but she knew he was focused on the woman approaching them. His trusty scanner came out.

"That's an automatic reflex for you, isn't it?"

"What do you mean?"

"Every time you feel you need to question something, you whip that out."

"I created this little gismo, and it has been very handy."

"Why are you using it now?"

"Because that can't be Heather. Look at the way she moves. It's too precise." He took the scanner, activated it and palmed it. "I think it's an android."

"What?" She found herself staring at it. "You think?"

"This will tell me for sure."

Heather stood in front of them. She was Heather, right down to the elder looking outfit she had on. She smiled at them. "Doctor, Toki, how are you today?"

"Fine, Heather. And you?"

She saw the device give a quick glow then shut back off. He looked at the readings and smiled at her. It might look and talk like Heather, but it was a machine. Toki didn't think her brother would allow his mate to be in harm's way while she carried their children. He wouldn't allow her to be in harm's way, period.

"I am fine. Al wishes to speak to you." She stepped aside and waited for them to move.

"I see our walk has been interrupted." He still had his arm around Toki, so she had to move with him. "I thought Al gave us permission to walk."

"He did, but he does have a few things he wishes to go over."

"Like where we're allowed to walk? I would think he has the whole compound under surveillance."

"The whole compound is under surveillance." The android led them to another building while she answered them.

"Miked and videoed?"

"No. Most of the outside is just video." She opened a door for them to enter. "But close to the buildings where the cameras are clustered can be given sound. They can scan your face so dialog can be added when needed."

"At least I know I can have some privacy with my bride as long as I'm not near the buildings."

"As long as you clear it through Ialog first." Heather escorted them to the main computer section. Toki had never seen anything like it. She looked around in awe.

"Doctor, why do you continue to push me?" Al was waiting for them.

"Because you think bullying will work on me and it won't. Why do you think you found me on that out of the way planet? I have had my share of people trying to tell me what to do."

"Maybe we should renegotiate."

"I never negotiated with you in the first place. You wouldn't take no for an answer." He had kept his arm around Toki the whole time. She felt the slightest tightening of his hold as he waited for Al to respond.

"Perhaps I did overstep my boundaries. Why don't the two of you join me for dinner and maybe we can work things out between us."

———

Heather came down to the main room of the compound once she finished her time with the elders. She and Storm had been spending as much time as they could watching what was going on with Kuarto and Toki. They hadn't been gone that long yet, but with their own workloads Heather and Storm didn't want to fall too far behind in the recordings.

Storm hadn't come down yet.

"How are you feeling, Heather?" asked the computer.

"Why?" She knew the computer was detecting something.

"You're slightly anemic. I'm also detecting a lower than normal blood pressure and your metabolism is a little sluggish."

"Thanks. All I need is for Storm to hear that and he won't let me leave our room."

"What is it you don't want me to know about?" He walked into the room and wrapped his arms around her.

"The computer is pointing out a few things my vitamins haven't fixed."

"Thought so. You still have those darkened areas under your eyes." He brought her to the chair and sat her down. "Stay there."

"Please don't treat me like a child. I'm fine." She stood and glared at him.

"Computer, can you give us a bigger chair? One I can sit

in with her so she won't escape so easily. It might be a good idea to allow it to recline so she can rest when need be."

It didn't take the system long to create something they could be comfortable in.

"Storm." He gave her one of his devilish smiles and started to stalk her. She darted away from him but knew there was nowhere to go. Turning to face him, she continued to back up as he came at her. "I am a full-grown woman."

"I know you are. You're *my* full-grown woman." The gaze in his eyes intensified as he spoke. "You are also the mother of my children. Something you know is rare and precious here."

"I can still function on my own."

"And I'm not saying you can't." He reached her then and scooped her up in his arms. "But you are as stubborn as your mate, and don't always do what is best for you."

He was right. He sat her in the newly formed chair, then joined her. "Computer, how about a light cover? My mate likes to snuggle."

She gave him a quick pinch. He wanted the cover to keep any fondling he might do out of the watchful eye of the computer.

"I can correct your health issues every time you pass through the doorway if you wish me to, Heather." A blanket appeared on their laps.

"I think that would be a good idea." Storm touched her face. "The stress of the pregnancy is showing a lot earlier on you than most women on our planet, and that worries me. There could be complications later that could harm you, and our children."

She couldn't fight with him when he got like this. He was only thinking of her safety. "That will be fine, computer."

"Then to get your first dose, I need you to go to the doorway."

"Can't we do this when we leave?"

"No." Storm stood, then helped her to her feet.

"You know I can walk, right? Stand up on my own and everything." Her sarcastic remark made him smile.

"And you know I'm bigger, meaner, and can push you up against that wall and have my way with you. Make you forget why you're so cross in seconds."

She thought about sticking her tongue out at him, but knew he would take that as a challenge, and she'd find herself up against the wall with him buried deep inside in an instant. A thrill ran through her at the thought, but she also knew she wasn't feeling one hundred percent and that did come first.

She entered the doorway and found herself encased in a force field that lasted a few seconds. Once the force field dropped, she felt a little lightheaded. Storm was at her side instantly.

"Going through the medical field the first few times does take some adjusting," the computer said. "She should be fine in a moment or two."

Storm brought her to the chair, and carefully sat her down.

She hated looking so fragile. Storm loved it. It allowed him to be the dominating male and when she complained, all he had to do was say he was only trying to help her. No one would argue her side.

It didn't take too long before she could feel her strength returning. "Thank you, computer."

"Are you ready to see the latest recording of Doctor Kuarto and Tikolean?"

"Yes." Storm settled down beside Heather and pulled her into his embrace. "Comfortable?" He pulled the soft blanket up around them, making sure she was tucked in. He ran his fingers up and down her spine, relaxing her.

Kuarto and Toki's images filled the screen.

"I can't believe he would be that belligerent." Heather

curled up against Storm, enjoying the heat of his body against hers.

"He talked the same way to me. It's part of his sparkling personality."

She shook her head as she rested her hand on Storm's heart. Once she did that, she rested her head next to it, letting the steady beat of his heart comfort her. "He isn't that bad. I think it's those wonderful male egos butting against each other."

"I don't know what you're talking about."

Heather saw the image approaching her brother and Toki and felt the blood drain from her face. She couldn't be seeing what she thought she was seeing. As it got closer, she started to feel cold. She sat up when she realized what the image was. "No."

"What?" Storm felt her agitation building.

"Can't you see it? That is me." She pointed at the screen. "He lied to me."

"Who lied to you?"

"Al. He said I wasn't what he was after, it was our children, yet here is a replica of me." Her brother had already said something about her duplicate being an android. "If he wasn't fixated with me why would he create something so exact?"

"There's only one way to find out." He held her close. "We have to continue to watch and hope he will reveal why he created a copy of you."

TEN

"Are you sure this is a smart idea?" Toki didn't want to dine with the crazy man who had an android that looked like her brother's mate. There was something wrong with the whole idea.

"We have to give him a chance." Kuarto held her hand as they walked toward the dining area. "He says I can say no and there will be no hard feelings."

"Right, which is why he kidnapped me in the first place." She didn't like this at all.

"I know, but I did promise to hear him out." He squeezed her hand in reassurance.

She didn't argue any more. Not knowing what was bugged and what wasn't had her being as cautious as he was. They entered the large room to find it empty except for one table dressed for them. There were four places set. Heather sat at one of them.

She stopped walking when she saw the android. The robot gave her the creeps, and she didn't want to be around it. Why would he have it join them at the dinner table?

Kuarto got her moving again. "Relax." He spoke softly.

She nodded and allowed him to bring her to the table.

"Where is Al?" he asked.

"He will be joining us momentarily. He had a few things to take care of before he could dine." Heather gestured to two chairs. "Please sit."

Kuarto pulled out her chair and waited for Toki to sit before he went to his seat. She wasn't used to someone being so chivalrous and couldn't stop the odd look she gave him.

"What?"

"Nothing." She hesitated for a moment. "Thank you." It wasn't a phrase Vespians used too often, but Heather, the real one, had used it all the time.

"You're welcome."

Al came into the room then, carrying a small box. He set it down in front of Kuarto. "Good to see you, Doctor. I have a gift for you."

Normally Toki didn't like being ignored, which was why she always annoyed her brother so much, but she didn't mind being under the radar with this man. Having his attention worried her.

Kuarto touched the button on the top of the box, waiting while it opened. Inside was a small container. "This is the real thing?"

"Yes." He smiled as he sat and placed a napkin on his lap. "You'll find it at your workstation in the morning, if you decide to help me."

Appetizers were brought to the table. Toki wondered if he did that to let his words sink in. Timing was perfect.

"You haven't explained why I should help you with this." He held up the small container to the light. The tiny egg floated in an amber fluid.

All of this trouble for one tiny egg. Toki didn't understand.

"I was hoping the chance to work on something so rare would pique your interest." He took a few of the small, breaded items on the plate and placed them on a smaller one in front of him.

"I've had my share of working on rare things, so they're not that rare anymore. But you should know that, since I know you did your homework before you approached me." He mimicked Al. Once he placed a few pieces of food on his plate, he also put a few on Toki's.

"True." Al took a few bites.

Toki wondered what he would say to convince Kuarto to stay. They hadn't had a chance to talk, but by the way he was behaving, she had the impression her brother was involved with his arrival. Everything he did smelled of Storm.

She also knew neither of the two men here were stupid. Whatever Al used had to be something that would grab Kuarto. And Kuarto had to be careful to not to take something everyone knew he wouldn't normally accept.

"This egg shows it is sterile, yet the woman who carried it is now pregnant. Don't you want to know why she was able to become that way when it shouldn't have happened?"

She had to give him credit. Al was trying.

"I do." He wrapped his hand around the glass in front of him, pausing. "But I could work with the owner and have that question answered."

"True, but then you have to deal with her mate and the rules of the planet." He picked up his napkin and dabbed the corners of his lips. His lips had thinned. He didn't like Kuarto's answer.

"You do have a point." Kuarto took that instant to focus on her, which she could have done without. "You're not eating."

"Not hungry."

"What is the problem?" asked Al.

She had a choice here, and she decided to be like Kuarto and be honest. "Heather, I have met the real thing and I'm afraid this version makes me uncomfortable." She pushed her plate away.

"Now, we don't want that." He turned to the android. "You may go."

The android stood and headed to the doors at the other end of the room.

"Tell me why you created her." Kuarto watched her leave, his fascination with the thing obvious.

"She is to carry the egg. That system is to be a walking incubator."

"Hmm." Kuarto tilted his head as he watched her walk through the doors and disappear from sight. "I'll make a deal with you. You let me study your android and I'll also do the research you need on the egg."

"Deal."

———

Toki stood in their room as Kuarto ran his scanner over the whole place. "Anything?"

"Looks like he removed everything as I asked." He shut off the scanner and put it in his pocket.

"But you still don't trust him."

"He's given me no reason to trust him." He gestured for her to turn around. "Let me check your neck. I want to make sure it is healing properly."

"This dress covers the skin." And it had been bothering her during the meal.

He did a twirling motion with his hand. She presented her back to him and felt his fingers undo the seals so he could get a good look at the back of her neck. Cool air brushed against the damaged skin making her suck in her breath.

"Does it still hurt?"

"Nothing I can't handle." She felt the heat of his hand

near her wound, but all she could think about was his hands on her and where she'd rather they be.

What was it about this man that made her think about sexual desires? She had never really cared before. When she wanted release, she found a pleasurer or a willing male, but she never had a man cause this type of reaction before.

"The tissue looks much better. Probably will be fully healed by the morning." He closed the seals on her dress and stepped back. "I can give you another shot if it is bothering you."

"Please don't." She turned to look at him. "The topical medication doesn't do that much and it doesn't really hurt that bad. It's like a badge for me."

"It never should have happened." He brushed his fingers against her skin.

She smiled at him. "I'm pretty strong, you know. I've been through worse."

"But I was never the cause of it."

"Stop blaming yourself." She felt her heart beat faster when he pulled her into his arms. His lips captured hers in a gentle kiss.

"I know you're strong." He watched her as he spoke. "You have more backbone than a lot of the men I have met. You speak your mind, which is so refreshing. Most women don't tell me what they really want, but what they think will please me. And you're beautiful, with such expressive eyes I almost know what you're thinking."

"Really?" He found her beautiful? She gave him a sultry smile. "What am I thinking now?"

"From the desire in your eyes, you wish I would shut up and kiss you again."

"Very good, Doctor."

Their lips met again, tongues dancing together. Toki felt he was too overdressed, so she started working on the seams of his clothes. When she felt his skin against her hands, she smiled again. That was much better.

"You don't get to control this, this time. I am." He pulled out a small bracelet and snapped it on her hands. "Now you can't do a thing until I'm good and ready."

"That's not fair." She tried to separate her hands but found the restraints tightening as she fought them. "And I haven't controlled anything but the first time."

"Oh? You don't think you took over when you felt you needed to?" He stepped back and slowly removed his shirt, then loosened the seam of his pants, letting them slip down his hips a little before closing the seal and stopping their descent.

"I don't think I did." She would have argued but found it hard to focus on anything but his trousers hanging precariously off his hips. All she would have to do was give it a quick tug and it would fall to the floor. Unfortunately, the restraints hampered her movements more than she thought they would. She couldn't move her hands at all now.

"Then I might let you control the next time, but not now." He smiled. He liked having her at his mercy. She fought with her restraints, trying to get some movement out of them.

"You know the more you fight that the more restrictive it will be on your movements." He backed her up to the bed. "Now first, I need to fix the way you're dressed."

She felt his fingers against her collarbone, tracing the indentations there. Each brush heightened her desire. If only she had her hands. With excruciating slowness, he eased open the seams of her dress. He stood so close she could feel the heat of his body. The soft brushes of his fingers against her skin drove her crazy. She wanted more.

Her dress opened all the way, exposing her to his gaze. "Never get tired of seeing you this way." His hand trailed over her breasts, down her abdomen, and across her hips. Goosebumps followed his fingers.

"Now, the last time I used my mouth on your body, you melted at my feet." He touched her in just the right spots to get her to lie on the bed. "Don't want that to happen again, so this time you will be in a safe position."

"But."

"Shhh." He pressed his finger against her lips. "I want you to relax and enjoy."

————

"What are you doing?" Heather stood between Storm and the intimate scene unfolding on the screen. "Computer, stop playing."

"Heather!" He stood and moved her out of his way, but the screen had already done dark.

"How dare you!" She couldn't believe his audacity. "You hated having him join us when we reached our release and now you're sitting here watching him and your sister like some sort of voyeur?"

"What does she see in him, anyway?" He started pacing.

"What does it matter?" She watched him, his agitation apparent.

"She's not supposed to be with anyone." He stopped and looked at Heather. "The position she is destined for is one of isolation."

"Really?" Heather jammed her hands on her hips. "I've done my research and there is nothing in any of the records that says the religious leader has to be celibate. I even spoke to your uncle. The man in the position right now. A long time ago, when this planet was warring amongst itself, the religious leader was mated, but his family was used against him, and in the end he lost them, and his will to lead. That was why the people who became the religious leader stepped away from mating until after they left the position, but it has always been voluntary."

"It became normal procedure, and she knows that." He gestured at the blank screen. "Yet, here she is acting like she found her mate."

"And what if she wants to change the old customs, because that is all it is."

"She can't." His words held a finality.

"You are being stubborn."

"So are you." He glared at her. "Old customs or not, she knows what her future is, and she has a certain path to follow."

"Have you asked her if she wants to follow that path?"

He stopped then. "Why should I?"

"No one has made sure she will fulfill her duty?" Sometimes she found their way of thinking strange. They just assumed so much.

"Of course she will. She's my sister."

"Who is now with a man who has shown her she can walk away from her destiny if she doesn't like the way people treat her." Heather wished she hadn't said it that way, but now it was out there and Storm would react honestly.

His brow dropped and anger snapped in his eyes. "I knew I didn't like him."

"That is my brother you are talking about."

"I know, but he isn't good for my sister..."

"Or isn't good for your plans for your sister." Her words stopped him again.

"There are times when you say things that anger me." He ran his fingers through his hair. She hated pushing him this way, but sometimes it was the only way to make him look at a situation differently. "Why?"

"Because you don't always look at things from every angle and I wouldn't be much of a mate if I didn't make you do that." She knew what she needed to do to distract him. She started to work on the seals of her clothes.

"I disagree. You could be one of those quiet mates who

never questions. I wouldn't mind." He gave her one of his heart-warming smiles when he noticed what she was doing. "Have I won the argument? You've decided to become one of those docile women whose sole job is to please her mate? Because I'm very pleased at the moment."

She laughed. "What do you think?"

"I think I'm in a lot of trouble."

Her dress hit the floor, and she had his undivided attention. "Now, why would you think that?"

"Because I have taught you too well. I know how to distract you, and now you're using the same tactic on me."

"Is it working?" She smiled as she stretched, closing her eyes for only a moment. Before she opened her eyes she felt the heat of his hands on her body. When she did open them, he stood inches away, devoid of his clothes. "How do you do that?"

"What?" His lips found his favorite spot on her throat.

"Take your clothes off like that. It always amazes me." She had hoped to make it to the chair before he was on her but found herself being backed up to the wall once again. "When I watch you undress you never move that fast, but if I look away for a second, you're like lightning."

"My desire for you makes me this way," he murmured against her skin. "When you're watching, I try to take my time, which can be excruciating by the way."

"Anyway we can utilize the chair?" She thought she might still get her way if she asked nicely.

"Maybe later." He pinned her against the wall. "You know I'm partial to our chair. Nothing can replace it."

"What chair?" asked the computer.

"One Storm had created for the ship we used to rescue his sister," Heather answered. Perhaps she should program it to remain inactive while they were being intimate the next time. It was disconcerting to have it ask questions when all they could think about was their joining.

"The one you brought Dr. Kuarto back in?"

"Yes." Storm had her right where he wanted her, nibbling his way down her throat.

"Searching." The computer was quiet as it worked through information, but Storm wasn't still. He had now nibbled his way to an ear, which tickled and made her giggle. "Is this the chair you are looking for?"

Storm turned to look at the spot where the other chair stood. It had been replaced with an exact copy of the chair he had created. "Oh computer, you and I can be best of friends if you keep this up."

He wrapped his arms around her and carried her to the chair. After he sat down, he maneuvered her so she could straddle the chair and join him. "You know why I like this chair so much, don't you?"

"No. The other one would have been just as comfortable."

"But with this one, there is no height difference. I can bury myself deep inside you and still nibble on your neck as I like to or lean you back and have my way with your breasts, which I know you like."

"I see." She tilted her head to one side so his mouth could find his favorite spot on her throat. Slowly, she slid down his length, easing him inside as she settled herself on him.

"Woman, I don't think I will ever get tired of this."

"I hope not." She pulled back to look at him. "Sex for you is like breathing for others. If you ever tire of me, you better be dying."

He laughed as he grabbed her hips and set a pace. "If you promise to never become docile, I promise to never get bored."

"Deal." She tilted her head back as the friction between them built to a point where she could feel her release just outside her reach. With their minds merging, Storm always knew how to move or what to do to push her over the edge.

It didn't take too long before she felt her body tighten and constrict as the orgasm took control.

Storm kept her body moving as she lost her bearings for the moment. Then he shifted their bodies so he could be the one moving and he pounded into her, each surge pushing them over the edge a little more. Each drive in brought them a little closer. Storm felt the tension in his body shake him just as Heather started to vibrate in his arms. Her body pulsed around him, sending her free-falling and taking him along with her.

The joy she found with him awed her. She looked up at his smiling face.

"I will never get tired of your mind touching mine. Having that ability makes each time stronger and more explosive." He touched her face with his fingertips. "Promise me I will be the only one you will ever share something so intimate."

"I can't see me sharing this with anyone else." She touched his face.

"Good answer."

———

Toki hated the restraints he put on her. Kuarto had moved her arms up above her head and locked it against the wall, so she couldn't use them.

"Why must you dominate?"

"Because any man would want a chance to prove he had what it took. This way, I will prove it without any interference from you."

She made a noise, which he chose to ignore. He watched her for a moment, waiting for her to try to get out of his hold.

"I have an idea." He sat back, letting her fight with the bonds he put on her. "Let's see how you do in total darkness."

He gave the command, and the lights went out. "Now you can't see me coming. You won't know where my lips will fall next." His words were next to her ear.

"How can you see and I can't?"

"I can't see any more than you can. This will affect both of us. But I will search for you with my mouth. I want to see if I can make you cry for more."

She felt him shift on the bed but had no idea where he was or what he was going to do. This was making her antsy. He did have a little advantage because he had a hand braced on either side of her body before the lights went off. The heat of his breath brushed against her collarbone before she felt his mouth close on the heated tissue. Not knowing where he would go next had her body reacting at the thought of where he could go. Warmth surrounded her nipple as he pulled it into his mouth. He teased it with his teeth and tongue, making it tighten and harden until she found her body moving under his ministrations. Just as she thought he would put her out of her misery and enter her, she felt his lips move south. Licking and gently biting his way down her stomach to her core. She felt his fingers enter her, stretching the tender flesh as his mouth closed on her mound. The double attack had her arching her hips off the bed. "Please."

He doubled his efforts. Drawing whimpers and sighs from her.

"Now. Please. I can't take any more." She felt him shift once again, and he entered her.

Everything shook at the invasion. Her body sang as he filled her. Muscles clamped down on him, giving him a snug fit. She felt him shake a bit too.

"I love how you grip me so tight like you don't want to let go." He pulled out and slid back in again. "It causes such wonderful friction for me. Does it for you?"

"Oh, yes." Her voice sounded deep and throaty in her ears. "I wish I had my hands."

"Not this time. You're supposed to lay there and take it like a woman. I'm setting the pace this time. My turn to drive you wild." His lips closed on an ear lobe, giving it a soft tug before he blazed a trail of kisses down her neck. His mouth moved to a collarbone and with his tongue he traced the indentations there.

She found her body arching against him, silently begging for something. She felt his lips curl in a smile before he lathed the tip of her breast. Toki sucked in a deep breath at the sensation that caused. "Oh!"

He moved faster then, filling her each time as deeply as he could. She knew he had to be close.

Everything splintered around her. She felt the slow build of the wave that would take her to heights she had never experienced before. Tears sprang to her eyes as her release grabbed her and flung her out to the stars.

Her own labored breathing brought her back to reality. "That was…"

"Unbelievable," he finished for her. He lay beside her and pulled her into his embrace. He kissed her forehead as he released the restraints. "I don't think anything can hold a candle to this."

She had to agree. The thought of ruining the moment wasn't what she wanted, but she had to ask him. "Why do you want to study that android?"

"I know she bothers you, but I'm fascinated by her." He touched her hair. "Have you touched her?"

"Ew, no." She rested her head against his chest.

"She's warm to the touch and the skin feels real. No one I know has the ability to create an android with realistic skin. A robot might look like one of us, but as soon as you touch it, you know what you are dealing with. The material used to make the skin is rubbery and has no elasticity. Other androids can't carry on a conversation the way she can, either. I want to know how he made her, if he made her. And if he didn't, who did?"

"But you knew it was an android the moment you looked at it. How did you know if she's so realistic?"

"Her eyes. There is no life in them."

She thought about that. He must have very good vision to notice that so fast. "I'm not sure what you're getting at."

"They sparkle with laughter, fill with tears when sad. It has been said the eyes are the window to the soul and I believe that. Life is in the eyes, without it they are flat." He brushed his fingers along her spine. "The technology of the Heather android is far more advanced than anything I have seen. Other than the eyes, he has perfected the creation of a synthetic body."

"And that is what has caught your attention."

"Yes." He gently brushed his fingers through her hair. "He said she was the incubator. How is that possible?"

"I'm sure you're going to figure it out."

———

Storm tried to play what he had been watching earlier but found the computer continued to skip over it. "What is going on?"

"Heather has commanded me to not show you anything intimate between Kuarto and your sister unless pertinent information was revealed and she has to be present for me to air it."

"Figured. Alright. Show me the next scene then. I don't want the recordings to get too far ahead of us."

He sat in the chair and watched as the next scene started up. His sister worked on a screen near Kuarto. Heather's egg floated in a liquid in a jar sitting on his desk. Storm wished he could reach into the screen and grab it, but he and the doctor had a plan and they had to follow it.

Heather walked in. "I see you started without me."

"Just did." He patted the spot in front of him. "You haven't missed anything yet."

She curled up against him. "My egg?"

"Yes."

"You two have made plans to bring it back?"

"That or destroy it. We will make sure he won't have it anymore."

"Good."

"Now, sit back and watch."

"Goodness. Did I interrupt?" She feigned shock.

"Sorry." He wrapped her in a warm embrace. "I guess I'm kind of caught up in this. Let's just sit back and watch. Since you blocked all the little naughty bits from me, all I can do now is gather information."

She laughed at his choice of words. "Had to. You were getting out of hand."

"Good thing there is no one to hear you or you'd be in trouble." He planted a soft kiss on her forehead.

"Since I like the way you punish me, you sure that's a good threat?" She snuggled against him, getting comfortable.

"As long as no one else knows how much you enjoy them, there is no problem."

The android came onto the screen and Heather wanted to bury her face into Storm's shirt. "I really hate that thing."

"I know, but we need to learn as much as we can about it."

Heather focused on her brother instead of the creature speaking to him.

"How are you to carry this egg once I fertilize it?"

She opened a small door on her stomach and exposed the compartment the egg would go in. "Once the egg is inserted, the area will fill with a liquid that will mimic amniotic fluid for the child to survive in."

"And what will happen when it starts to grow? That space isn't big enough to accommodate a full fetus."

"This area will grow with the fetus."

"Fascinating." He picked up his scanner. "May I?"

"Al doesn't want my information accessible."

"Of course." He set the scanner down. "It just makes it so much easier for me to study you, which he promised I could do."

"That is true. I guess that would be permitted since he did give permission to study my system. I will have to remove the data when you leave here, though."

"Of course." He picked up the scanner and ran it over her.

Within seconds, the information loaded onto the computer system on Vespia.

"That's all her data?" Heather stood and looked at it.

"Whatever his scanner picked up."

"We're going to need an expert, you know."

"Already working on it." He patted the chair. "I miss your heat."

"Which heat?" She asked it innocently enough, but saw his eyes darken when he realized what she was asking.

"What kind of question is that?" He stood and walked to her side. In seconds, he had her in his arms and captured her lips with his. His tongue dipped into her mouth.

Heather closed her eyes as a thrill raced through her. She sighed and returned the knee weakening kiss. When the kiss ended, she leaned back and smiled at him. "That was very nice."

"There's more where that came from."

"You know, the only thing I was getting at was the universal translator didn't get that word right for you. The word should have been warmth."

"If I get to feel you surround me more often because of a faulty translator, I'll make sure yours goes out on a regular basis." He grinned. "I had planned on being a gentleman when I asked you to join me on the chair, but after your comment I can't guarantee my hands will behave."

"I'll take my chances." She followed him to the chair and sat in front of him once he had taken his seat. "Computer, please resume play."

"Of course."

———

Kuarto found himself distracted by Toki's presence. All he could think of was their amazing time together. He had been with his share of women but none of them moved him the way she did. Even now, only a few hours since they were together, he wanted to come up with an excuse to be with her again. He now understood why Storm was always after Heather.

He wondered what Storm thought of their relationship since he couldn't interfere. He sure didn't seem happy about it before.

"You okay?" asked Toki. She had stepped up to the table he worked at.

"Me?" He touched his chest. "Sure. Why?"

"You seem to be far away right now." She played with the cuffs of her dress.

"Just reliving some wonderful memories." The smile he gave her should have told her what memories he was reliving.

"I seemed to be having the same problem." She gave him a shy smile.

"Then we'll have to make a few new ones later." He went over the readings he had gotten on the egg. "Can you please pull up the file on the clone? It's part of the stuff I had you separate and mark before."

She walked to another station and loaded the information he wanted quickly.

"Thanks." She started to wander about and he knew she didn't know what to do with herself. "Would you like me to explain what I'm looking at?"

"Sure." She stood next to him. He could feel the warmth of her body.

"The information you just loaded is this section here." He pointed to one side of the screen.

"And what is all of that?" She pointed to another set of data.

"DNA information." He pulled it forward, so it was the most dominating item on the screen. "This is what I have learned about the egg. It shows this one is sterile." He pointed to one of the files. "This one shows all the different tests I ran on it."

"And the real egg?"

"I've just started the same tests on it. So far it looks like I'm getting the same information."

"That one is sterile too? Then how did Heather get pregnant?"

"That I don't know. If all the tests turn out the same as the clone then that's something I'll have to look at." He sat back. "These tests will take some time to run. Maybe we could try taking that walk again?"

"Sure."

He offered her his hand and led her out into the bright sunshine. "I've wanted to talk to you without interruption."

"And you're not afraid of him overhearing?"

"No. What can I say that would worry him?"

"True, but he thinks the Vespians got to us."

"I know." He wrapped an arm around her shoulders. "But he'll just have to trust me."

Once they were far enough away from the cameras, he spoke again. "Why did you leave the room on Vespia?"

She took a deep breath. "I guess I was feeling a little sorry for myself."

"Why? Did I say or do something to upset you?"

"No." She paused as she chose her words. "I was reminded of my obligations and it upset me."

"Camera." He didn't point but gave her a playful nudge.

"How long will your tests take?" She gave him a bright smile, but he could see a slight spark of fear in her eyes. Had she said too much?

"It should be done in a moment or two." He gave her a curious look. "Why?"

"No reason. Was just thinking about those memories we were reliving earlier." She didn't make eye contact. "Thought maybe we could make a few more."

"Now?"

She nodded.

"I would love to." He changed his hold on her so their bodies touched as he held her in an intimate embrace. Their mouths met, and their tongues danced. She melted in his arms. He moved his lips to a cheek before he found the tender flesh of an ear.

She tasted so good to him.

He worked on the seam of her dress, opening it up so his lips could explore her some more. They were both breathing hard when he spoke again. "He has cameras everywhere here. Unless you don't mind putting on a show for Al I suggest we move to our room and finish this."

"I don't really care right now, I want you so badly." She licked her lips. Her hands slipped into the top of his trousers so she could wrap her fingers around his hard length. "I can't wait for us to make it back to our room, can you?"

"Not when you do something like that." He spotted a nice little copse of trees nearby. Picking her up, he took them to the shaded area as fast as his legs would allow. By the time they made it she had freed him from his pants and wrapped herself around him. Just as they reached the trees he felt himself enter her. She meant it when she said she couldn't wait. He almost dropped to his knees as her sheath gripped him. It took a nearby tree to steady him enough to maintain his feet.

"Oh, much better," she murmured in his ear. He felt her teeth graze his collarbone before she nipped and bit him.

"So you paying me back for tying you up earlier?" He backed her to one of the smoother trees. "You keep this up and I just might have a small seizure. My heart is already pounding in my chest."

"I'm sorry. I can't help myself right now." She tightened against him. "I need you. Please."

The frankness of her words spurred him on. He braced her back as he started to drive into her. Finesse wasn't part of the equation. She didn't care about tenderness at this point, she just needed to feel her release and he wanted it to be a heart-stopping one. Each time he pounded in a little deeper. Her breath hitched and her head dropped onto his shoulder. She shook as the constant in and out motion built the friction between them. He felt her nails on his back as he pushed her harder and faster, then her muscles tightened around him like a vise and she hit her orgasm. He felt it milk him, it was so powerful.

He followed her over the edge. If their releases were always going to be like this, he might not be able to walk away from her when this was all said and done.

He stood there deep inside, holding her close while he waited for her to come back to him. He heard another sigh escape her before she blinked and looked at him.

"You are beautiful." He eased her to her feet.

"I am so sorry." She had a problem making eye contact with him.

"You have nothing to be sorry about." He put a finger under her chin so she would look at him.

"I seem to be a bit aggressive when it comes to you." She brushed her fingers against his collarbone. "I bit you for goodness sake."

He laughed. "I know and I found it very arousing."

She buried her face in his neck.

"You don't strike me as a woman who second guesses the way she does things, why are you suddenly doing that?"

She patted his chest before she lifted her head and looked at him. "You make me lose control. I've never done that before."

ELEVEN

Storm growled when the scene jumped.

"You are the worst." Heather had her eyes closed. He thought she was asleep until she spoke. "Why can't you give your sister a break?"

"Because there is something between them. I can see it from here."

"You didn't have to send him." She lifted her head to look at him. "You could have gone and gotten your sister back."

He growled again. "Sending the doctor made more sense at the time."

"So I'm right."

"You are walking a fine line, woman."

"I know, but I'm good at it." She sat up and turned to face him. "You were able to find your mate, why can't she?"

"I've already explained that." He was trying to keep his patience.

"Yes. A stupid argument."

He growled as he pinned her to the chair. "Why do you push?"

His domineering attitude might frighten other people, but she knew his heart and he would never hurt her. His anger wasn't always the most pleasant thing to deal with, but she had faced it many times and had survived. "If I didn't, who would?"

"Be glad you're my heart."

"I am, every day. Every moment I'm awake." She pressed a soft kiss to his lips.

He gazed at her intently for a minute or two before he captured her lips with his. He controlled the kiss, drawing her tongue with his. She remained docile, letting him control, understanding his need to dominate.

The video continued. Heather half listened as her brother and Toki walked back to the area where they were working earlier, while Storm nibbled on her neck. If she had to choose between sex and Storm's anger, sex would win every time.

"I was right," her brother said.

"What do you mean?" asked Toki.

"This egg is just as sterile as the clones."

"How is that possible?" asked Storm. He lifted his head to look at her.

"The computer told us you have a catalyst in you that fertilizes my eggs." Heather looked up at him.

"Yeah, but it hasn't explained what that catalyst is." He watched the screen intently, his anger forgotten.

"Then how did Heather get pregnant so fast?" asked Toki.

"I can't answer that yet. According to my readings, she shouldn't have. Perhaps they went to a specialist."

"They don't strike me as people who would do that." Toki stood next to him as she looked at the readings he had just gone through. "They had just started their life together, and they were just as surprised about her pregnancy. Didn't they mention they were both sterile, yet she is now with child? That was why they wanted you in the first place."

"True." He took the egg and duplicated it.

"Now what are you doing?"

"Making my own clone. This way I'll know no mistakes were made, and I can see if I can duplicate what Heather and Storm have done." He had his cloned egg and moved it to another container. "I'm not sure what we'll do with it if I can duplicate their situation, but I need to try."

"What DNA are you going to use?"

"Good question."

———

"Is he out of his mind?" Storm screamed at the screen, his anger back.

"Storm, relax." She knew he wouldn't like the next thing she would say to him. "Kuarto mentioned this when he was here. He wanted a DNA sample from you to see what made you so special, and I made sure he had one."

"What?" He glared at her. She was still pinned beneath him, or she'd be trying to put some distance between them. "You went behind my back?"

"No." She felt her anger start to boil. "Why is this all about you? That is my egg, not yours. It was my body it was stolen from, not yours. I have a say in this and no amount of posturing from you is going to make me back down."

He remained quiet, but the glare didn't disappear.

"You two made plans to send him to rescue your sister. Did you think through what would be expected of him once he got there? Because I did," she snapped. "Al would want him to fertilize that egg and I wanted to be sure that if he was successful, I had a hand in whose DNA was used. Do you want him to use Al's DNA? Or some total stranger?"

"No." He realized then why she did what she did. "So how did you get a sample?"

"Left that up to the computer."

———

"I'm not sure what Al wants me to use, but I have a few DNA samples in my bag. We can try those first and see what happens." Kuarto pointed to the bag he had leaned against a table leg. The one he had kept with him most of the time. "Let's use four samples and see what takes."

"If you are sure."

He nodded. The DNA he had gathered was from several races, including one of the guards in the elder's hall. The one Heather had given him from Storm would be the last one he would use because he was positive it would fertilize the egg and he didn't want to give his hand too soon.

He took the bag she handed him and got to work. If he was right, Al or the Heather android should be showing up at any moment.

Kuarto took the cloned egg and made four more. He inserted the DNA into the first egg and waited to see what would happen. This DNA was from a human he had met a few months ago. The man was pretty normal and, as he suspected, it didn't take.

"Nothing?"

"Nope." He moved the egg aside. "Didn't think it would either. I have another sample from that same donor, and I'm going to try to add an enzyme to work as a catalyst to see if it would make a difference."

―――

"Please tell me he hasn't had time to study my sample."

"I don't think so." She shook her head.

"You don't think so? Heather, what kind of answer is that?" His temper started to rise again.

"I trust my brother to do what we need him to do. I didn't babysit him, so I'm not sure if he ran any kind of tests before he left here."

"He did not." The computer answered for them. "There

was no data on his scanner when I erased the information requested."

"Thank you, computer." Heather glared at her mate, waiting for him to say something she would make him regret. He had the potential.

"I would be one hundred percent happier if our siblings were here instead of there. His research could be compromised where he is now."

"And he's smart enough to keep that research to himself." She didn't like this any more than he did. "You have to trust him. I know you don't like it when you're not in control, but you have to let him do the job you sent him to do and you have to trust he will do the job right."

"I know." He still had her pinned beneath him. "I thought he would be able to get in, get my sister and your egg and get back out again."

"And the fact that it hasn't worked out that way upsets you."

"I understand that things don't always work out the way you plan, and you have to go with contingency plans." He brushed one of her stray hairs back into place. "But now there are people I care about involved. That changes everything."

"I am right here, my heart. Safe in your arms." She pressed her hand to his heart. "Your sister can take care of herself, and you know that. You trained her like you trained me."

"And what if Al decides to change the rules again and use her as leverage once more?" He shifted his weight so he could place his hand on top of hers.

"Then we'll have to deal with that, but I don't think he will." She twined her fingers with his. "He needs Kuarto too much."

"He is suspect of his time here on Vespia. If I were in his

shoes, I would be too. I don't think he trusts Kuarto and is just waiting for him to make a mistake."

"Which my brother is aware of. You can tell by the way he speaks to your sister. He has yet to let her in on the plan because he knows Al is watching."

"And my sister can be as stubborn as my mate and cause problems because she isn't focusing on what is going on around her." He shifted again, this time taking her into his arms and settling back in the chair with her.

"Your sister isn't here where she feels safe and wants to annoy either one of us. She knows she could be in danger if she isn't careful." Heather snuggled against him. "And I think your sister is as stubborn as her brother, not your mate."

"I'm not sure about that one. My mate likes to argue with me. I keep waiting for her to do it in front of people when she knows she shouldn't, but that hasn't happened yet."

"That's because she's very smart. Something I'm not sure you give her credit for."

"Oh, I do. She is my mate, after all. That was probably the smartest thing she's done." He bent his head and nibbled on her neck.

"Oh." She smiled as she tilted her head. "You sure you don't mean her mate? I think taking her as his mate was probably his smartest move."

"Sounds like something we'll have to discuss at length." His lips worked their way down her throat to the collar of her dress. "You know this thing gets in my way so often."

"What you want me to do? Walk around naked all the time for you?"

"It would make it easier." He brought his hands forward to work on the seals of her dress.

"Okay, but it wouldn't allow me to wear some of those little outfits you like so much."

He stopped and looked at her. Like a child who had been

handed a present, his eyes got wide and a smile spread across his face. "Do you have one on now?"

She smiled back. "You're going to have to look, now aren't you?"

His smile deepened as he gently opened the seal of her collar. A flash of red caught his eye. "One of my favorites?"

"Keep looking."

The red was a ribbon sewn into the top of the cream top. He eased the dress off her shoulders to reveal the thin straps holding the soft lace against her body. The dress slipped onto the chair and revealed a one-piece outfit. The lace cupped her breasts and hugged her stomach.

Storm traced the edge of the material with his fingers, softly brushing skin in his exploration. "This one is a lot different than the others." He pulled her to her feet and walked around her to see the whole effect. The back had very little to it.

She had debated about this one for a while. It covered so much of her body she wasn't sure if he would like it as much and right now she didn't think he did. He hadn't said anything and he seemed to be a little distant.

He came up behind her, wrapping her in his embrace. His hand slid down the soft lace covering her front to her core, and found it opened like the others. He teased her just enough to make her want more but he still hadn't said anything. He moved around her once more, so he stood in front of her. Then he went to his knees. She felt the heat of his mouth on her core, his tongue causing an exquisite contraction of her muscles. Her knees weakened at the passionate attack.

His hands braced her waist, helping her maintain her feet as he continued his ministrations. He played her body like a beautiful instrument, drawing sighs and making her want to purr for him. Her body shook and she could feel her orgasm closing in on her.

In the blink of an eye, she found herself back on the chair with him naked, surging into her. The orgasm he started with his mouth exploded all around her when he slid in as deep as he could. Her legs locked around him, holding him still as her muscles rippled against him. A gasp escaped her has a second wave crested. She floated for a moment before returning to reality.

"Woman, your climaxes are so powerful I have trouble keeping up with you."

"You started it with that wicked tongue of yours."

"You started it with that outfit, but I promise to finish it." He drove into her, a quick pace that would give them a nice, strong shared release. She could feel his orgasm building, sending little shivers down his spine. She sensed desire swirling in his belly through their mind meld.

Heather pushed against his chest. He stopped moving, wondering what she was up to. "I want to be the one controlling this."

He grinned as he allowed her to ease him back onto the chair. She shifted her hips and legs, then placed her hands on his chest. It took her a few moments to set the pace, but once she found the right rhythm, they sighed in unison. His hands settled on her hips, helping her to keep the pace up.

"You don't need to hold me."

"You tend to lose control when you feel some of those precursors to your orgasm."

She shook a little then. Her eyes closed as every fiber in her body felt a quick increase of heat focusing in her groin. "I'd argue that point, but you know me too well."

"I know." He gave her a smile. "And I know you want to be in control, but I also know what you need to hit that point." He grinded her hips against his.

Everything caught on fire with his movements, then she felt the flames of desire consume her. All she could do was feel. Her release washed over her, causing all her nerves to react.

Storm was right. She lost it when she had her orgasm. But since he shared her release, he couldn't complain. Just as she started to come back down again, she felt his orgasm start. He shook at the intensity, her sheath keeping a vise-like hold on him as she moved up and down his length.

His hand pulled her down into a deep kiss. The intensity of their combined orgasm had them gasping for breath.

Storm planted soft kisses all along her cheek and neck. "Yes, I like this one too."

"You like them all." She chuckled. "I have found it is more the excitement of not knowing what I am wearing than what I have on that gets you."

"I've already said you could be naked all the time and I would be very happy."

"Only because you'd have easy access." She brushed his hair out of his eyes. "But you like the not knowing too."

He drank from her lips. "I do." She was still on top of him and he was still buried deep inside her. "I also like how you defused the situation that could have pushed my anger high."

"You needed a little stress relief."

"I'll remember that the next time I feel you need a little relief." He nibbled against her throat.

"Just look for the lace. That will tell you when I'm planning something."

"Really?" He gave her a sultry smile. "Then I have permission to rip your clothes off you whenever I want to see what you're wearing, or not wearing underneath?"

"No."

"Excuse me?" He pulled back to look at her.

"I mean, not in public." She gave him an apologetic smile. "That didn't come out right, either. I was hoping it would be another one of those sexual games we like to play. You'll never know what is under the demure outfits I wear and your job would be to discreetly try to see if there is something extra under my clothes. Something to get your motor running, so to speak."

"Just being around you has my motor running." He pressed a kiss against her throat, then touched her face. "But we need to focus on how to get our family out of harm's way."

"I agree, but they are safe for the moment. Even though Kuarto and I have built a shield so he's not with us, I can feel his confidence. If they were in real trouble, I'd know it."

"So I must trust you."

"Don't you, anyway?" Such a simple question.

"Of course I do. But you know how I like to control things, and this is one of those instances where I don't have what I want."

"Does this mean you're going to be dominating me a lot?"

"Possibly." He smiled as he started to nibble again. "You are a tasty treat and do keep me sidetracked enough not to worry about what I can't control."

"Guess that means I need to keep coming up with new outfits." She sighed as he lathed her throat.

"As long as you are near me, we'll be fine." He looked at her. "Ready to get back to the video?"

"Are you going to keep your temper under control?"

"You going to keep on that outfit and not cover up?" His fingers traced the lace around one of the cups hugging her breast.

"Will it keep you from getting angry?"

"Only one way to find out."

"Computer, start showing us the recordings again. Where we left off at, please."

The image picked up where they left off. They watched Kuarto insert each of the DNA's into the eggs he had cloned.

The readings from them filled the screen, and he shook his head. "Nothing, which is what I expected."

He decided to clone a few more eggs. Once he was done, he noticed four new specimens sitting on his desk. Compliments of Al he was sure. He scanned each of them to see what type of DNA he sent. He logged it into his system and tried each of them with the same effect as before.

"I know you're listening. They didn't work either."

"I noticed." He walked into the room. "And that doesn't surprise you. Why?"

"It was something Heather and Storm said. They told me they were sterile before Heather became pregnant. I'm assuming you acquired it right before she became pregnant, so it could be from the same group that ended up having one fertilized. If that is true then any egg from her would be sterile. Including the one which is now carrying life. So how is her coming child possible?"

"So you think it is something with them, not the egg?"

"I'm not sure, which is why I want to run the tests I have set up, but I suspect it." He stood. "Unless you have other plans." Kuarto was taller than Al and planned on using it to his advantage. "You haven't trusted me since I got here."

"That isn't true."

He pointed to the cameras in the room. "You already have the computer wired to give you any info I learn on the egg. Why would you have so many cameras in here and out in the hall outside our room if trust wasn't the problem?"

"I am worried about the egg. That is all."

"The egg isn't inside our room."

"Didn't you have a security system set up at your home? Something to make you feel safe."

"I did." He grinned. "And I was as paranoid as you seem to be. Look, you don't trust me. I get it, but either let me do my work the way I'm used to or lock us up and find someone else. The way you're doing it right now is driving me crazy. I feel like a prisoner, not someone you hired."

"Trust is a very hard thing to give. I have trusted before and was betrayed."

"So was I." Kuarto watched him. He knew so little of the man he was forced to work for. "Who betrayed you?"

"It doesn't matter." Al moved then, breaking eye contact. "I will remove some of the security, but I want you to understand I need to feel safe, so some will remain. Your room has already been cleaned, as you requested. I'll also pull the security sensors from the hallways near your room so you can have your privacy, but this room will remain the same. This is my life and I don't want anything happening to it. I'm doing that for my protection."

Kuarto didn't like all the cameras. If he had his way, they'd all be gone. Al knew he couldn't escape. He had made sure they didn't know anything but the few buildings they had seen of the compound. But at least he would feel more comfortable talking to Toki in the lab. "And if we prove ourselves?"

"Then more freedom will be given to you."

————

Toki walked into the room first. She wrapped her arms around herself and turned to look at him. After he stepped in, the door was sealed and they were alone. "So you trust him to remove the security near this room?"

"That's what he promised." He walked to where she stood and pulled her into his embrace. "It falls into the 'we'll have to see' category."

"Do you trust him?" She leaned into him, needing his warmth and strength for comfort.

"Are you okay?"

"Frightened, but fine." She loved the feel of his arms around her. "Sure would like to know what is going on."

"Would you believe I'm here to rescue you?" He spoke to her softly, just in case.

She laughed. "I think you're doing a terrible job."

"I know, but there is a second part to why I'm here."

"The egg."

"You got it."

"I would think you would want to get us away from here before you started your research."

"The situation didn't work out that way." He remained quiet while he figured out what to say. "Once I got here, I knew I couldn't just walk out with that egg. It doesn't matter what Al said, that egg doesn't belong to him. Heather and Storm trust me to bring it home or destroy it. I can't fail them."

She hoped the system outside had been cleared before they started talking, even if they were speaking softly to each other. Kuarto was revealing things she didn't expect.

He let go of her and pulled his scanner out. Changing the setting to a security one, he checked the hallway near their room. "It's clean."

"Why didn't you do that before?" asked Toki.

"Because it was a test to see what he would do with the information."

"So you're sure we're safe now?"

He nodded.

"Will you tell me what is going on, then?"

He turned the scanner on once more and set up a white noise to block recording devices outside the room that might be close enough to pick up what they say. "I'm wired."

"What?" She hadn't noticed anything, and as often as they had been intimate, she was sure she would have seen something, but she did a quick look again just in case.

"You remember the old tales of an underground

compound?" At her nod, he continued. "Heather found it and the technology there rivals anything here. They can see and hear us like they are here."

"Everything?"

"I'm assuming they aren't watching every minute." He frowned at the thought. "That will be something we'll have to ask when we get back."

"I will kill him if he is watching."

Kuarto grinned. "Not her?"

"I know better. Heather would give us our privacy. My brother wouldn't." She crossed to the small bed.

"Your brother is the least of my problems right now. I'm worried Al will push me to move on this faster than I want to."

"Why are you dragging this out?"

"Because I haven't figured out how to get us out safely yet. And have no clue where we are so they can come and get us. So until we get more information we're kind of stuck here at Al's whim."

"If that computer is so advanced, why can't they have it track us?"

"Heather hasn't been able to activate the entire system, so it will only do so much." She gave him an odd look. "It's a long story. Right now, we're on our own and need to find a way to let them know where we are."

———

Kuarto sat at his desk, waiting to see if Al did hear anything they had said. He had a few tricks up his sleeves so he would know if they had been overheard. If Al said anything about the compound he would know the man had been listening in. Heather and Storm had kept the compound under the tightest of securities. Nobody knew about it but the four of them.

He got up and stretched. Toki had been too quiet since learning her brother could hear and see everything that they did. She sat nearby, never too far away from him. He walked by a shiny surface and noticed a slight discoloration on his collarbone. "Hmm."

He walked to another spot where he could get a better look. "What is that?" He pulled his scanner out and ran it over the area.

"What?"

"I seem to have a new mark. It's nothing that will harm me, but I wonder where it came from?"

She came over to look. Her face didn't show any emotion, but her eyes shined with fear. He felt a little jolt when she ran her fingers over it. Did she know what it was?

"Is that where I bit you?" Her voice a little high pitched for her.

He had to think. "I think it is. You saying you caused that?" He looked back at the surface to see it again before he turned his gaze back to her.

"Um, it's possible." She wouldn't look him in the eye.

"Well?"

"Well what?"

"What about this has you so frightened?"

TWELVE

Storm watched the screen in shock. "She marked him?"

"Isn't that what you did to me?" Heather touched the side of her neck where her mark was. It was something she wore with pride.

"Yes, but that was different." He pressed a soft kiss against her mark.

"How?" Heather sat in front of him, so she had to turn to look him in the face. "If I remember, your sister yelled for quite a while when she realized what had happened."

"That's because I didn't follow protocol. We were blessed by our religious leader. He's not there with them, is he?"

"You're not getting it, are you?" He could be so dense at times. "Let's try this a different way. When we were first told we were to marry, did you plan on taking me as your mate as well?"

"My uncle—"

"Don't care about him right now. Deep down inside. What did you feel?"

"I was attracted to you." He touched her face gently.

"I was a new toy to play with."

"You had the stamina to put up with my voracious appetite.

No one could do that. You also didn't fall all over yourself to get my attention the moment I met you. I found that intriguing."

"And this?" She exposed the little mark on her neck. "Did you plan this?"

"No. It just happened."

"Exactly." She pointed to his sister. "It just happened. I think they are destined for each other, even though your sister knows her duty. She isn't very happy about that mark. Just look at her face."

Her face was frozen on the screen because the computer stopped the video when they started talking. Stark fear shone in her eyes.

————

Toki wasn't sure what to do. Lying wasn't part of her nature, but he might not be very happy about what that meant. She took a deep breath. "Um, Vespian mates receive a mark like this when they go through the mating ritual."

"We haven't gone through a ritual."

"I know, but the mark has shown up on people before the ritual was done as well. That is very rare, but I know of one instance that happened recently."

"Really?" He watched her with curiosity on his face. "Who?"

"Heather and Storm." She stole a quick glance at him.

"The one on her neck?"

"Yes." He didn't seem to be too upset with this. She wasn't sure how to handle that.

"I wondered what that was." He was quiet for a moment. "Does this mean we're mates?"

She found herself studying the floor a lot. "I don't know."

"You mean you don't want to commit, even though you were driven to mark me as yours."

"I'm not supposed to mate." This was going to be very hard to explain.

"What are you talking about?" He walked to where she stood. His hand slipped under her chin and lifted her head so she would look him in the eyes. "Don't look at the ground while we're talking about this."

"I am to be the next religious leader of the planet. It's a position I'll hold for fifty years and I'm not to look for a mate until after I have served my term." She watched his face as her words sank in.

"Why?"

"That's part of the job." She shrugged. "Why aren't you upset about this?"

"Did you do this on purpose?" He touched his collarbone.

"No." She looked at the mark. Good thing he didn't ask if she was proud of it because in a way she was, but for all the wrong reasons. A mate wasn't part of her life right now, and she wouldn't dare ask him to wait until she had fulfilled her duty.

"Didn't think so." He studied her, making her nervous. "You don't seem happy about this."

"It shouldn't have happened." She had been groomed for her upcoming position. All the training, all the studying, was done. No one could do it but her. It would take too long to get someone else ready.

If only she could speak to her uncle. He would know what to do.

He wanted to press it further, but the door to their room opened at that moment. Their guards ushered them back to the lab.

She was grateful for the reprieve. It would give her time to think everything through.

Kuarto walked beside her, quiet. She wondered what he

was thinking. Then he whispered in her ear. "Do you have one too?"

She didn't know. That would be something they would have to look for when they went back to their room.

———

"Told you."

"Told me what?" Storm refused to acknowledge what his mate was driving at.

"She knows her duty." Heather gave him a smug smile.

He grunted. Kuarto was right when he told his sister things weren't going as planned. The computer hadn't been able to track Kuarto once he left the bar because of some sort of security scrambler. It was still working on a way to decipher the data to try to get a fix on their location but hadn't been successful yet. The mention of the binary stars helped, but none of the planets they saw when Kuarto and his sister went for their walk was helpful. They still needed more information.

And now his mate was proving she knew his sister better than he did.

Storm chose to let her comment go.

Heather watched him with that grin on her face. His lack of reaction seemed to work for her, as well as any comment he might have made.

———

The readings always came back the same. Nothing would fertilize the sterile egg. "I need to speak to Al." He knew the room was bugged, so waited for one of their guards to answer.

Al came into the room within a few minutes. "Have you found something?"

"Nothing. No matter how I manipulate any of these samples the results are the same."

"You feel this egg can't be fertilized." For some reason he didn't seem surprised.

"Not by any normal means."

"Use this and put it in the real egg." He handed him another sample.

"I need to run tests on it before I can do that." Kuarto looked at the sample. "We only get the one shot."

"I know." Al didn't say yes, but he didn't say no right away, either. "I'll allow you to run your tests, but I want to make sure the data doesn't leave this compound. I'll want to wipe your scanner before you leave this planet."

"That is fine." He picked up his scanner and held it out to Al. "You want to check it before I run my scans?"

He looked at the scanner for several seconds before he shook his head. "I'm going to have to trust you sooner or later, so why not start now."

"I'm touched." He hoped his hand wouldn't shake as he used it. The scanner pulled the data off and loaded it to the screen. It didn't take long for the scan to finish, but he knew it would take him a few days to work his way through all the information. He frowned as some of it caught his eye. "Whose DNA is this?"

"Mine."

"You have a lot of the same markers the egg from Heather does. I've never seen anything like this." Heather had a high percentage of ancient in her. What he saw showed this man as one hundred percent ancient. How was that possible?

"I wouldn't worry about that." He headed to the door. "You do what you need to get this egg fertilized."

Toki came to his side once Al left. "That sounded like an ultimatum."

"I know." Kuarto stared at the data. What did this mean?

Heather looked at Storm. She had walked in right before Al handed his DNA over. "How is that possible?"

"I don't know. We've never had any records of an ancient being amongst us."

"That is not true. He lived on this planet for several years. He found this facility and utilized it while he was here." The computer gave them the information. "His knowledge is the reason I wasn't able to track the doctor the way I should have."

"And you didn't think that was pertinent information?"

"You never asked if he had come to the compound."

"It is still a computer, Storm." She could feel his anger starting to grow. "Volunteering information might not be part of its program."

The glare he gave her would have made anyone else cower, but she understood. "Are you saying there are ancients living amongst us without our knowledge?"

"He and Heather are the only ones who fall into the category of ancients, but the elders are aware of both people."

"The elders didn't know of Heather's ancient blood and I doubt any of them know of Ialog."

"They were the ones who woke him up."

"Excuse me?"

"I think we need to speak to your mother," said Heather.

"You think she's been keeping information from us?" He had that 'I'm not in control and I don't like it' look on his face.

"I think she's following the basic need to know basis your planet runs on." Heather knew she needed to handle this properly. "We haven't told her about Al, so she doesn't know who has been causing all of our problems. I would think she would have told us about him if she suspected him to be the threat to us."

"You're right." He slipped an arm around her waist as they headed out of the compound. "You always give people the benefit of the doubt."

"There's no reason to get mad until you have all the information." Heather had to walk fast to keep up with his long legs.

"How was she today?"

"Pretty normal. She's worried about your sister, but I didn't see a break in her armor this time."

"Wonder how she's going to take our questions." He nodded to one of the men guarding her rooms.

"We'll know in a moment." Heather stepped in first. "Anseri?"

"I'm in here." She came out with a hopeful smile on her face. "What brings you here? Do you have news?"

"We have a few questions." Heather looked at Storm. He needed to let her ask the questions or he could end up upsetting his mother more than he planned. She took Anseri's hands and led her to a nearby couch. "We have found out who took my egg. He is the one holding your daughter and my brother. We think you know him."

She looked from Storm to Heather. "You think he's Vespian?"

"No. He's an Ancient. We're sure of it." Heather let the words sink in. "His name is Ialog. The same man who kidnapped me several months ago."

"Ialog?" She acted like the name didn't ring a bell.

Heather looked at Storm. "Could he have done to her what he did to me?"

"Possible." He touched Heather's shoulder. "You think you can go in and release the info?"

"Me?" The thought of entering Anseri's mind made her nervous. "I've never done anything like that. I don't know where to start."

"Uncle. He would know." Storm pressed a quick kiss against her forehead. "I'll be right back."

Heather watched him leave before turning her attention back to Storm's mother. "Ialog did something to my mind, so I wouldn't recognize him if I saw him. We have proof he was here and interacted with the council of elders, so we're thinking that he did something to your mind, too. Storm wants me to go inside and see if I can help you unlock the information you can't seem to remember. Is that okay?"

"If you think it will help you."

"I do." Heather held her hand.

Storm came back with his uncle in tow.

"I understand you need me." He stood there, smiling.

"Storm said you could help me to get into your sister's thoughts. I have no idea how to do it."

"I wondered when you would ask about this. You have just started using your mind, so wouldn't know your full potential yet, Heather." He pulled a chair up to where the two women sat and parked himself. He laid a leather pouch on his lap. He pulled a few items out and handed them to Heather.

"And what am I supposed to do with this stuff?" She looked at the items he handed her.

"Nothing." He laughed. He pulled out a fist sized crystal and held it up to the light. "I have found when I work with people who are just learning to use new talents like this, it helps them to focus on something. This should work for you. I just needed you to hold those things so I could get to the crystal."

She shook her head at his humor and handed everything back before she took the crystal. "What am I supposed to do?"

"Relax." He set his bag on the floor beside his chair. "Think of something pleasing."

She closed her eyes and thought of Storm. Her mind released itself a little.

"Good. Now, focus on the crystal. Nothing else but that."

She opened her eyes and looked at the rainbow of colors that flowed out of it. They moved around her, enveloping her in their soft glow. Her mind began to reach out. It happened too easily, and she found herself pulling back.

"Don't fight that, Heather. Natural instinct would be to hold back but you need to open your mind more. Allow yourself to touch other minds besides your mate's. You can see into the thoughts of anyone you want. Good or bad. At first, you'll probably enter only those minds you know well. But as time goes on and you continue to use this mental ability, you will be able to enter anyone's consciousness." His voice spoke to her softly, methodically. It lulled her into a deeper state that blocked out the rest of the world. All she could see was the crystal. All she could hear was his voice. "Now, reach out with your thoughts. Contact those around you."

She felt hesitant, knew she needed strength. Her mind searched for Storm's. His strength would help her do what was asked of her. The next mind she encountered was a little quirky, filled with so much knowledge. Uncle? Anseri? She wasn't sure. She probed some more and found the psyche to be female. A whole new world opened for her. Information she never wanted spilled into her head. The reasons why things were done a certain way. It was like a vast library and all she had to do was touch an image and all of that data was hers.

"I feel like I shouldn't be here."

"That is very natural. But remember you were invited in. There is no reason to feel like you're invading." His soothing words calmed her. "Now, you're looking for a memory."

It looked like a vault to her. A lot of small drawers with

no markings that she could see. "I have no clue how to do this. Her mind is so different than mine or Storm's."

"Not unusual. You know what you are looking for, put that thought out there, see if it draws you to any particular spot." He continued to speak in that soft, monotone voice. "If the memory is buried, it might be different in design. Maybe a different color or size."

Heather followed his suggestion and looked for something like that. On the bottom of one of the many drawers was one that didn't fit. It was dull and darker than the rest. She touched it and a rush of memories flowed around her.

Heather looked out through the eyes of a much younger Anseri. The whole council stood around as one man spoke. It was taking her some time to acclimate herself to the memory. She was also having trouble understanding them without her translator. Suddenly everything clicked into place and she was Anseri.

"So what do you think is behind this wall?" Heather heard herself ask.

"I'm not sure, but everything I read points to an ancient device. Each time we have found some of their technology we have gained from it as a whole."

The wall they stood in front of had ancient writing on it, which Heather could read. She let Storm and Hynna know what she was seeing through Anseri's memories. "I'm in front of a tomb."

"What sort of tomb?" asked Storm.

"One built by the ancients. We'll have to see where this place is afterwards. Maybe it is still intact and we can get more information from it. There's lots of writing on the walls nearby and from what I'm getting whoever is entombed was put here on purpose. He or she tried to destroy the ancients through his own greed and desires." Heather quieted as the vision continued. "They're getting ready to open it."

The wall shimmered and faded from sight. It revealed a

room empty except for a rounded box up against the far wall. As they approached it, the thing came to life with lights and noises, startling them all.

"What is that?" asked another person. Male this time. From the joy surging through Anseri, Heather assumed this was her mate. Storm's father.

"I'm not sure. I'll have to study it and let you know."

The memory faded then.

"It's gone."

"That is normal. Don't break the contact and the next one should start momentarily. Think of it as the old films they used to watch on Earth and this is an intermission."

"Something is starting to happen now." Heather watched as the next scene unfolded in front of her eyes. They were in front of the box she saw earlier, but now she recognized some sort of cryo-chamber. Voices floated around her, Storm asking questions and breaking her concentration, forcing her to fight to stay in the memory.

"He's still alive in there."

"Who is he?"

"From what we could decipher, he is an Ancient. His name is Ialog, but we couldn't figure out why he was put in this chamber." The man speaking held a pad. He kept glancing at it as he explained the story he had uncovered. "If he had some sort of disease we could be jeopardizing his life."

"Do you read any illness in him?" asked the same male voice she had assumed was Storm's dad. Heather had never seen any images of him. She tried to turn Anseri's head but wasn't able to get it to move. The scene continued to play out in front of her.

"Nothing we can detect."

"Then revive him and we'll hope for the best."

Heather watched as the chamber opened. Her heart beat faster when she recognized the man inside. Everyone else stood in awe as Ialog opened his eyes and looked around. The memories came a little quicker as she moved from one to another. She also found she could slip through memories if she found they didn't have anything important for her to learn.

She felt hands on her. Releasing her mind from Anseri's, she looked at the faces gathered around her. "Yes?"

"Time for a break, my heart. You've been at it for several hours and you're pushing yourself too hard." Storm knelt in front of her.

"What? But there is so much more to go through." It didn't feel like it had been that long to her. She found herself slumping against the back of the couch instead of sitting upright like she had been when she first started. "Okay. So maybe I do need a break."

"Here." Storm's uncle handed her a glass. "This will help build your energy back up fast."

"That's not that foul tasting stuff you gave me when I was going in and out of Heather's mind, is it?" Storm grabbed the glass and took a whiff before handing it to her.

"No. She doesn't need any of the things you did to keep the link open. She has that ability naturally. This is nothing more than an energy boost."

Heather took the glass and took a hesitant sip. A nice fruity flavor filled her mouth, and she downed the whole content in one swallow. Energy started to return. "Thank you."

"Your mind will get stronger as you push it like this, but never push so hard you're vulnerable." He took the glass from her. "That can be very dangerous. Especially since we don't know what you're up against yet."

"The elders were the ones who released him from the stasis unit he had been trapped in." She smiled at her mate. "I'm looking for a section of the palace or compound where they freed him." She shared the image with him. "Do you know where it is?"

Storm shook his head. "No, but I think I know something that would. I'll go check with the computer."

"Perhaps we should all go there," suggested Heather. "It might be safer while we work through her memories."

"You sure?"

She brushed her mind against his. If they couldn't trust their family, then who could they trust with this?

Anseri sat immobile.

"Anseri?" Heather touched her arm, but she didn't react.

"What have I done?"

"Nothing," said uncle. "This happens when you open old memories. She's between the memories and the conscious world. Once you finish going through the memories, she should be fine."

"Can she walk?"

"Her body will respond to what we ask it to do, I'll make sure she makes it there." He stood and took her hand. "Come, sister. Let's walk."

Anseri stood, waiting.

Storm scooped Heather up in his arms. "Let's go."

"I can walk."

"I know, but I want to hold you close."

She sighed but didn't say anymore. She knew she had pushed herself too hard, and this was his way of protecting her, but the porcelain doll treatment would get old.

Storm led the way to the underground compound. Everyone but his uncle had been cleared for the main complex, so Storm was surprised when the computer allowed him entrance. "Thought everyone was stopped the first time by the force field to wait for Heather's permission to enter."

"Hynna has been here before," said the computer.

"I have?"

"Yes." The computer was quiet for a few moments. "Your mind has been altered, your time here has been blocked."

"Why was I here before?"

"You were learning about the ancients and Ialog allowed you entrance."

"He had full run of this compound?" asked Storm.

"He knew the question to ask."

"What question is he talking about?" asked Hynna.

"My blood allows me to access this compound, but there is a question I'm supposed to ask in order to unlock the system." Heather felt kind of stupid because she hadn't figured out what the question was. "Until then, there's a lot the computer can't tell me."

"If I leave, can I get back here?" Hynna asked.

"Yes," the computer said. "I can also free your memories if you'd like."

"In a few minutes." Hynna headed out of the area. "I think I can help you."

"Computer, make sure he makes it back here okay." Heather wondered what he had that could help her.

"I have already set up everything he'll need to find his way back."

"Thank you." Heather looked around the area, noticing the only piece of furniture was Storm's chair. "Can you give us a little comfort? I need to work with Storm's mother while he does research."

"What is it you need?"

"Furniture. A couch or several chairs." It took only seconds before she found a couch and several comfortable chairs. She led Anseri to one of the chairs. "We are also hoping you could also tell us where Ialog was found."

An image appeared on the screen. Directions came up next.

"Storm, will you stay with your mother?" She knew he

wanted to go with her, but she wasn't sure if they should leave his mother alone.

"Anseri will be fine here." The computer enveloped her in a colored light. "Her mind is trapped in the memories you have started, Heather. She won't be released until you finish. I can keep her in this healing wave until you come back."

Heather looked at Storm. Would it be safe for them to leave her? He put his hands on her shoulders and steered her out the door toward the area where they found Ialog.

"You trying to tell me what to do again?" he asked once they were alone.

"I know it seems like that, but no. I knew I needed to read the writing around the wall near Al's chamber, and I wasn't sure if we should leave your mother alone. I was asking, not telling."

"Sometimes it's hard to tell."

"I'm sorry, my heart. I guess I was focused on finding out why he was trapped and how that is affecting him now." She wrapped an arm around his waist. "Guess I was being like my mate."

"Flatterer." He stopped in front of a small alcove. "This looks like it."

Heather nodded. She stepped up to the wall and ran her hand over it. The faded letters glowed before they darkened and cleared for her to read.

"Didn't know you could do that."

"I didn't know either." She looked at him in shock. "What else am I going to learn about myself haphazardly like this?"

"Let's see what would happen if you were to wave your hand over me like that."

"Normally, all I have to do is look at you and I get a reaction." She studied the wall, moving about once she finished one section. "But if you want to test a theory, I'll help."

He stepped up behind her and wrapped his arms around

her. "That's my heart." He looked at the writing curiously. "What does it say?"

"Ialog was locked in here because of his crimes."

"What sort of crimes?" His lips were close to her ear so she could feel his breath against the tiny hairs as he spoke.

"Still working on that." Desire unfurled deep inside her, then like someone dumped ice all over her, she felt cold. "Oh God."

"What?"

She didn't speak, just broke his hold on her, and marched back to the computer room. Uncle had returned with a tattered old book.

"Ialog is the one who created me?"

THIRTEEN

"Yes."

"For what reason?"

"You must ask the right question."

Heather wanted to scream in frustration. "I am ancient, and I was created by that man for a purpose, so why must I ask you for this information? It should be available for me because of who I am not because of some stupid riddle."

Storm's uncle handed her the book. "Try this."

Heather read from the page he had it opened to, and then looked at him. "Really?"

"Have you spoken to the computer in ancient at all?"

"No." The computer hadn't spoken to them in ancient, so she never thought twice about using the language.

"Would it hurt?"

He was right. The language flowed out of her so easily. The beautiful cadences filled the air as she asked the computer what was in her heart.

Nothing seemed to happen. That didn't make sense.

"Perhaps you asked the wrong question," suggested Storm.

"The passage in the book said each ancient had a different

question. Like a password, and it was normally the question of their heart. You know mine. I want to know why I was created." She looked at him with hope and fear in her eyes.

"How would the computer know what is in your heart?"

"Because my system was designed that way." The computer spoke. "I am programmed to know what every ancient is thinking. To anticipate their wants and needs without them having to ask for it. The first time Heather entered this installation she was installed with a chip that would allow me to do that. Now that she has given me the correct password, she can program me to give it to anyone else non-ancient that she wishes to have it. It will allow me to give them data without getting approval from Heather each time."

She looked at Storm. Did he want the computer to have access to his mind? He gave her a slight nod. Since the computer said it would be able to pick up her thoughts, she decided to put it through a test. Without a verbal command, she gave it permission to install the chip in Storm.

He arched a brow at her. Her mind brushed against his letting him know what she had done. Storm had to ask for something outrageous so they would know it worked. The smile he gave her sent a shiver down her spine as she felt a weird sensation against her skin. She pulled her bodice out so she could peek inside. The black lace outfit encased her breasts. Five seconds ago, she didn't have it on. The heat of a blush filled her cheeks. At least no one else knew what he had done.

Storm was beside her in seconds. He wanted to see for himself. Knowing how easily she blushed, he slid his fingers inside her bodice to see what he would find. The grin on his face made her wish they were alone.

Just as she got ready to ask the computer to show her the rest of the compound, doorways and other rooms attached to the one they stood in started to appear.

"What about your mother? I have to free her from whatever I trapped her in before we can do anything else." She looked at Storm.

"I agree." He looked at the newly lit areas, then back at her. "And you don't want me to go without you, do you?"

"Do you mind?" She sat next to Anseri and took her hands, needing to focus on her. Now that she had entered her mind once she felt more comfortable with the process and slipped back in easily. The file was still there, its darkened color standing out from the rest. It amazed her how easily she could see it now when earlier she hadn't noticed it at all.

She found the memories easier to sort through too. There were several with interactions between the elders and Ialog which Heather skimmed over. Her mind seemed to know what was important and wasn't. He lived amongst them for quite a while, never asking for anything and helping whenever they needed it. They started to trust him with everything. He even came up with a special injection when one of the elders became ill and gave it to all of them, explaining it was designed for their unique blood type and would help keep them healthy.

Only a few months later the first ruling family became pregnant. Within a year or two Anseri turned up pregnant. Heather knew there had to be a link between the pregnancy and the shots they were receiving.

Anseri had questioned it too. She spoke to her brother about it and asked him to see what he could find out.

Memory after memory filed through, the information her brother gathered and told Anseri. He found Ialog working on some sort of scientific experiment he had done years ago. The excuse Hynna got from Ialog didn't sit right with him. Then some of their people were able to translate more of the words around the area where they found Ialog. Evidence started to mount against him.

They found out he was using them as guinea pigs, trying different things on them to see what would help him recreate the race he wanted to design before. The ancients had destroyed all his research, so if he was accidentally reawakened, he would have to start from scratch, and the elders had allowed him to have free rein to do just that.

The elders worked on a way to stop what he was doing, and Heather found their plan ingenious. Hynna befriended Ialog. His job was to find a way to get the material he was using to create this race and destroy it. He had access to the computer, and with his knowledge as religious leader, he knew more about the ancients and how to stop him than anyone else. Once they destroyed the material, Streya would command the computer to erase all data and block Ialog from being able to use this computer ever again.

Heather worked her way through the files and found Anseri didn't have the knowledge she needed. Hynna kept her in the dark about what he did so she would remain innocent of all of it. Heather also learned it wasn't Ialog who blocked the memory from Anseri's mind, but Hynna, who did it as a protection to keep it from surfacing accidentally. Heather resealed the file, making sure she put it back the way she found it. After sending her healing waves of love and support, she eased herself out of Anseri's mind. She continued to hold her hand and waited for Anseri to rejoin them, not sure if what she did would bring her back.

Anseri blinked and looked around. "Where am I?"

"You're back in the ancient compound," said Heather. "How are you feeling?"

She smiled. "Refreshed."

"Good."

"Did you get what you needed?"

"Yes." Heather was happy to see her back to normal. She was afraid she had done some real damage when she first started this. She looked at her mate. His mother should go lie down. He nodded and escorted her out of the area.

Once they left, she stood and walked to where Storm had been. "Computer, can you fill in the gaps with this information?"

"Of course." The information she learned started to stream across the screen. Then the system loaded the visual aspects with sound so they could see and hear everything that happened.

Storm came back as quickly as he could.

First, the system caught Storm and his uncle up to what Heather had learned about Ialog through Anseri's memories.

"I don't remember any of this," commented Hynna.

"Not surprised. He has this ability to make you forget you ever met him," said Storm.

"It's possible Hynna blocked this himself. He was the one who buried the memory in your mother," Heather said softly.

Storm looked at Heather with concern. "You think he has done it to others?" He kept his voice low.

"I'm sure it was used because of the circumstances," she murmured. "If you wish I can check you later."

He nodded.

The image on the screen centered around Ialog. It showed him in a room in the complex, working diligently on something. Hynna walked into the room.

"What are you working on?"

Ialog looked up from what he was doing and turned the system off. "Did they ask you to come down here and check up on me?"

"I am the religious leader." Hynna shrugged. "I had a vision about knowing your research and they suggested I come down and learn from you."

"You don't have to do everything they say." He turned the system back on and went back to work.

"They mean no harm." Hynna walked around. He studied the screen when he could without being caught. If Ialog looked at him, he pretended he was looking at some of the gadgets on the different tables. "I've only been in the position for ten years. There is still a lot I need to learn."

"That sounds like something you have been fed." He pressed a few buttons. "Ten years is a long time in one position, I would think you'd know it all by now."

"It's taking the learned info and converting it into the practical. I feel like I'm still very new at this." He grinned. "But it is only fifty years of my life. Only forty more to go."

"You could have told them no."

"It's what I was trained to do." He leaned against the counter Ialog worked at. "Look at what my sister had to give up to become leader. Thank goodness that worked out for her."

"She does seem to care for her mate." He looked up.

"She does, now and with the twins on the way they've never seemed happier." Hynna smiled, the proud uncle shining through.

"I need to check her to make sure they are all doing fine."

"I'll let her know." He hesitated, wondering what the man was actually doing to her. "Do I need to do that now?"

"No, but it should be soon. Maybe the next time you come down here you should bring her."

Hynna nodded. He looked around the compound. "Guess I should leave you since you're working. Didn't mean to interrupt you."

"You didn't." He sat up. "It's just this part is a little tricky."

"Is that an embryo?"

"Close. It's hard being the only ancient, so I'm hoping to create a companion. This is the beginning of what I hope to be a womb."

"You plan on growing someone in there?"

"One day I hope to."

Hynna nodded, keeping his features masked.

"That bothers you," Ialog said it matter-of-factly.

"Wouldn't it bother you?" Hynna had to be honest. It was part of his nature. "You're playing around with things the ancients have told us not to."

"That's because they hadn't perfected this the way I have." He studied Hynna. "I promise I'm not trying to create a massive army that will take over the world, just a companion for me to grow old with."

Heather wondered if he suspected anything. He had already been stopped once.

"Why not create an android?"

"They don't age and they don't have real emotions." He turned to face Hynna. "You know how you feel about this leadership position you must now fill? You don't relish the idea of going without companionship for so long, do you?"

Hynna shook his head.

"Imagine how I feel. I am the only one of my kind."

The image changed at that point. This time it showed Anseri and two toddlers in her rooms. "You seemed distressed, Hynna."

"I'm just not sure about this. He has done a lot for us. Look at your children. I don't think you could have had them without his help."

"I know." She ruffled the hair on her son's head. He looked up at her with a big smile.

Heather felt that smile all the way to her toes. "You've had that heart stopping smile all your life? No wonder you are the way you are."

He shushed her as he wrapped an arm around her.

"But he needs to be stopped. He now wants to give the injections to the entire population and as much as that would end our lack of children, I'm afraid it would cause adverse effects." Anseri looked up at him. "Storm is a lot more aggressive than any other child his age. Thank goodness he has the mind to temper it. He's already reading and learning to write. Other children his age are just learning to control basic body functions and have a limited vocabulary."

"We were advanced, too, you know."

"I know." She sighed. "Guess I'm just frightened over all of this and seeing these signs in my precious ones just breaks my heart."

"They are fine healthy children and you have nothing to fear." He picked up his niece, who promptly started to chew on his hand. He laughed. "I see someone is now teething."

"And she chews on everything." She held out her hands for her daughter and put her in a small enclosure to keep her out of the way. Storm sat at their feet calm and quiet, so she let him be. "Have you figured out when he's going to create this being of his?"

"He keeps saying soon. Ialog does seem to have everything he needs now to finish his experiment." He touched his sister's arm. "He is growing this woman. It will be nothing more than a fetus when we remove it."

"You want to give it to someone? Are you sure that is safe?"

"No, but if it is brought up in a loving, nurturing environment, won't that make a difference?" he asked.

Storm tightened his hold. They were discussing her future, and they could have easily ended her life before it even started.

"Let me speak to the elders and see what they wish us to do."

The image changed again and brought them back to the lab where Ialog had been working. He had a stream of information loading on the screen in front of him. Happy with what he saw, he took the two specimens he had in the two units on his table and merged them.

"Now all I can do is wait and see what happens." He walked away from the computer then.

Heather stared at the screen. Did she just watch her creation? The whole thing made her ,feel cold inside. Knowing she had been created was one thing, but to see it happen had a bone chilling effect on her.

The computer focused on three different events then. One was the creation of life in the lab. It followed Ialog to the elders' chamber, and Hynna. He had waited until Ialog left for the chamber before he entered the lab. He walked up to the small cylinder that held the possible life force and checked the readings. He looked once more before walking away from the container and heading to the elders' chambers as well.

Ialog stood in front of the elders. "Why did you call me here? My experiment is almost ready, and I need to get back."

Anseri spoke for them all. "We're not sure if allowing you this creation is right."

"Now? You have second thoughts now, when I'm so close? After all I have done for you?" His anger radiated through the screen. "I don't need your permission to do this."

"You used our DNA to create this being of yours. The DNA of my children."

"What makes you say that?"

"The fact that all three elder families have either had children or are carrying one. That has never happened before. We know you manipulated us to get what you needed to create this thing. We're the ones with the most of the ancient blood in us, and you needed that to make your creation."

"How are you going to stop me? Your weapons don't work on me. You don't have the mental power to stop me the way the others did, and if you think I'm going to walk back into that chamber and be refrozen, you're crazy."

Storm's uncle came into the room holding an ancient manuscript. Quietly, he started to read from it. The words filled the chamber, making Ialog react violently.

"What are you doing?"

"We found this in our records. It's supposed to bind you and banish you from our planet."

"It won't keep me away forever." He struggled against the words, his energy failing him.

"It might not, but it should keep you away long enough."

He fell to the floor. Hynna continued to read from the book, completing the binding. Once he finished with that, he started another to erase the memory of where Ialog had come from, and why he had been there.

"I don't know how long that will work on him, but we will have enough time to destroy his work, maybe for good." Hynna went down to the lab then with Streya. Storm's uncle programmed the computer to destroy all the research Ialog had done. He nodded to Streya, who gave the command to wipe the system completely in ancient.

A light flashed on the control panel as something flashed on the screen. "I think it wants an access code."

Hynna repeated the code Ialog had used in his presence and watched as the data disappeared from the screen. He went to the container and picked it up. It slipped from his fingers as he stared blindly ahead. He stood, frozen, as a vision flashed through his mind. Streya caught the container before it hit the floor.

"Hynna?"

He blinked and looked at Streya. "We can't destroy her."

"I thought I dreamed that," Hynna murmured.

"What?" asked Storm.

"My first vision of you two. I saw flashes of your life together. The joy you will bring to each other. I knew Heather needed to be protected then. I knew it the moment I touched that cylinder."

"It looks like your suppressed memories made sure you didn't forget that," commented Storm.

"Hynna asked me not to suppress that memory when the time came. He knew it was an important one," said the computer. "That was when he knew he had to save her."

"But how did we insert the baby into Heather's birth mother? I don't have that kind of medical knowledge."

"You knew the danger of having that knowledge, so requested that I take care of that while you blocked the memories of the ruling council. I never saw you after that, until today."

Heather had been very quiet. Her mind was having trouble coming to terms with everything that had happened.

Storm hadn't let go of her. "Uncle, do you think you could give us a few minutes? I need to help my mate right now."

"Of course." He touched Storm on the arm before he headed out of the compound.

Storm turned to Heather. She seemed to be lost in her thoughts. "My heart?"

She looked up at him, sadness etched on her face.

He wanted to help her but wasn't sure how to do it. He touched her face in his usual manner. It comforted her before. "You know, none of this changes the way I feel about you."

A sad smile spread across her face. "I know, but it's hard to learn how you came into these worlds. It's one thing to think you weren't loved enough to be kept by your real parents, but to find you were a creation from a madman isn't something you can prepare for."

"I don't care how you came to be, I'm just happy you're here."

She touched his face. "You are my heart."

"And you are mine."

"Computer, I want to see that lab." Something deep

inside urged her on. "I'm assuming Ialog has been there since he came back to the planet, and I want to see what he was trying to do."

The way to the lab lit up as they walked through. Heather held onto Storm like a lifeline. Everything about this frightened her, and he knew it.

The room didn't look that much different from the main room they had been in. The computer loaded the data he pulled up since his return. Since most of the information when she was created had been erased, there wasn't a lot he could do. He was able to get her life history, though. Everything was there. What she found interesting was all of Storm's info had been pulled as well.

"Computer, we were told Storm has a catalyst. Can you explain that to us now?" She rubbed her fingers against the bridge of her nose.

"Are you sure you want this information now?" the computer asked.

"Why?"

"Your blood pressure is elevated, your eyes are dilated and your heart is racing. You are on the verge of hysterics."

"The computer is saying you need to calm down." Storm agreed.

She gave Storm a look. "I figured that one out on my own, thanks."

He smiled. At least she hadn't lost her sense of humor. "It's just looking out for you."

"My heart." She looked like she wanted to hit him. "I do understand. I need to calm down and I will. It's just a little overwhelming for me."

He backed her up against the wall. In a thought her dress and the lace he put on her, plus his clothes, were gone. The soft curves of her body pressed against his. He grinned when he realized he could get real used to that. He gazed into her eyes. "There is only one way I know that will make you forget everything but the here and now."

She was torn. Part of her wanted the physical act to show the strong bond between her and her mate, yet she also wanted to know the answers to her questions, no matter what they might be.

"Storm."

"I am here, my heart." He picked her up and braced her against the wall. In an instant, he was buried deep inside her. She quaked in his arms as she rested her head on his shoulder. This time, he would be the one in control. She needed to forget for just a moment or two.

FOURTEEN

"You have a thing for walls." She loved to feel his steel length driving in and out of her body. He knew what she needed and made sure she had it.

"No. I have thing for you. The walls just come in mighty handy." Muscles tightened at the delicious friction building between them.

Heather's mind let go of the overload of information in her and allowed the wonderful sensations to wash over her. The movements of their bodies freed her. Flesh against flesh. Heartbeat against heartbeat. Her whole being relaxed and she became mindless. All she knew was him and her, the joining of their bodies and their souls. Heather needed this more than she realized. Reacting to the buildup inside her, she felt the wave of release circle around and sweep her away.

He did this for her. Her mate gave so she could have a few moments' peace.

Storm had left her mind alone this time. He missed the shared release but knew she needed to think of nothing more than the moment, and his thoughts could ruin that. She deserved a few moments to herself.

Slowly, she came back to him. Tears sprang into her eyes.

"Why are you crying?" What was upsetting her now? He hoped the reality of their situation hadn't come crashing in already.

"Because of you." She placed a soft kiss against his chest. "As much as you enjoy our intimacy you always think of me first."

"What kind of mate would I be if I only cared about my pleasure?" He eased himself out of her and put her feet on the floor.

"Pretty normal." She looked down at her state of dress. The black lace he had thought of was the only thing she wore. Heather was surprised to see it. "When did this show back up?"

"I'm not sure." He ran his fingers along the edges hugging her waist. "But I like it. Maybe I should make that mandatory dress for down here."

"Really? Then let's give it a trial run and see how long you can handle me wearing only this." She turned and faced the computer. "Am I calmer now?"

"Much better," said the computer. "The ancients always believed that everything happens for a reason. The reason they stopped Ialog the first time was because they knew you would be created too early."

"Are you saying they knew Storm and I were destined for each other?" Heather placed her hands on the console, arching her back so she could lean forward comfortably.

The tiny little skirt inched up on her, revealing a touch more skin. The image she presented him went right to his groin. Was she doing it on purpose?

"Yes, and I have the records to back that up, if you would

like to see them." The computer loaded the data on the screen, which filled with the images of people Storm had never seen before. They went about their day working in the compound.

One stood not too far from where they were looking at the information. "The data is exact. We have to stop him from creating her now. She is far too important to the future of this planet. The catalyst won't be born for another thousand years."

"You are sure about this?"

"Yes. We know our days are limited. Have for a long time. The people on the surface, though, are strong enough to populate this planet and thrive. As they grow there will be those among them like us. More our race than theirs. Our blood will flow through these people. They will be our future. It is the only way."

"What about Ialog? He doesn't believe in the prophesies you have seen."

"Won't stop them from coming true." He turned from the screen and looked at his companion. "He has never believed in the spiritual and never will. He's too marred in the sciences."

"He looks like me," Storm said.

"Yeah. I noticed that too." Heather straightened her frame and Storm watched.

He found he couldn't keep his eyes off her as she shifted and moved while they watched the images on the screen. "You think he's one of your ancestors?"

"He is. Storm is a direct descendant," said the computer.

The two men they had been watching on the screen continued talking as they went back to their workstations. "What have you told the others?"

"The truth. She will be born to members of the ruling class here. The people will call them elders and she will be sent from this planet to another one. They're doing it for her protection and it will help shape her into the woman she needs to be."

"And what about the catalyst?"

"He will be born to members of the ruling families as well. A leader among men. From what I can see, he will win her heart quickly." He pressed a few buttons. "I feel for Ialog."

"Why?"

"Because these people will wake him, and because he still feels the desire to create this companion he wants so bad, he'll have a hand in creating this catalyst. The one thing that will come between him and his ultimate goal."

"And you're sure of this?"

"Very sure, I have run the scenarios hundreds of times with the same results. He is the one who creates the woman, wanting her as a mate. He also inadvertently creates the catalyst."

"How?"

"He uses these elders to further his research, using enhancers to see if that will allow him to create the woman. One of those enhancers creates the male who will be her true mate."

"But I thought we were going to block him from accessing his work."

"That won't stop him. He'll have plenty of time to recreate what he is doing right now." He pulled up the information on the screen. Mathematical equations sat next to his predictions. "I have put all of this information in books for them to be given when they learn of this."

A drawer opened in the desk they stood next to. Inside held a large, well-worn leather book. Heather leaned over and pulled it out. The front of her top fell forward, exposing her breasts. The small bit of lace hugging her hips inched up a little more. Storm wanted to forget everything except their flesh together. It was driving him crazy.

She turned to look at him with a sultry smile. She *was* doing this on purpose. He stepped up to her, his need for her strong, but before he could touch her she handed him a smaller leather book.

"This one has my name on it." Heather looked at the cover bearing her name. The age of the book and the lettering made her look at Storm. "This looks very old." She set it down and backed away from the book. "They knew about us?"

"Your destiny is a lot older than you realize," said the computer. "Ialog didn't believe in the prophesy even though he played a big part in it."

Heather found she needed to sit. "This is all a little farfetched."

"Read the book. It will explain everything."

———

Kuarto sensed something wrong with Heather. He didn't know what it was, but she was definitely upset. Not wanting to break the seal between their minds, he let it go. She wasn't in any kind of danger. He would know if she was.

He had her egg in front of him, debating on what to do. The research he had done on Ialog's DNA came back inconclusive. There didn't seem to be anything special about it. The computer had told them his genetic code wouldn't fertilize the egg. Did Al know that and add something he couldn't find? He had seemed awfully confident when he handed over the sample. If he took a chance and it did nothing, Ialog could get violently angry, and that wouldn't be good. If he used Storm's sample and he got wind of it, that wouldn't be good either.

Toki worked nearby. She seemed to sense his hesitation. "Problem?"

"I'm not sure what to do. I can't see how his DNA is any

different from anything I have already used. It doesn't look like it will work."

"Tell him."

"As angry as he has gotten lately?" He looked at Toki. "Not sure if I want to take my life in my hands like that."

"He'll be twice as angry if you don't."

"I know, and that's my dilemma." He pushed back from the desk. "Let's go for a walk."

She stood as well and followed him out of the room. "You seem to be a little distracted."

"The link. Even though we closed it off, very strong emotions can still slip through. There's something going on at home that has Heather upset."

"It's not the children, is it?" She voiced her concern.

"No. Nothing life-threatening, but it does have her emotions in turmoil." He grinned as he took her hand. "It's weird having this link with her, but I'm getting used to it now."

"As long as they don't share their orgasms with you?"

"Exactly."

"Have they figured out where we are?" She kept her face away from any camera that might pick up what she was saying.

"I don't get that much detail. It's like being in another room. Sometimes you might hear their voices raise, but you don't know what they are talking about." He led her past one of the cameras, talking about the egg. Once he was sure they were in the clear, he went back to their conversation. "We need to figure out more about where we are."

"It must be a recognizable sky at night."

"What makes you say that?"

"Because he never lets us see it."

He laughed and pulled her into his embrace. "You are wonderful."

———

The worn leather book sat in her lap, but Heather couldn't bring herself to open it. "Have you looked at yours yet?"

"No, my heart. I figured we'd do it together." He stood across from her, leaning against one of the counters, his book tucked up under his arm. "I must say you pose quite an arousing picture sitting there in nothing but the lace."

"I know better than to cover up. I see you haven't changed your lack of clothing either."

"Have to be ready to please my mate at a moment's notice."

She couldn't help but smile. Setting the book aside, she stood and crossed to the main console of the computer system. "Please load all data Ialog had been working on."

The system loaded the information as she requested. She stared at the data, confused. "Is this all he looked at?"

She felt something strange happen before she lost control of her body. It started to move on its own, quickly accessing information she had no idea how to look for. She found she couldn't speak or stop herself.

She reached out to Storm, just touching his mind when her body went limp and she fell to the floor.

———

Heather dropped to the floor and his heart stopped beating for a moment. He raced to her side, shouting at the computer. "What is going on?"

"The sentry woke when she approached this console. It was able to pull up some files before her self-protection program overrode what the sentry tried to do."

Storm looked up at the screen, looking at the files opened. "Why did he wait until now to open these files?"

"They were blocked to him before. Heather has access to all data and he used her to get to sensitive information."

"Did he get anything he shouldn't have?"

"It depends on what he plans on doing with the information he did get."

———

Kuarto heard him screaming before he saw the angry face of Al. He wasn't sure what just happened, but he sure didn't seem happy about it.

"They trained her too well." He slammed his hands on the table. "Have you figured out how Heather became pregnant?"

"No. I don't have what I need to do the research."

"What do you need?"

"Storm's DNA." He couldn't lie. Al would know if he was trying to avoid fertilizing the egg, and he wasn't about to say he had his DNA with him already. Without it, he couldn't do anything.

"I'll have it within twenty-four hours."

———

"We spend more time here than anywhere else. Why don't we move in here?" He found he couldn't keep his eyes off the lace, and he didn't want her to cover it up just so they could return to their room.

"In the compound?" She gave him an odd look. "After all the work your mother did to free those rooms upstairs for us?"

"For now." He came within inches of her, his fingers sliding under the lace wrapped around her shoulders. "Then we can use it as we need it."

"You just love that damn chair, don't you?"

"This computer can anticipate my every thought wherever I am so I can have that chair anywhere. I was just thinking between watching the data stream on your brother and my sister, and reading these books, we're going to be here all the time anyway. Why trek back to our rooms every night?" He tried to give her an innocent smile. "You can accommodate us, right computer?"

"There are rooms set aside for that purpose."

"See? I think it's a good idea for now."

She shook her head but saw no reason not to go along with it. "We do spend a lot of time here."

"Good." He spoke to the computer then, asking to see the room they should use and then taking off to help set it up for them to live in.

Heather held the book in her hand again. She still hadn't quite gotten the nerve to open it up. Not knowing what was on the pages had her second guessing herself on a regular basis now. Her life had been turned upside down since she met Storm and each day it got just a little bit stranger. "My heart, why are our lives in such turmoil? Why can't we have one normal day amongst the chaos?"

"Now what fun would that be?" He took her hand and pulled her with him. "I have done my share. You need to add your touches."

"Fine." She walked into the room and was not surprised to see a huge bed dominating it. Heather shook her head. Was that the only thing he worried about? She half expected to see the chair in here.

Tomorrow she would bring down the things they would need while staying here. She sensed her mate behind her and she turned around. "I see you got the most important piece of furniture placed."

"Wanted to be sure you were comfortable." He gave her one of his heart-stopping smiles as he crowded her backward toward the bed. "Want to try it out? Make sure I got it right?"

"You are incorrigible." She had to laugh as her knees hit the edge of the bed. "But you're going to have to wait. We've been asked to join your mother for dinner. She wants an update on your sister."

He eased her onto it and started to nibble on her neck. "We don't have to eat with her. I can call her right now and give her three words. I don't know."

"And then your mother would lecture you on having to change your ways if you're going to be the leader of the council for about an hour or so." She said it softly, not wanting him to stop either, but knowing his mother needed their company. "Personally, I'll get hungry waiting, so why not just play nice and have dinner with your mother?"

"Because I don't know what to tell her." He pulled up and looked at Heather as he helped her to her feet. "We have no idea where they are so can't get them out and their time there is starting to run out. Especially after he tried to take over your body to gain information he had been shut out of."

"So he didn't get anything?"

"Not much." He looked at the bed one last time before he looked at his mate. "He pulled up information on the injections he gave my mother, but none of the chemicals that he used were able to load before you shut down."

"So he knows he needs a catalyst and has figured you're it." She touched his arm with her hand. "He's now going to come after you."

————

Kuarto and Toki sat in their cramped room, trying to figure out how they could get out while it was dark. There had to be a way. He decided to try the direct approach. Banging on the door, he waited until someone answered. "Is there any way we can go for a walk? We've been cooped up in here for hours and I'd like to, you know, be kind of romantic and a walk might help me out a bit."

"You're not allowed out."

"Come on. Ask the boss, see if he'll let us out for a little while." He leaned against the door and dropped his scanner into the man's pocket with it on. Hopefully, he dropped it in the right direction and it would scan the sky, not the ground, as he walked to Al's office. Assuming his office was in another section of the compound. The amount of time it took for him to get to them made Kuarto think it was.

The guard seemed to be caught. He wasn't sure what to do. Kuarto just hoped he'd be able to get his scanner back.

He contacted another guard who just about laughed in his face. Well, that got shot down pretty quickly. Kuarto pretended to stumble so he could get his scanner back and thanked the young man. He came back into the room and shrugged his shoulders.

"No?"

"He didn't even leave my sight. We'll have to come up with something else."

"It can't pick up the stars during the daytime?"

"It's not designed to do such long-distance scans." He set it on the table. "I don't have what I need to modify it and if I try to get the part, he'll know what I'm up to. He hasn't been the same the last few days."

"I noticed it too. What do you think happened?"

"No idea." He walked over to her side. "I'm more worried about him. He seems more volatile now. One wrong move and we could be in real trouble."

———

Dinner had gone better than expected. Storm escorted Heather down to the ancient compound. The moment they walked into the main part, he worked on ridding her of her cumbersome dress. He grinned when the dress disappeared and left nothing but lovely skin for him to look at.

"Storm!" She turned to look at him. "I can have that thing deactivated if you abuse it too much."

"What?" He was just as naked as she was. She couldn't help but smile at his innocent look. "I'm just more comfortable this way and I thought you would be too."

A beep filled the air before an image came on the screen. Heather scrambled to stay out of sight. "Sir, you're needed at headquarters."

"Now?"

"Yes, sir. We just got a communiqué from your sister."

He glanced at his mate. "On my way."

The screen went black.

"Why didn't you just think your clothes back on?" He was fully dressed again.

"I'm not as good at it as you are. My brain said 'hide', not 'clothes'." She watched him for a moment. "You're not going, are you? You know it's a trap."

"One I'm not supposed to know about." He touched her face. "I have to do this."

"He's too dangerous."

"My heart, I felt the same way when you knew you were going to be kidnapped. I know he's going to try to ambush me, and I'll be ready. I'll be back before you know it, and we'll make sure that bed is the right one for us." He pulled her to him, lowering his mouth to hers. His tongue begged entrance, which she gladly gave. The fruity flavor of the wine they had shared with his mother after dinner still lingered. He drank his fill of her, then broke the kiss. "There's more where that came from when I get back."

He walked out into the night and headed for the security office. His senses told him he was safe enough at the moment. Walking into the main office, he found no one there. Oh, that couldn't be good. He had his weapon with him but had a feeling that it wasn't going to do him much good.

Methodically, he worked his way from room to room. They had to be here somewhere. Just as he crossed through another archway, his world went black.

FIFTEEN

Heather contacted the people in her team the moment she felt Storm fall unconscious. Not being able to touch his mind frightened her a lot, but she tried to stay focused so she could get him back.

She called them to meet her at the rooms Storm and she shared at the palace. Before she left, she spoke to the computer. "Computer, follow him. Don't lose my mate. I need to bring everyone home."

"His vital signs are good and the ship he has been loaded into has left the atmosphere."

"Thank you. I'll be back as soon as I can." Her snug fitting uniform helped keep her focused. Once everyone had assembled in the main room, she filled them in on what was going on.

"You can't go."

"Excuse me?"

"I'm sorry Heather, but you know the deal," said Fridon. "Anyone involved with the extraction of family isn't allowed on the assignment anymore. The commander put that out after your kidnapping."

"Which one of you is going to stop me?" She looked at

each of them, daring them to try. "If I have to take all of you on at the same time, I will."

"We know what you're capable of, Heather," Fridon said. The two of them had bonded after he had been wounded because of her. "And none of us will stop you, but the commander will not be happy with any of us."

"I know, but he will know who was in charge. I'll make sure of it." She laid out a plan she hoped would work and sent them to get whatever supplies they might need for the journey. They would all meet up within the next thirty minutes near the main hangar where Storm landed their vessel.

Heather hurried back to the underground compound. "Have you been able to keep tabs on Storm?"

"Ialog did use the scrambler, but I was able to get direction and speed before they took off. With the information I have from what the doctor had given us, I have the data to show you where the ship should be going. I believe I can pinpoint the location once your ship is in close enough to the planet they are on."

"And how do you plan on doing that?" Heather didn't think her link to the computer would work that far away.

"There is a way to transport me. There is a portable unit I can be downloaded to." A section of the main computer slid aside so she could see the unit it spoke of. "Put it in the alcove I have highlighted for you and we'll begin the process."

"What will happen if this unit is destroyed once I download you?" She pulled the unit out. "Will I lose you completely?"

"No. Only the version in this system. Majority of my memory will remain here, but you will have what you need with you."

"Good. I've gotten used to you now. Sure would hate to lose you." Heather loaded the unit into the slot the computer recommended and waited for it to download. Once done, she slung it over one shoulder and headed to the hangar where the small ship waited. It was the same one she and Storm had used before. The thought of her sitting in the chair without him hurt, but he had shown her how to fly it, so she felt better using this one more than any other ship.

She attached the computer to the main frame and set up the communication system so the computer could control the ship. "You have the data on the people I wish to bring with me?"

"Yes."

"Good." She started the engines. "We have no clearance to leave, so make sure you get out undetected. I'm going to be in enough trouble over this, and if we're not successful it will just compound the problem."

She felt the ship lift off. "Once you're in orbit, you have permission to bring my team aboard. I have spoken to them and made them aware of what I wanted to do, so they'll be ready to be transported up."

The moment the ship hit orbit, her security team stood in front of her.

"I know this ship is small, so it will be a bit tight for us, but our destination isn't far. Our goal is to retrieve Storm. There's a lot I can't tell you about what you might see and hear, but I'm sure you're used to that." She gave them a sad smile as she turned to the computer. "You have his coordinates?"

"Yes. We're following the trail at a discreet distance."

"What was that?" asked Fridon.

"It's a prototype."

"And when can I get a look at it?"

"Fridon, you know I can't let you do that." She looked at him.

"Sorry. Habit." He put his hands up in front of him,

knowing his mistake. "You know how I enjoy tinkering with computers."

"Let's get ready," said Heather. "I have research for all of you to look at."

———

Kuarto walked into his office and stopped short when he spotted the body lying on the table near his workstation. Toki stopped right behind him.

"What?"

"It seems we have company." He pointed to the table as he tried to shield her reaction from the camera.

She peeked around his shoulder to see her brother lying there. "Is he dead?"

Kuarto pulled out his scanner. "No. He is in deep stasis."

"And why is he here? I thought all you needed was a sample of his DNA, not him."

"I felt this way you can't tell me you didn't get enough sample material," said Al. "Find out why he was able to impregnate Heather."

Toki practically jumped out of her skin when she heard Al's voice very close to her. She hadn't expected him to be there.

Kuarto nodded. He wasn't happy about the situation. The one person he thought would be able to rescue them was lying on the table. This put an unwanted kink in their plan.

The uniform encasing Storm was just like the one Toki had been wearing when he found her. "I'm going to need something to cover him when I remove this uniform."

Toki didn't question as she handed him a cloth from a shelf near her station.

He pressed the seam of the uniform and watched as it opened for him. Draping the cloth over Storm's waist, he pulled the uniform from under him. He held it out to Toki. "Can you do something with this?"

She took the uniform, folded it up, and placed it on a shelf. He noticed she kept herself from looking at him, probably afraid she would give something away.

He took a blood sample and ran it through his equipment. He thought of talking to her but decided to leave her be. Al was still in the room.

"You two always this quiet?"

"When we're focused, yes." Kuarto looked up from his computer, waiting for his readings to come back. How was he going to be able to stall with Storm here? His DNA would fertilize the egg before they could escape with it.

"And your mail-order bride seems a little uncomfortable with our guest." His intense gaze rested on her.

"Well, he's naked, and the cloth isn't really covering anything properly." She pointed to the table. "Wouldn't you be a little uncomfortable? The only naked body I've seen has been Kuarto's and I don't want to compare."

Kuarto tried not to choke on his laughter. "You can look if you wish. I'm sure I'll do okay."

"Really? So you've already done the math?" She arched a brow at him.

"I'm just saying I should be able to measure up." The computer made a slight ping sound. He went to the screen to see what the data said. The information made him frown. "This can't be right."

He walked to Storm's side, pulled another sample, and ran it again.

"Something wrong?"

"Um, no. I think the sample got contaminated, so I want to run it again."

"How?" Al walked to his station and looked over his shoulder. "This is all new equipment."

"I've had it happen before. Just being cautious." He ran

the same test as before and got the same readings. Now Storm's readings were changing. He had read about Heather's device, how her DNA started to change when she met Storm, and the device began its disintegration.

Everything was off the chart, and he had no idea what to do about it. "I'm not going to be able to find out why he was able to get her pregnant."

"Why not?"

"Look for yourself."

Al looked at the readings on the screen showing constant changes to his DNA sequence. His changes were happening a lot faster than Heather's did. There was no evidence of any sort of inhibiter, so why wasn't this detected before? And why was it happening now? What set it off?

He looked at the small machine sitting on Storm's forehead. It was what kept him under without pumping chemicals into his system so his DNA wouldn't get contaminated. Could it? "How is that keeping him under? Could it be what was causing all of this?"

———

Heather rested in the command chair, slipping into slumber without planning it.

"Heather."

She heard Storm's voice so clear in her head. She spun to see where it came from. He stood behind her, looking very confused. "What happened?"

"You never came home, my heart."

"So where am I?"

"I don't know yet. I'm assuming you're with Kuarto and Toki." She tried to move toward him but found herself rooted to the spot. No matter how hard she tried, she couldn't get closer. "We're following you through your computer insert, but Al used the scrambler, so we have to get closer before we can pinpoint your exact location. Don't you know where you are?" She didn't like this at all.

"No. I was in the main security area and it was empty, so I knew I was in trouble. I don't remember anything since then."

"Could you be unconscious?"

"I am able to join you in your dreams, so I'd say no. Maybe kept under by something so I can't cause trouble."

"Okay. I can check with the computer to see what Al might be using. Maybe there is a way to beat it."

"Don't leave. Not yet. I don't know if I can come back again."

"I will find you, my heart."

"No." Anger laced his words. "You need to protect you and our children."

"My mate is in trouble and needs me. He would do the same thing for me. He has done the same thing for me."

"Yes, but he isn't carrying our children." He watched the determination on her face and knew she wouldn't back down. "At least tell me you didn't come alone, and that you have a plan."

"Our team is with me. You know they are the best."

"And the plan?"

"I was trained by the best. I would never disappoint my trainer. He is everything to me."

He tried to reach for her and found he couldn't move, either. "Why can't I touch you?"

"I don't know. Maybe it has something to do with the dream state we're in. I haven't been able to move here either." She wished she could. "I have tried to touch your mind several times before, but you didn't respond. If you hadn't contacted me, I'd probably be frantic soon."

"In other words, you were already frantic, and this helped."

"Yes," she smiled at him. "A lot. At least I know you're safe for the moment."

"Have you tried contacting your brother? See if he knows what is going on?"

"And what if Al didn't take you to where he's been keeping them? Didn't want to give our link away until I was sure. I have to assume Al is watching them like a hawk."

"Have you asked the computer for updates from the recordings? You might find what you need there."

"I've been so worried about you, I didn't even think about checking on that. Besides, the team is with me now, and I know you don't want them to know that much about the computer."

"And what do you mean by that?"

She knew he wasn't going to like what she said next. "I brought it with me. Before you get too mad, understand the computer suggested it. The only way to track you with Al using that scrambler was to bring the underground computer's tracking device with us. It had a portable unit I could tie into the main computer of your ship."

"So you're flying my ship as well?"

"Yes. I also took off without clearance."

"Do you know the consequences for that?"

"I do. I have spent time in the brig before. I had to rescue you, and time was of the essence. I'm willing to pay for my crimes when I get back if it's going to save my family." She felt someone touch her shoulder, which made her image shift a little.

"You're going to go now, aren't you?"

"You will see me soon, my heart, and you can yell at me all you want for everything I've done wrong. If I could touch you, my hand would be on your heart, letting you know I want my mate back in one piece, anger and all."

"Promise me you'll be careful."

"I promise." Heather opened her eyes and sat up. Fridon knelt next to her. "Your computer is asking for you."

Heather nodded and swung her feet to the floor. "Computer?"

"I have some new data that you need to see."

"Not now." She knew she couldn't allow any of her team members to see what the computer was capable of. No one had technology like that. It would raise too many questions.

"I can send the data to your link." Seconds later, she found herself staring at the data Kuarto had been looking at, but it was inside her head so no one else could see it.

"This doesn't make any sense. His DNA can't be changing." She could hear her brother's voice in her head.

Storm's DNA was changing? Heather could see the information Kuarto was looking at like she was the one reading it. Why would it start changing now? Then she realized this wasn't something she needed to worry about now. She needed to know where her mate was, bring him home. Once that was done, they could find out what was going on with him.

The problem was she couldn't get a visual on the room. Her brother kept staring at the screen instead of looking around the room. Finally Kuarto looked up at the table and Heather saw the prone form covered with the cloth. Her heart stopped for just a moment. She'd know that body anywhere. The image stopped, and she found several set of eyes watching her.

"You okay?"

"Yes." Heather smiled, happy to know she had what she wanted. "We have three to bring home."

———

Kuarto stared at the data. This just didn't make any sense. He took another sample, this time setting the tests to see what caused his DNA to start changing.

Toki sensed his frustration. She moved to his side and placed her hand on his shoulder. "You okay?"

Al had left the room in anger when he saw the information on Storm.

"I don't understand." Kuarto stared at the screen until the heat of her hand penetrated his concentration. He placed his hand on top of hers when he looked at her concerned face. "I'm fine. It's just a bit strange, that's all."

"What is going on?"

"I'm not real sure. Storm's DNA is changing and it shouldn't be."

"What is he changing into?"

"Have no idea." He looked back at the screen. "I also don't know how long this has been going on. Could this be why he and Heather were able to produce? Because their DNA changed?"

"Is Storm sterile now?"

"That came back inconclusive. He's changing too quickly for the readings to settle." He leaned back in his chair. "One minute it will show him sterile then the next fertile. Is that what happened? A shift in their DNA made them go from sterile to fertile? I wish I had an old sample to compare this to." He did, the one he took when they first met. He didn't remember anything like this going on when he first looked at their DNA, but he couldn't let Al know he had that with him. He needed to keep the egg unfertilized as long as he could. Give Heather time to find them.

He knew she was probably the only one who would be looking for them.

"Or you could ask Al to wake him and ask Storm yourself." She looked at her brother's unconscious form.

"Al would never do that. You know how intimidating the man is when he is awake." He wasn't sure why she suggested it since she knew Ialog wouldn't go along with it, either.

"Just thought I'd suggest it."

He pulled up the new changes in Storm's DNA and studied them. What he wanted to do was get moment by moment readings to see what he was going through every second. Storm wouldn't want to go along with it, but he knew Heather would. She had been through the same thing and had allowed those readings to be recorded.

The doctor in him wanted to compare the sample he had with the ones he just took, but he made a promise to Heather and he would keep it. He looked at the reading again. There had to be a pattern to this. And Storm might be able to shed a light on what was going on.

Al came back into the room and glared at him. Kuarto wondered what he did to get such a look. Al walked over to Storm's unconscious figure, snapped on some restraining straps around his wrists and ankles, then ripped off the device on his forehead.

"Wish you wouldn't do that." Kuarto stood and crossed to Storm, checking the nasty gash on his forehead before sealing it and accelerating the healing process.

"Why should I be kind to the one man who has done me wrong?"

"How did he do you wrong?" Kuarto checked Storm's eyes as they fluttered open.

"He stole what was mine."

"Are you talking about Heather?" Kuarto stood between him and Storm. The angry look on Al's face had him wondering if he would cause bodily harm to Storm.

"Of course I am." He slammed his hand against the wall. "I created her for me, not him. She was to be my companion. But his parents decided I was a menace and took her from me. They turned my creation against me. Changed her so she would be his, not mine."

"Changed her? How?"

"They inserted her with some of his DNA and vice versa, so they would have each other's markers." He pointed to Storm. "It was so they would find each other no matter what."

Storm was now fully alert and listening intently to the conversation.

"I'd say it worked."

"Yet it took my threat to get the ruling families to force them together. If it hadn't been for me, they never would have met."

"Why did you want that? You probably knew where Heather was. Why not go after her then? Before they could meet."

"Tried that. She had no interest in anyone." He paused for a moment. "I knew the only way to get my companion was to make them meet."

"How would that make her your companion?"

"Because I had planned on killing him off. I thought once they met and her device had disintegrated, I could take her away and kill him when he tried to rescue her. It would break the bond. That would leave her free to be my companion." He started to pace. "I didn't expect their relationship would become deep rooted so fast. Their bond with each other was too strong. That's when I knew killing him wouldn't help me get her back. That's when I decided to settle for her daughter."

"But she tricked you into taking the wrong egg."

"Yes, that was very skillful of her. Hadn't thought she'd be that mentally strong so soon after getting her powers."

"It sounds like you underestimated them at every turn." Kuarto got a hateful glare for that comment. "I'm just saying each time you have tried to get the best of them you have failed."

"Kuarto, please don't make the man mad." Toki crossed to his side and placed her hands on his arm. "He might try to hurt us."

"I'm only being honest."

"I did underestimate them, but not because I wasn't smart enough to figure out these things. I made them. They were supposed to be as brilliant as I am, but I knew they hadn't been trained by me. Never thought the inherent abilities would be the thing to make them best me." He was proud of what they did, even though they beat him at almost every turn. "Now I have the chance of fertilizing the egg I do have to create another companion, and the one person who could have helped us is no good to me anymore." He turned to Storm. "I knew you had been altered just like she had been, but you should have already been through any changes that could have happened. Your mate had that inhibitor, you didn't."

"What are you talking about?"

"Your DNA is changing." Kuarto spoke this time before pointing to a screen near Storm.

He read the data there but kept his thoughts to himself. "So this is stopping you from using my DNA to fertilize the egg?"

"The egg is sterile. You and Heather were sterile, yet she's with child. Can you explain it?"

"No." He looked at his sister, then Heather's brother. "But he's the doctor, not me."

————

Heather felt it the moment he regained consciousness. "He's with us again."

"Are you sure this is the best way to get them out?"

"No, but Al's not going to just let them walk out. We'll have to get into the compound and take out the guards one by one."

"We?"

"Fine, you will. I stay here at the command post and watch for any changes or issues that could crop up." She hated not being able to go but knew everyone was right. She needed to protect the children inside her. It would also give her time to listen to what else the computer had learned.

She programmed the ship to send them down close to the compound. As the computer gave the layout of the compound to her, she loaded the data into their helmets. Information where each guard stood loaded as well. Now they had everything they needed to protect her loved ones and hopefully bring them home.

Then she sat back and spoke with the computer. "Can I have live time now?"

"Yes." The computer brought up the images she had seen in her head not too long ago. "They have been discussing you and your mate in great detail. Storm's DNA has changed more than fifty percent in the last two weeks."

"Is that how long this has been going on?"

"Yes. It seems when I had him place his hand in the receptacle that first time so I could download the data on the ancients, I caused a reaction in his system."

"Great." She hated this. "Is he going to be okay?"

"He might have a few moments where the changes cause some slight trouble for him but nothing life-threatening."

"Why didn't this happen before?"

"He had never been in the compound before."

"Let me try that one again." She ran her fingers through her hair. "What is it that activated whatever is happening in him now and not before?"

"Unknown. I need to run several deep scans on him to see what is happening so I can pinpoint the cause."

Having gone through the same thing, she wondered why Storm was also going through DNA changes. It seemed to be more than a coincidence. She hadn't been paying attention to the screen while they were talking, but she found herself trying to figure out what was going on.

"Your mate's sister wants Storm to put his uniform back on now that he's awake and has asked for him to be dressed."

"That's because she knows the uniform can protect him."

"If she can get the android to do it, I might be able to overtake its system. She could be beneficial in the future."

"I'll let Storm know." Heather centered herself and touched Storm's mind. Hoping he would figure out what she wanted him to do, she sent the suggestion to him. "Now back up the video so I can see what was said."

———

Storm didn't like sitting on the table naked. Normally, his state of dress didn't bother him. His mate had pointed it out many times. But knowing how well his uniform would protect his body if things went bad had him wishing he was in it.

Looking at his sister, he kept cutting his gaze to his uniform. The first few times she didn't seem to understand, but then her eyes widened, and she gave him a slight nod. He knew she had figured out what he wanted.

"I'm sorry, but I can't handle this anymore. Can you please let him get dressed?" Toki averted her gaze. "I'm tired of the little peep show I keep getting from him sitting here."

"Don't like what you see?" He gave her a heated smile.

She glared at him.

"If you dislike it so much, dress him."

She blinked at the thought. "Ew. Why can't your robot do it?"

The Heather android moved to the uniform and brought it to Storm. Since Al didn't stop her, she proceeded to help Storm stand and climb into the uniform while wearing the restraints. Once done, she stepped back.

"Can you please fix the collar?" Storm moved his neck. "It seems to be tucked under, and that will drive me crazy."

The android slipped her hand behind his head and under the collar. Her skin touched the tissue where his link was. Storm looked at her oddly when he found her touch warm. It felt like she was real. He had to look in her eyes to know the truth. He shivered for a moment.

"She touched you, didn't she?"

"Yes. I've never known an android to have a body temperature before." He looked at the Heather look alike. "How did you do that?"

"My advanced circuitry allows me to mimic the heat of the humanoid body."

Storm watched as a flash filled the robot's eyes. There was no way he could be sure they were successful unless the computer took over the android's body.

He moved his shoulders and shifted his hips so he could get his suit to settle on him properly, then sat back down on the table. "You know someone is coming to rescue us."

"I assume your mate will be leading the charge."

"You want her here." He didn't answer, so Storm knew he was right.

"She is still important to my plans."

"You had your chance." Storm couldn't believe he thought he could still take Heather from him. "There is no way I'm going to allow you to get within ten feet of my mate."

"You aren't in the position to stop me."

"Are you sure? I'm head of Vespian security so if you want to test that theory I'm game." He got to his feet once again. "I have been in worse situations and gotten out of them, so I know I will stop you before you can harm her again."

"I never wanted to harm her." He looked at Storm like he was a simple child. "I created her, and she is perfect."

"She is mine." Storm didn't mean to sound so territorial about his mate, but this man didn't seem to understand their lives were intertwined.

"I know that." He glared at Storm. "You heard part of what I said earlier. What part didn't penetrate that thick skull of yours?"

"If you think your sad story is going to sway me, you're wrong. I don't care how Heather came to be. All I know is she's my mate and carrying our children."

"Children? You mean she's carrying more than one?" A spark entered his eyes.

"Yes." Storm looked at Kuarto. "You never told him?"

"He never asked." Kuarto shrugged. "Guess he was too focused on this egg to worry about anything else."

He smiled at their interaction. "I figured Storm had convinced you to come here and try to get the egg back. He's a little too predictable." He turned to Toki. "I also never believed you still had amnesia, but since it worked in my favor, I pretended right along with you."

Toki inched over to Kuarto.

"I understand you are to take your uncle's spot as the religious leader." He looked pointedly at Kuarto. "Have you explained the rules to him? Or is this just a fling until you take your position?"

Her lips thinned, but she didn't respond.

Storm decided to bring his focus back to him. "We've learned a bit about you too, but you know that. You tried to take Heather's body over while we were in the compound. How'd that work out for you?"

"You think you know everything, don't you? You and

your mate have no idea what I was looking for, so how do you know I didn't get it?"

"The system showed me what you were after and you never were able to open the files all the way. Heather's protective protocol took over."

"Was that when you were stomping around here angry earlier? Right before you took Storm?" Kuarto crossed his arms over his chest. "It makes sense now."

He glared at Kuarto but didn't respond. "Looks like we're at a stalemate. You're all in here with me and the one thing that will free you is out there with about eight people slowly taking out my guards. Heather is going to have to deal with me on my terms if she wants to see any of you alive."

SIXTEEN

Heather heard that, and a chill ran down her spine. She knew what he wanted and if she planned on keeping her family safe, she would have to give it to him.

Life was less complicated when she didn't have anyone to worry about. Less than a year ago, she would have gone in with her weapons blazing and not worried about who would get hurt. And nine times out of ten, she would save the person in trouble without anyone from her team getting a scratch. But this time, she knew she couldn't do that. The chance that anyone one of them could get hurt was one she wasn't willing to take.

She contacted her team and made them aware of a change in tactics. She transported herself to their location to see a group of concerned faces staring back at her.

"You shouldn't be here," one of them said.

"I know, but he won't negotiate with anyone else." She set her uniform at one of the higher settings to protect her womb and looked at them. "I know Storm will berate every one of you for allowing me to do this. I know how angry he will be at me for even considering this as a viable option, but if it will bring them home safe I must. None of you have to accompany me."

"Your mate would tear us apart if we let you go in there without our protection."

"I'll secure you in the ship, and he'll have no reason to be upset with you."

"You can't go in there alone."

"I'm not." She snapped on her helmet and sealed the suit.

"He means without our protection," Fridon said. Her team did the same thing, so they all looked the same. "We won't let you go if you don't take us with you."

"Are you sure?" She knew the size of Storm's anger but wasn't sure if they did. They were in for the dress down of their lives once this was done.

"Yes, ma'am. I would rather be in trouble for accompanying you than be in trouble for letting you go alone," said Fridon. All of the squad nodded.

"Okay, but be warned, you have never seen the level of anger you will today, and I hope you never see it again." She headed to the main doors of the compound.

"How do you plan on getting in there?" one of the team asked.

Just as she stepped up to the door, it opened for her. "I plan on walking right in."

"I don't like this." Fridon walked at her side.

"He is expecting me. I have a feeling he knows I have been watching everything that has transpired. Nothing gets by him." She stopped in front of another set of doors and waited for them to open.

"Very astute, Heather." He stood on the other side of the door.

Heather felt cold when she saw him, but she came to rescue her family and the first thing she needed to do was search the room for her mate, his sister, and her brother. They walked in as a unit, helmets on so no one would know which one she was. Everyone pulled their weapons and trained them on Al.

"I see you brought your entourage."

"Never leave home without them." She knew he expected her to be the one in the middle of the crowd, so they had made sure she wasn't. "Is everyone here?"

"Yes. Ma'am."

"Heather." That was all Storm needed to say. Anger laced his voice, but her heart soared when she heard it.

"I know. This is about the dumbest thing I could have done, but leaving you here was out of the question." The squad shifted positions. "What do you want, Al?"

"You know what I want." He sighed. "If I promise not to give them a reason to shoot me you think we could actually be able to see you?"

"Sorry." They all shifted again. "I'm already in enough trouble with my mate, so I'm not about to push that anger up a notch."

"Fine." He watched them move around in amusement. "You think this little dance is going to make me forget which one is really you?"

"It couldn't hurt." She paused for a moment. "You made me come here. What do you want from me?"

"I want a trade."

"Don't do it, Heather." Storm's voice sounded like music in her ears, but she couldn't let him sway her.

"What sort of trade?" They all shifted again.

"Your daughter."

"No." She fought the urge to touch her stomach, a habit she had gotten into early. That move would give away where she was in the group. "You already tried that one and failed. You don't get a second chance."

"I understand you are carrying twins."

"And who told you that?"

"Your mate." He turned to look at Storm. "I was surprised he revealed that little tidbit."

"Doesn't matter. This is my daughter. The mother-daughter bond has already happened. If you were to take her it would hurt her and I couldn't have that."

"You'd leave your mate behind? Let me do what I want to him?"

"You will not harm my mate. That I swear, but my daughter isn't negotiable, so you need to come up with something else."

"Fertilize the egg."

"You took my mate for that reason. You do it."

"Can't. His DNA is changing too much, but I'm betting you were prepared for that when you sent your brother here. I know a sample of Storm's DNA is in that knapsack of Kuarto's." He nodded to her look-alike, who walked to the bag and picked it up. She carried it to Kuarto's desk and sat it down. "What do you think of my little creation?"

"She's a machine." His smile faded a bit at her words. "What? Did you expect me to be upset over this? It's actually kind of flattering."

"Back to the DNA."

"Right." The sample they had was after Storm had started changing. She wasn't sure if it would work any better. She heard the computer explain it had pulled any of the odd strands out of the sample before the doctor took it. It should be good. It also reminded her that Kuarto took a sample of Storm when they first went to rescue Toki. That would be clean. "Kuarto, you still have that sample from when we came to find Toki?"

"Yes." He still stood between Storm and Al.

"And if you fertilize the egg can you specify the sex?"

"Yes." He crossed to his table.

"Then do it."

"Heather." Storm growled her name, showing he didn't like what they were about to do.

"And what would you do if I were there, and you were here?" She was met with silence. "I know he'll take care of her and at least he's not asking for me, which is what he really wants."

"What am I doing here?" asked Kuarto. He was met with silence for a few moments.

"Do as she asks." Storm's voice was terse, but at least he went along with her.

Kuarto went to his table and pulled out the sample. "You're sure?"

"Yes." Heather closed her eyes and waited. She hated doing this but hadn't figured out a better way. This child would be just like her, created in a tube, not from the love of two people.

Kuarto worked in silence. It weighed heavily on her.

"I'm done."

"How long before we know?" She heard a ping, and a computerized voice stating the egg was now fertilized. This hurt so bad. Giving him this child was not what she wanted, but she wanted the rest of her family safe. "Understand Ialog, you may have won this battle, but you won't win the war. I will be coming for my child, and I will stop you once and for all."

She thought about the android. One word and it would stay with them for them to study, but she could let it go with Ialog, so they would be able to keep tabs on him and her newest daughter. It would give them the chance to utilize her in the future.

They did run the risk of AI figuring out the underground computer was in control of the android Heather, and that could cause trouble, but she decided to take the chance. He had created the thing to carry her child, and once the egg was fertilized, she had already started thinking about it as her daughter. She wanted to give her child every chance. She would be getting her back.

"Now you have a few seconds to get out of here before I change my mind."

He didn't wait for her to speak again. The android opened its stomach and inserted the egg. Once the container had filled with the amniotic fluid, she nodded at him and they were gone.

The moment Al was gone, Storm was off the bed and standing amongst them. He still wore the restraints, but they didn't seem to hamper his movements.

"Don't anyone move." She knew they had kept moving so no one would know which one she was. Her lack of height was shielded by the uniform. She wanted to see if it had worked. If they could fool Storm, then she would know she had been relatively safe.

They surrounded Storm, waiting for him to make the first move. He studied each uniform, trying to figure out which one was his mate.

"I watched as you shifted. And if I was paying attention properly I believe you are Heather." He pressed his fingers against the seals on the helmet and released it. He laughed when he had guessed wrong. "Okay, best two out of three."

Heather felt his hand wrap itself around her arm and pulled her to him.

"But I'm pretty sure I have it right this time." He hit the seals again. This time, he found violet eyes gazing back up at him. He pulled her closer to him so he could pull her into his embrace and lowered his mouth inches from hers.

"I know." The relief of knowing he was safe released a stream of tears. "He could have killed you."

"He could have taken you from me." He dipped his head to capture her lips. The salt from her tears mingled with their kiss.

———

"Are they always like that?" asked Kuarto.

"Their mating bond is very strong," Fridon answered as they secured the area. "You'll get used to it."

He wasn't sure about that. Whatever it was between them was unique. Kuarto had never seen anything like it before.

He noticed Toki hadn't said two words to him since Al disappeared. He wanted to touch her, take her into his arms and kiss her the way Storm was still kissing his sister, but it was like she put up a shield he couldn't penetrate. He went to Toki's side. "You okay?"

She nodded, keeping herself busy with whatever she could. "Can't believe she let him go like that."

"I'm sure there was a reason." He touched her arm, finally drawing her attention. "I'm assuming we need to talk?"

She nodded a second time. Toki couldn't look at him and he wondered why. "Can we do it privately? It's not some-thing I want to speak about with all these people around."

"We could go for a walk." Kuarto wanted to get to the bottom of this as quickly as he could. Ialog had said things that upset her and confused him. They had already talked about her position as religious leader, so why was she so upset? Had she left out something?

"I'd really like to wait until we're back on Vespia, unless you don't plan on going back there." She didn't look him in the eyes.

"I can wait." He didn't want to, but he would to find out the truth.

———

"Why? Why would you take such a chance?" Storm couldn't believe her audacity. He also couldn't keep his hands off her. Part of him still wanted to prove she was okay.

"The computer had every angle covered. I was just as safe here as I would have been on the ship." She ran her hands over him. "If he tried to take me, he wouldn't have gotten very far. If his ship was in orbit, the computer would have blocked any beaming he would have tried. If the ship was on the ground, he might have moved us there, but the computer would have targeted his engines so it wouldn't have been able to take off."

"That is no excuse." He held her face in his hands.

"What would you have done?" She looked up at him. Proving her point was important, but she knew she'd be aggravating the situation if she did it while everyone watched.

"We'll talk about this when we get home." Storm saw the look on her face and knew her determination was strong. She would try to make him see her way when they were alone.

———

They arrived on Vespia without incident and were greeted by the council when they exited the ship.

"We wish to speak to all of you in the council chambers." Storm's mother didn't wait for them to agree. She turned and left.

"I'll talk to them," Storm said.

"I made this mess and I plan on cleaning it up." Heather straightened her uniform and walked after Anseri.

Guards stood on either side of the doors of the council chambers when she walked through. Shoulders back, she faced them with no shame. "I was in charge. These people had nothing to do with anything that transpired since Storm was kidnapped."

"Heather, you broke I can't count how many of our laws." If she was surprised with Heather's confession, she didn't show it.

"Yes, ma'am, I did." She stepped forward, separating herself from everyone. "Let them go home. I was responsible. They helped me rescue Storm but weren't aware of my transgressions."

Anseri watched her for a moment before looking at her fellow council members. With a nod, she released the rest of her team. One by one, the members of her team walked out, leaving Heather and Storm to face the wrath of the council alone.

Storm stepped up and took her hand. He was there to support her.

"Storm, why can't you control your mate?"

"Because she doesn't need controlling. She did what any one of us would have done if we were in her situation." He wrapped an arm around her waist.

"I don't need to be protected." She knew what he was trying to do and wouldn't allow him to take the punishment for what she did. She spoke to the council but found herself looking at Storm while she spoke. "I am ready to pay for what I did. Storm is my mate and I would do it all over again to bring him home safe."

Her comment won her a glare from her mate. "What are you doing?"

"Being honest. You won't pay for what I did." She hoped she kept her voice soft enough so they wouldn't be overheard.

"Heather."

The elders spoke amongst themselves while Heather tried to explain her feelings.

"Storm, I have always stood up for what I believed in, and this is no different." She placed her hand on his heart. "I made it to commander twice before they busted me back down for what my old government felt was insubordination. What I did was right, even if I did it the wrong way."

"As the mate of the future leader, you need to think about how your behavior might be seen by others." His words were harsh, yet he placed his hand on top of hers. She wasn't quite sure how to take what he said.

"I will remember that the next time you do something like this." She glared up at him, forgetting all about the council.

"We have made our decision." Anseri brought their attention back to the people watching their heated exchange.

Heather turned back to face them. It took every ounce of her training to keep her anger under control. Storm had said the one thing that she had thought about the entire time she worked on getting her family back. To have him act like she didn't think about how her actions might be perceived upset her.

"We all agree that it wouldn't look good for the future leader's mate to be under arrest, yet your violations can't go unpunished."

Heather expected that. She would probably have to do some sort of community service to pay for her crimes.

"We also know that if you hadn't broken our laws, we could have lost our future leader and you could have lost your mate. You jeopardized your life and the life of your children to rescue him." Anseri looked at the other members of the council before turning her attention back to Heather and Storm. "Therefore, it is the decision of this council to turn you over to our head of security who will decide what your punishment will be and enforce it."

Heather wasn't sure what just happened. "I'm sorry—" Storm's hand covered her mouth so she couldn't say anything else.

"I will make sure she pays for her crimes. I know the

perfect punishment." He bowed to them and escorted her out before anyone could change their mind.

"What just happened?" She looked behind her.

"They went easy on you. Be happy about it." Storm had a strong grip on her elbow and kept her moving.

"I don't understand."

"Don't question the decision of the council." He continued to propel her toward their rooms. He walked so quickly she was practically running to keep up with his quick stride.

"My heart, if you don't slow down, you're going to be dragging me along very soon. I can't keep this pace up much longer."

"Sorry." He slowed down so she could walk at an easier pace. "I just wanted to get out of there before they changed their minds."

"About that. I feel like I missed something back there."

"The council left your punishment up to me."

"You? They said the head of … oh." She grinned. "Didn't make the connection."

He turned away from their rooms and toward the underground compound.

"Taking the long way around?"

"Had too. Couldn't reveal the opening to the rest of the council." He looked down at her. "But we still have a bed to break in."

"And what about my punishment?" They had just crossed into the main entrance of the compound.

"It starts now." With a thought, their clothes were gone.

"And I'll be a good little girl and take my punishment."

He gave her a heated look. "What makes you think you will like your punishment?"

"I have all the other times you punished me." She tilted her head at him as she looked into his eyes. "So have you felt any different since the changes started in your DNA?"

"No. Why?" He touched her face.

"Because your eyes are glowing right now." She leaned her face into his palm.

"Just thinking about the punishment I'm going to give you."

"I mean glowing like a cat's. I've never noticed it before." Joy raced through her as he touched her. Heather didn't realize how much she needed his touch until he wasn't there. She rested her hands against his chest, reveling in the beat of his heart against her hands. "We should go and speak to my brother."

"Where did those two get off to, anyway?" He traced the line of her jaw.

"They have things they need to talk about." The warmth of his skin penetrated her palms. "Al sort of dropped the bomb on him."

"Good. I have other things on my mind right now." He captured her lips with his. Their tongues danced with each other, happy to be back together again. "I have missed you."

"And I you." She closed her eyes as his hands roamed her body. The feel of his fingers sent little shivers of desire down her spine.

The chair was there, and he backed her up to it. "Forget about the bed. I don't think I can wait for us to walk the few steps to take us to it."

She looked into his eyes as she slid her fingers over his chest. His eyes closed at the soft contact.

"Your punishment should be no chair, but I missed it, so that would be more of a punishment for me than the other way around."

She sat on the chair, watching and waiting.

He crawled onto the chair with her. "I also thought I would try to keep my hands to myself and make you wait, but again I have missed you, and that would be punishing me as well as you."

Heather laid back on the chair as he crept up on her. He dropped a kiss on her abdomen.

"But I have promised the council I would punish you." His lips closed on one nipple, suckling it until it pebbled in his mouth. "Right now though, everything I can think of that could punish you will also punish me. I need you so badly I can't focus on anything but your luscious body in front of me, begging for my touch."

"You know best." She looked up at him because he was now over her.

"I do, don't I?" He nibbled on her neck, but he hadn't pressed his weight into her. He was torturing her, and he knew it.

"I believe you have found a way to punish me, anyway." She decided two could play this game and she let her hands roam over him. Knowing what got a reaction and what didn't, helped. The first few moments were for her, she slid her fingers over the muscles that sculpted his chest. She loved the feel of the hard planes there. It was her way of proving he was there with her, not some fantasy in her mind.

His eyes dilated as a smile slid across his face. "I see you don't want to fight fair."

Her fingers worked their way down his well-sculpted stomach. "I learned from my mate."

He growled as he pressed his weight down, trapping her hands between them.

"You know that won't stop me, right?" She wiggled one hand down until she came into contact with the velvet hardness of him. "Ah, that's what I was looking for."

He grabbed her hand and moved it up above her head. To be sure she didn't try again, he took her other hand and brought it up with the first one. Once he had her hands pinned, he grinned. "You know I might like it this way."

She felt his hand sliding across her stomach, then up over her breast. His gentle touch caught her skin on fire.

"With your hands otherwise occupied I can explore you all I want." He teased one peak with the tips of his fingers as he worked on the other one with his tongue. Heather started squirming as each touch sent little spirals of heat deeper into her.

"You are punishing me." She felt every little thing he did like it had been amplified a thousand times. If he didn't fill her soon, she was pretty sure she'd explode.

"Of course not, but if you wish me to start the punishment, I can." He lifted himself off her.

"No." She knew she said it a little too quickly, but it was too late. Knowing he could still change his mind, she shifted her weight so she could move her legs. With deliberate slowness, she slid them up his body until they rested on his hips. "If you punish me, you will also punish yourself. Is that what you want?"

"No." He surged into her. They sighed together as her heat accepted him.

"Thank goodness." She closed her eyes as he started to move inside her. She bit her lip when she felt everything heighten. "Oh, this is going to be very quick."

"You're going to kill me if you take off too quickly." He slowed down his pace, changing his penetration as well. "I thought the crazy multiple orgasms were only that one time?"

"They were, but I have missed you." Her breath hitched, and she arched her back.

"You are no help, my heart." He ground his hips against hers.

"Oh, my! You aren't helping either." Every fiber of her being felt that. Her body shook. "You keep that up and I'm not responsible for what happens next."

"And what are you threatening me with?" He watched her face, looking for signs.

"This." She rolled him over and took control. Her body

rode him hard. Muscles contracted and spasmed as she found the right tempo and angle to make them both explode. Each time she accepted him deep in her body, she felt the tension build a little more. It didn't take long before she wasn't doing anything but feel.

The orgasm blossomed up from her toes. Heather felt it in her fingers, then arms and legs, before it centered in her core and exploded outward. She screamed at the intensity as it overpowered her. Storm surged into her two more times before he felt the same overpowering sensations, his mind leaving his body as his release took control.

"You know I'll have to start your punishment all over again."

"I promise, this time, I will behave."

"I hope not." He kissed her deep and hard.

———

"So we had talked about you being the next religious leader, yet since Al mentioned it, you haven't been the same. You want to explain what he said that upset you so much?"

"That." She had brought Kuarto back to her place so they could talk. This was the moment she had been dreading. How was she going to explain this properly? "My tenure will start in about six days and will last fifty years. Part of the protocol is that the person who holds the job isn't supposed to take a mate until they retire."

"Why?" He sat down on the couch.

She blinked. That was a good question. Heather had asked her the same one. "Because that's the way it has always been."

"So you're just going to go along with it? No questions asked?" He didn't seem to be upset, but his complacency wasn't what she expected, either. It bothered her.

She frowned. "You're taking this very well."

"You've already decided for the both of us, so who am I to question your decision?"

There was something in his voice. "You're mad."

"Of course I'm mad." He stood up. "I thought there was something between us and now you're saying it meant nothing to you." He snapped his fingers. "Al asked you if this was a fling and that was what upset you. Is that all I am to you? A fling?"

"No." His words hurt. How could she get him to understand the good of the planet came before her personal desires?

"I don't believe you. You're not willing to question any of these rules you have to obey." He threw his hands up in the air. "Does this job mean that much to you?"

"No. I don't even want to do it." She looked away. She couldn't handle the emotion swimming in his eyes. "Especially now."

"Why now?" He stepped up to her.

"Because I've met you." She looked at him.

"Then what are you going to do about it?"

———

The ceremony was one of the most boring things Heather ever sat through, and she had been through a lot. Because of the delicacy of the whole process, Hynna spoke softly so no one could hear him. She fought a yawn. When Storm caught her, he discreetly pinched her.

"I'm sorry." She straightened her shoulders. "I don't mean to show any disrespect."

"Then save those yawns for later." He leaned toward her and spoke softly. "Uncle is shooting us evil looks, and I'd like those to stop."

Heather clasped her hands and placed them in her lap. She started a little game she had used when she had to sit through boring meetings on Earth. It worked, keeping her attention alert until the ceremony ended.

Once everyone started to mill about, Heather got to her feet. She hadn't seen her brother and wondered where he was. People stood in line to congratulate Toki, who looked slightly unhappy, but quiet. She thanked them and smiled at all the right times, but Heather could sense something was wrong.

Family was the last of the people to speak to her. Uncle Hynna whispered in her ear, which had her nodding.

Heather waited for her turn. She said all the right things the way she had been taught and hovered until she could speak to Toki alone.

"Have you seen my brother?" she asked quietly.

"No." She nodded to another person who had whispered in her ear, then was finally done with the receiving line. "I sent him home several days ago."

"What?" Her voice got loud.

"Heather." Storm, always close, warned her she needed to be careful.

"What do you mean, you sent him home?" She lowered her voice but still had to find out what happened between them. "You marked him as your own."

"Yes, I did." She kept her voice soft and looked Heather in the eyes.

"Why?" Heather didn't understand.

"I'll explain later." She smiled at her, grasping her shoulder for a moment. "I promise."

She didn't want to wait, but she plastered a smile on her face, and went along with it. No need to embarrass everyone by losing the tight control she held onto her anger. There was plenty of time for that later. She wasn't quite sure why she was upset about this, but she was.

Storm sensed her boiling anger because he became twice

as attentive and kept giving her looks. Finally he asked. "You okay?"

"Nothing a good temper tantrum couldn't cure."

"Ah, you're angry because of what my sister said." His calmness just pushed her anger up a notch.

"What makes you think that?" she asked sarcastically.

"You said it yourself. She knew her obligations and has kept them. Now you understand why I was upset when they first got involved."

She wanted to hit him. Heather never felt this angry before. Was it the pregnancy causing this? She needed to get a grip. "Don't patronize me."

"I'm not." He touched her face with the back of his hand. "You feel a little warm. You feeling okay?"

"I'm fine." Her voice snapped with anger.

"No. You don't get this emotional." He took her hand and brought her to a chair. "Sit. I'm going to find a doctor."

"There is nothing wrong with me." She took a step.

"You better sit down or you will see my anger." He gave her a look that told her to listen or she would make matters worse. "The council did release you to me, and I'm supposed to be keeping you under control. Any outburst from you could make them change their minds."

"Alright." But she didn't mean it. She crossed her arms in a huff and turned her face so she wasn't looking at him.

He wasn't gone very long before she felt hands on her forehead. She slapped them away. "Stop that."

"Is that the way to treat your brother?"

She looked up in shock. "I was told you had gone home."

"I had. I needed to get my things before returning. Wasn't about to leave my truck." He pulled his scanner out of his pocket and ran it over her. "I was supposed to be here before the ceremony, but I was delayed."

"Why are you here?" she snapped at him.

"My, we're a little testy, aren't we? Your mate asked me to

stay to take care of you while you're pregnant, and I agreed." He looked at her. "But I can leave if you want me to and you can find another doctor."

"You are the only one I would trust with this, and you know it." She sighed. "I just don't understand."

"What?" He checked his scanner.

"What happened between the two of you?"

He looked around. "Can we talk about this later?"

"Why does everyone want to talk about this later?" Her anger started to boil again. "Why doesn't anyone seem to care?"

"Come on. I think you need to get some air." He helped her to her feet and practically dragged her outside.

"Kuarto, I'm fine." She tried to pull herself from his grasp, but he had a lock on her arm and wasn't letting go.

"You want to start a fight and I'm not going to let you." Once they had walked far enough away from the main hall, he let go of her. "Okay, now. What is it that has you in this state?"

"You two!" She stomped around. "I don't understand how you can just walk away from her."

"That is what has caused this?" He looked at Storm, who had followed them outside.

"I don't know. It did start when she questioned my sister about you two." Storm stepped up and watched in awe as she grew angrier.

"Is that all you can say?" She was hyper-focused on Kuarto and Toki.

"Is it any of your business what happens between Toki and me?" He crossed his arms over his chest.

Storm just grinned.

"And what are you smiling about?" She turned that anger on him.

"You. You're glorious."

"What do you mean by that?" She felt warm and started to fan herself.

"My heart, I've never seen you so mad. I'm not sure why you're so angry, but it does something for you. You're glowing."

"They say that about all pregnant women."

"I know, but I mean it literally." He took one of her hands and pulled it to where she could see it. It glowed a bright pink. "Doctor? Why does my mate look like the aurora borealis on Earth?"

"I don't know." He glared at Heather. "I was trying to find out when she went supernova on me. I figured I needed to let her burn some of that steam off before I could continue with my examination."

"Kuarto?" Toki sighed in relief when she found them. "Here's where you all got off to. You are needed inside."

"Not another ritual," grumbled Heather.

Storm chuckled as he escorted her back into the building. The glow hadn't faded, but the bright lights of the hall should keep people from staring too much. "Just try to remain calm."

She pinched him. "I am calm."

"No pinching. I pinch back." He stayed beside her, ready to drag her back out the moment she became unruly.

Toki stood in front of the crowd and thanked them for all their well wishes. "You have made this transition easier for me, and I hope to serve the planet well." She looked around at all the faces staring back at her. "I do hope to change some of our more outdated laws so we can function better as a society. One of those laws pertains to some of the non-mating clauses that have been attached to some of the positions we have in our society."

Heather listened a little more intently now.

"I have spoken to the council and our newly retired religious leader about this and we are going to start making the changes immediately. The first one is this position. In the past, our religious leaders abstained from taking mates because of one person's misfortune. But that happened while the planet was at war with itself and we have been at peace for hundreds of years."

Storm's demeanor changed subtly. She felt his body stiffen for a second before he forced it to relax again.

"Recent circumstances brought my life mate to me before I took my vows. Once I realized this, I knew I had very few choices, our happiness," she looked at Kuarto. "Or my planet's happiness. It was my brother's mate who made me look at the laws. She couldn't understand why I couldn't have both. I was groomed for this since I was a child. My dilemma then was, why should I force my planet to allow me to have a mate, when many were in the same situation but didn't have the power to make the changes needed. The position they hold was one of danger years ago, but not anymore, yet they still can't mate. That isn't fair to them or to me." She looked at Kuarto again and held out her hand. He stepped to her side and put his arm around her waist. "I have spoken to the council and we will begin working on this at their next meeting. We will also be looking at some of the other restrictions on other positions, like the ones only men can hold, those that only allow mated people to be in. I know this will upset some of you. We've all been taught certain ideals as children. But we need to grow as a people, which means we need to look at ourselves from time to time and make changes that are for the good of the planet."

"So did you know about this?" Heather turned to Storm.

"You are still glowing." He led her outside.

"You didn't answer my question."

"I know. I wasn't about to in front of those people and you know that. What made you ask me a question like that in public, anyway?"

"I don't know. I feel strange." She touched her cheeks.

"I'm not sure what is causing this, and I think it is affecting the way I'm thinking."

"Thought so." He brought her to a bench. His Uncle Hynna was close, so Storm called him over. "Please stay with her. I need to find her brother."

"Of course." He sat next to her. "So what did you think of the big announcement?"

"I'm happy, but I don't understand what the big secret was all about." She stared at her hands. "I really am glowing, aren't I?"

"Very much, but it is pretty to look at." He took her hand in his. "The secret was they had to get permission from the council before they could do anything about it and that permission only came just after the ceremony."

"That's when you whispered in Toki's ear."

He nodded.

"Then they haven't been bonded? Went through the cere-mony?" Heather couldn't believe the council would be that cruel to them. "They have to wait until her term is up now before going through the mating ritual?"

"Didn't say that." He gave her one of his secretive smiles.

"What are you saying?"

Storm showed up at that point with her brother in tow. "Help her before she angers too many people. Including me."

"Your mate is fine." Hynna patted her hand. "And if you paid any attention to Vespian physiology you would know she has eaten something that doesn't agree with her. It will pass."

Storm and her brother looked at each other. "What are you talking about?"

"An allergic reaction? Ever heard of it?" He looked at the two men. "What? You feel this can't happen to Heather because her ancient blood is stronger than her Vespian blood? That's where the issue came from. Most Vespians don't glow, although they do turn a very becoming pink." He stood. "Don't forget what I know, boys. My knowledge of the ancients is vast and now I have two students to pass that knowledge onto. Four if I teach the two of you as well." He pointed at Storm and Kuarto.

"They'll be there, Uncle," said Heather. "I'll be sure of it."

"You need to stay away from the luswenda plant." He kissed her cheek. "Pretty sure that's what caused this."

She nodded and stood. Once Hynna walked away, she turned to her brother. "So, you going to explain his comment or am I going to have to make a scene to know what's going on?"

"Heather."

She totally ignored her mate and stared at her brother. "Properly or not?"

"Why is this so important to you?" Kuarto looked at her oddly.

"Because I care." Now she was on the verge of tears. "Oh, my." She walked away. She was losing total control of her emotions, and she didn't want anyone to see it.

Storm came up behind her. "My heart?"

"I'm fine." She wiped her eyes. "Just a little emotional."

"I hate seeing you like this." He wrapped his arms around her.

"What was that plant he mentioned?"

"Uncle? A berry, I think. It is used as a seasoning most of the time."

"Great. Now I have to be careful what I eat." She rubbed her stomach. "Anyway you two want to come out early?"

"Stop." He walked her back to where her brother stood. "Can you give her something for the reaction?"

"I can try."

Heather sat down. Fatigue started to set in. "I don't want anything injected unless you're sure it will work. This isn't doing anything more than messing with my emotions and skin." She looked at her hands again. The glow had faded just a little.

Her brother knelt in front of her, scanner in hand. He got the reading he had been after and gave her a quick injection. Within minutes she returned to a nice healthy tone with no glow.

"I have made promises to my mate and the council that keep me from answering your question. You have been a member of this race long enough to know there are things they want kept a secret. Toki gave you a hint at the reasoning in her speech earlier." He ran the scanner over her once more. "You should be fine in a moment or two."

"So I have to wait for the changes to start before I get my questions answered?"

"Yes."

"Then you have already answered it." She closed her eyes as the medication finished clearing her system. "I feel much better, thank you."

"You're welcome." He helped her to her feet. "I'm going to learn how good a doctor I truly am working with you, aren't I?"

"I fear you will," said Storm. "But it's one of the reasons she's my heart. It's never a dull moment around here."

"That I believe."

"You three have got to stop taking off like this or I'm going to have to put bells on you so I can hear when you disappear." Toki looked at Heather. "I see the glowing has stopped. Feeling better?"

"Much." She took Toki's hand. There was no invisible bond wrapped around her wrist. "We were just coming in."

"Good." She looked at Kuarto. Her formal dress shifted as she leaned into him for a moment. It was all Heather needed to see the mark her brother sported now on the soft swell of Toki's breast.

Heather grinned. Feeling much better, she hugged her mate and smiled up at him.

"What?"

"You were there, weren't you? The witness they needed."

"You have very good eyes."

"I know." She rested her head against his chest, happy to know they had been able to go through the mating ceremony before she took the position over. If they hadn't, Heather wasn't sure who would be able to do the ceremony for them.

Now all she had to do was get her daughter back.

———

Coming Spring 2023
Animal Desire
The Desire Series, Book 3

———

Don't miss out on your next favorite book!

Join the Satin Romance mailing list

THANK YOU FOR READING

———

Did you enjoy this book?

We invite you to leave a review at your favorite book site, such as Goodreads, Amazon, Barnes & Noble, etc.

DID YOU KNOW THAT LEAVING A REVIEW...

- Helps other readers find books they may enjoy.
- Gives you a chance to let your voice be heard.
- Gives authors recognition for their hard work.
- Doesn't have to be long. A sentence or two about why you liked the book will do.

ABOUT THE AUTHOR

Writing for Barbara Donlon Bradley started innocently enough, like most she kept diaries, journals, and wrote an occasional letter but she also had a vivid imagination and wrote scenes and short stories adding characters to her favorite shows and comic books.

As time went on, she found the passion for writing to be a strong drive for her. Humor is also very strong in her life. No matter how hard she tries to write something deep and dark, it will never happen. That humor bleeds into her writing. Since she can't beat it, she has learned to use it to her advantage.

Now she lives in Tidewater Virginia with a cat who thinks he owns everything, her husband and daughter.

www.barbaradonlonbradley.com

ALSO BY BARBARA DONLON BRADLEY

Novels

Love Is…

A Portrait in Time

Love on the Run

Love's Quest Series

A Quest For Love

Magical Quest

Desire Series

Dominated by Desire

Passionate Desire

Animal Desire (Coming Spring 2023)